Series Titles

The Clayfields
Elise Gregory

Kind of Blue
Christopher Chambers

Evangelina Everyday
Dawn Burns

Township
Jamie Lyn Smith

Responsible Adults
Patricia Ann McNair

Great Escapes from Detroit
Joseph O'Malley

Nothing to Lose
Kim Suhr

The Appointed Hour
Susanne Davis

Praise for
Elise Gregory

"Elise Gregory's novel in stories, *The Clayfields*, made me feel like I was part of a Wisconsin farming community. The novel is layered with both the complexity and simplicity of farming life, the danger and the beauty. It helps us understand what hard work is and what it means to those who do it. This novel is layered with emotional tension, tied to the people and the land and animals they care for and work. The language is both simple and poetic, the stories compelling and linked and revealing more with each season that passes. I am in awe with Gregory's ability to tell a good story and make me want to be there with them, standing in the manure, all that comes with it. I wanted to know these people. They felt as real to me as anyone I know. A beautiful, beautiful book."

—Laura Stott
author of *Blue Nude Migration*
and *In the Museum of Coming and Going*

"A lush, evocative, and beautiful book. In prose both lyrical and precise, Elise Gregory introduces us to an upper Midwestern community that cultivates a host of complicated and interconnected relationships between a cast of unforgettable characters, all of whom are authentically rendered with disarming clarity, while set against striking locales and landscapes. From bluffs perched over farmland, to the local tavern, to potlucks, to milking goats, to harvesting crops, to wandering cornfields at night, *The Clayfields* is a sensual and heartfelt debut."

—Keith Lesmeister
author of *We Could Have Been Happy Here*

"Elise Gregory beautifully captures the heartbeat of rural Wisconsin life, where news travels fast, beer is served in pitchers, and bakers vie for ribbons at the county fair pie contest. But there's enough space even in the smallest of towns to hide family history and secrets, both of which unravel with the rhythm of Wisconsin's seasons. *The Clayfields* is charming, poignant and thought-provoking."

—Shelley Tougas
author of *Laura Ingalls is Ruining My Life, A Patron Saint for Junior Bridesmaids, Lily and That Guy,* and *Finders Keepers*

"*The Clayfields* is a fully imagined novel in stories driven by lunar cycles of growth and decay, grief and joy, birth and death, waiting and renewal—not to mention goats and milk and cheese and corn and love and blueberries and memory and pie and everything else that sustain us. Elise Gregory has brought a world to life in this beautiful, engaging book."

—Samuel Ligon
author of *Wonderland, Among the Dead and Dreaming, Drift and Swerve,* and *Safe in Heaven Dead*

"Elise Gregory's novel-in-stories, *The Clayfields,* is an utterly absorbing, charming, and original work. Its focus on family, food, farming, and all the generational disjunctions and conflicts of Midwestern agrarian life today is so exactly rendered and compellingly nuanced the reader ends up feeling like part of the family and its larger community. One warning: you may find yourself getting hungry more often than not as you read!"

—Gregory Spatz
author of *Inukshuk* and *What Could Be Saved*

THE CLAYFIELDS

A Novel in Stories

Elise Gregory

Cornerstone Press
Stevens Point, Wisconsin

Cornerstone Press, Stevens Point, Wisconsin 54481
Copyright © 2022 Elise Gregory
www.uwsp.edu/cornerstone

Printed in the United States of America by
Point Print and Design Studio, Stevens Point, Wisconsin

Library of Congress Control Number: 2022940329
ISBN: 979-8-9861447-3-3

Cornerstone Press titles are produced in courses and internships offered by the
Department of English at the University of Wisconsin–Stevens Point.

DIRECTOR & PUBLISHER   EXECUTIVE EDITOR
Dr. Ross K. Tangedal   Jeff Snowbarger

SENIOR EDITORS
Lexie Neeley, Monica Swinick, Kala Buttke

PRESS STAFF
Rhiley Block, Alyssa Bronk, Grace Dahl, Patrick Fogarty, Ava Freeman, Angela
Green, Brett Hill, Cale Jacoby, Hunter Kiesow, Adam King, Jeremy Kremser, Amanda
Leibham, Leo McEvilly, Abbi Rohde, Abbi Wasielewski

Also by Elise Gregory:

Aftermath
Domestic Spiral
All We Can Hold: Poems of Motherhood (with Emily Gwinn)

Contents

It's all I have to bring today—
This, and my heart beside—
This, and my heart, and all the fields—
And all the meadows wide—
Be sure you count—should I forget
Some one the sum could tell—
This, and my heart, and all the Bees
Which in the Clover dwell.

—Emily Dickinson (#26)

SPRING

Milk Moon

Terrain

If she had known what lay ahead of them, Terra wouldn't have fed her anger. She'd torn open the wool fabric, which wouldn't repair.

Woken at five from dreams of weed-picking to a day of chores, she battled over carrots and onions, pinching off purslane, and lamb's quarters. The crab grass had her seeing double. Dirt wedged under her nails, and sweat formed at her hairline. She swiped it with her damp wrist, leaving dirt. She was the dirt.

She looked up through the garden fence and scanned her alfalfa field and beyond. Corn threaded out in geometric patterns beside the bluffs—farmland as far as the eye could see. Sometimes all that working land felt like a vice grip tamping down her heart. She took a moment to breathe.

She carried the sprout bucket to the compost. Hens pecked at something white. She leaned over the wooden slats. Fatty white on their beaks. Cheese. Creamy goat cheese that took months of fermentation. Simon had blown the batch of Cabra al Vino. This was the second trashed in six months. She felt like screaming.

Aiming herself at the red bungalow, she loped downhill and flung open the door. Chopped garlic, onion, and mint stung her eyes. Simon kneaded ground lamb at the wood island. Bulgur wheat cooled on the green tile counter.

He looked at her but kept mixing meat, "Hey I was going to ask what you'd like to open tonight. You think a Zin or a Malbec?" He hadn't even thought about the cheese loss. Wasn't he concerned for their survival? They were living in different planes of thought: she in the reality of their economic crisis and he in the midst of another project.

"I saw the cheese." She froze on their mat with dirt-covered shoes.

"Oh yeah. Had trouble with that one," he smiled at her.

"Did you forget it?"

"Complex recipe," he turned and grabbed the pan of bulgur wheat, emptying it inside the bowl. He went back to manipulating the meat more forcefully and didn't look up.

"Couldn't you have revived it?"

"If you want to pick the chicken shit off, be my guest."

The bowl he used was a large ceramic piece she'd thrown years ago. She had an urge to break it. He didn't even apologize, moving past all the hours and money lost with the cheese. They were barely making it these days.

"You know I was talking with Sue at the library," he said. "She's into wines. Maybe we should invite her over for dinner tonight."

"Sue has a baby you know."

"Well, they could bring it."

He looked at her. Stopped kneading. The meat climbed past his wrists. Wet clots of wheat littered the floor.

"Is something bugging you?" he asked.

"People with babies don't just come to dinner on a whim."

"Huh, guess you forgot I raised three daughters?" He looked straight at her.

It was a punch to the gut: how could she know anything about babies. Secretly Terra wondered if his ex-wife had done most of the rearing while he'd worked with their sheep.

"Are you mad about the cheese?"

"Listen, could you get me a glass of water? I just need a glass of water."

He wiped off on the clean dish towel. She bit at her lip. She couldn't bear to think about their accounting books. And that baby comment hurt, though she didn't know how to admit that to Simon.

"Throw the towel downstairs would you," she snapped as he carried the full cup over to her.

"You're mad about lost cheese," he brushed back strands of her wild hair. "It's just cheese."

She grabbed the glass. "We're losing money."

"Welcome to farming," he said.

The water quickly cooled her, and she wanted to swim or drown in it. She pushed the glass into his hand and was out the door before he could ask if she wanted another.

The western tomato and pepper garden could use cages soon. Beets could be thinned, but she'd already spent hours bent over plants this morning. Stables could be mucked. Dead birch cut and cedars in the animal area wrapped again. It was an endless list of projects needing her hands. After some twelve-hour days she'd fallen asleep on their kitchen floor without removing her boots. Several city restaurants and regional cooperatives sold their cheeses, but they were still just breaking even. The work spanned out ahead of her, and she didn't know if she could manage it.

What was Simon doing when he was supposedly monitoring the mold growth on the Cabra al Vino? She bet he'd been fiddling on the stupid, new irrigation system for the tomato and pepper gardens. Not exactly stupid, but the putzy way he did things made her wonder. It wasn't like she'd ever botched a big batch of aged cheese.

There was her one, small mistake that turned out fine once she'd worked with it, which was exactly why she was mad at Simon. He was onto the next thing, unbothered. Her anger always rolled off him. He never overheated.

Enough of his easy-going attitude. She wanted him to get mad too, get worried, shocked, something.

It was a good time for her to go on a bike ride. An adult time out. Get off the farm. Let her anger soften. She needed time to ponder why she was mad at Simon in the first place. She rinsed her feet and hands in the hose, working dirt from her callused fingers, her cracked heels. Her breathing slowed as she let her anger go. If she'd invited him to ride with her then when her rage had subsided, perhaps everything would have turned out differently.

Inside, she ran past Simon to change into biking clothes. He was singing off-key with Marvin Gaye as he swiped counters. He was so irksome.

"Going on a ride?" he asked, walking down the porch steps after her as she fastened her helmet and pulled out her bike from their garage.

"You're gorgeous when you're mad," he swatted her ass. Inside she let it go but grimaced at him. Call her pretty and make her feel silly about being upset.

"What're you doing then?" she asked.

"Think I'll down that boxelder today." He said this with that impish smile that showed he knew exactly how irritated she'd be.

He knew their verbal agreement was no solo chainsaw work. So, he'd gone and wrecked her bike ride too. She wouldn't let him.

"Fine," she gritted, "Wear your helmet."

He should have known how enraged she was as she sped away. Just let him drop a tree on his foot. *What a jack wagon,* she thought.

It ruined her ride. Rather than take the gravel ridge and swoop down the river bluffs to Painted Turtle Lake, she chose the quicker, two-hour, trafficked route into town and past the Hollows' Creamery. She couldn't enjoy the trilliums, just a hint of pink now. Right at their peak before the next wildflower opened face. She had to get home to him. Her head wasn't in it. She couldn't enjoy pumping uphill or feeling her quads and hamstrings burn. Her brain burned and worried about cut arteries and blood where the boxelder stood. Maybe the tree was down, but down on Simon. Some trees were called widow makers. She worried about the idea of his accident like a stone in a shoe until she found her way into an earlier memory on the farm when the burden hadn't consumed her.

It was her first year with Simon. After morning milking, Simon pressed her back with his palm. They were placing pails of fresh milk in the fridge to cool. His hand was like a heartbeat outside her spine. She turned and pressed his fingers to her throat so their hearts could hum together. The one in his hand; the one in her throat.

He wanted to skip weeding. She thought he might take her there in the milking shed in front of the small, white fridge. But he meant he wanted to canoe together. She remembered his face then: small creases gathered at his eyes and mouth. The gray hairs only slivered through the red near his temples. It was a small display of his aging. She'd liked that he was older, that his life held an entire first life before her with grown daughters and wife. Now his age was something that concerned her, the absent daughters a sore.

Terra pushed and lifted her cleated toes, forcing her bike tires faster. She reimagined the canoe on her ratty car. That day she'd followed Simon's truck along the river road on potholed asphalt and gravel, through swaths of wooded land and then corn. Simon parked his truck alongside a foxtail grass covered embankment. Jumped inside her car. Even now, biking, she could find that thrill between them as they drove and spoke like new lovers. The excitement of playing hooky. They weren't aware of the river level. Gold mixed in the summer grasses.

After they parked beneath a glade of soft maples, they undid the canoe straps. She lifted from the stern and he the bow. They brought the aluminum up over their heads where Simon worked his way up to the center and rested the wooden yoke on his shoulders. He walked ahead of her while she grabbed the paddles, life jackets, bag of wine and bottled water.

She dropped the gear onshore, ready to help him bring down his awkward aluminum hat. But he reached out one long arm, cradling the canoe like a baby, then lowering the metal belly to his thighs, then water. She remembers this because it was the first time she noticed the small green and purple handprints on one flank of the canoe, and his daughters' names scrawled below. She'd thought about how Simon's family took up all the metal openings. Almost nothing else but his family could fit inside. Now she and Simon were at either end. Two whole spaces between them.

He mentioned the water looked low. This is a line he restates each time they've relived this story. It's his way of showing he warned her. She replies that it implies he knew the river was too low since she'd never canoed it.

At the time, they eyed the rocks but were too excited to skip work, to drink warm wine and stop at a sand bar on their lazy path downriver. "We'll lift it over stones, drag it when needed," they said to each other.

They had no idea then the trip back to his truck would take them over six hours. Six hours of climbing out, lifting or dragging the waterlogged aluminum. Later they'd joked about how their canoe trip spanned a marriage: their beginning joy, the heavy lifting, literally on the rocks, and the quiet cooperation to see the trip to its end.

All they could think of was cold water once their wine buzzes faded—their water bottles drained. They were already brown from work, but the sun's reflection burned. Terra could feel her skin tightening; the bridge of her nose and brow felt raw. She remembered touching her blistered hands to her face, remembered feeling stupid for forgetting hats and sunscreen.

They'd become silent when before they'd pointed out redhorse sucker. The rounded silver bellies tight to the bottom as they sucked in crustaceans. Tired of the limestone bluffs which began as millions of soft-bodied worms and mollusks. The clinging roots of dwarfed junipers ready to fall with sliding stone.

Her biking become more languid the deeper she thought about their canoe ride. She half-watched the cars pass her.

It had been her first year around the Clayfields. It had surprised her to see people sitting in their submerged lawn chairs along their route. The people laughed at them and said, "Can't believe you're canoeing in this soup," Koozie-covered beers sat on their bellies.

Beside a deep hole, they watched a young boy in underpants arc over the pool on a rope swing and splash inside. They portaged around a beaver dam, through nettles and thistles. Cool limestone walls rose behind them. They would have swum if they weren't so spent and the boy's small face wasn't hard as he swam and stared.

They dragged and paddled through what seemed to be an extension of people's backyards, their whirly gigs stuck inside the river, pink flamingoes beside. They worked around drinking cattle. They ducked under barbed wire that spanned across and some that rusted beneath them. They glimpsed a dead cow that looked like stretched leather over bones.

And they began to speak again as the canoe nudged the final bank. Terra looked at the embankment covered by wild parsnip, something she hadn't noticed as they'd parked Simon's truck. It was a last note.

They emptied the canoe. Tipped it over to drain. Then hefted it up to thigh, overhead, and onto Simon's burned shoulders. Terra followed him, hugging their supplies. Her legs brushed the bunched yellow crowns and celery-like stalks of the wild parsnip. She knew she'd bear the sores later, wouldn't be able to wash off the toxic sap until it'd reacted with the sun. The marks would be on her legs for years before they faded under new skin.

She instinctively looked down at her calves as they pushed her forward along the highway home, past the Creamery again. She used to explain the pink scars as an example of how they put their relationship on the rocks. How she knew they could endure.

But as she turned onto their long gravel drive, destruction is what she imagined. Destruction is what she saw when she looked at the big hollow middle of the downed tree as she stopped her bike. The heartwood eaten clean by insects. She'd miss all those woodpeckers heaving head into the trunk to get at grubs. There was the gaping square hole from a pileated and smaller ones cut by red bellies, hairy, and downy. No red-headed woodpecker this year.

She was looking for him under the girth. Not exactly looking, but she did scan for blood. It's what she did: worry about the worst possible circumstances and plan ahead. She'd tried convincing him once, folks like her more regularly escaped burning buildings or planes. They already expected it and memorized their escape route.

"Good ride?" He came up behind and hugged her sweaty back to his sweaty front. Her bike helmet knocked into his wood cutting one, making them both laugh.

"What if I had a baby?" she said.

He pulled back. She almost wished she hadn't spoken since she wasn't really sure what made her say such a thing. Maybe she just wanted a reaction from him. She didn't know if she really wanted a baby, but in a couple years she might not be able to have one. After remembering their canoe ride, she wondered if maybe this next step was what she needed (as if life were a series of steps).

"I'm kinda old to be having kids," he said.

She faced him and hated the black, mesh guard blocking his face from her. She couldn't see his eyes.

"You're not too old."

She couldn't stand when he used their age differences against her like she couldn't understand such important life questions yet.

"Yes. I am. I'd be nearly 80 when the kid entered college. If I lived that long."

"That's a big stretch. Try seventies," she tried to sound light.

"I got grown kids."

"Yes," she wanted to yell, "from someone else." But she didn't. Wouldn't. Tired of fighting today. She stuck out her tongue, partly in earnest and partly to make him laugh, and rode like hell up to the garage.

It wasn't like this normally, her irritability. His callousness. It was just the day. When you live and work with the person you love most, arguments are bound to happen. It's like the saying from some talk-show pastor: he'd never ever thought of divorce, but he had thought of murder (a strange comment from a pastor). Still there was nothing truer in her mind. That day she wanted to murder Simon. Or at least throttle him simply because he was Simon.

When he left on his own bike ride late afternoon, nearly supper time, she didn't go. She'd already biked. He'd trashed her ride, so why make his fun. Besides, her emotions were still raw even after they fed the goats and sheep together. They'd milked without talking. He sang every Prince and Madonna song he knew.

She waited for him for over an hour, but then ate his *kufta* kabobs with hummus, cucumber sauce, and spinach. She nibbled olives and cheese. The Zin was spicy. She almost wished she'd biked again with him. Ate a late dinner together.

He wasn't home by nine. He probably met up with some friend, she thought. Caught a ride to the Junction Bar or the farm bar that she always refused after that first time. She had to be up early to milk. It wasn't unusual for him to be "lost" for hours. He'd come home after fishing with a friend or a new person with whom he'd made a connection. It was charming when she wasn't irritated.

At two she woke to an empty bed. She told herself he'd spent the night somewhere; she'd get a call the next morning. She hoped he'd be ready at 5:30 to milk Surly since he was the only one who could stop the doe from kicking. Enough of her premonitions, she thought. She read and reread the same page, trying to get back to sleep. The story wouldn't stick. She kept thinking about the big, downed tree, the never-baby, her absent husband. She tried not to think, but she had a head-full. Like an expanding balloon-skull, the thoughts pressing outward until her head floated off into the night. In the early morning, she fell asleep—arms and legs flung across the whole bed, filling Simon's spot.

At five she was startled by pounding. Strange, she thought, since she didn't remember locking the door. Down the stairs, hand on the rail. The diffused early light. Red dawn coloring the walls, the table as she walked by the big eastern window, and her body on her way to the front door. Later she wondered if it was protocol to have two officers. One to break the news. One to soften it with a hug or whatever the hell happened to her after the worst possible words were said. Everything began sharp and then blurred into an unknown, irretrievable place.

The cops asked if there was someone to be with her. Terra squinted at a lint ball stuck on the male officer's face. Kleenex perhaps. A cold. Spring allergies. The white lint. She couldn't think.

The female officer asked, "A neighbor?"

Terra shook her head. The lint grew. Or maybe it was a sunspot in her eye. She was confused by what was real.

One officer said, "How sorry I am to report… words, words, words …Simon was found…" more words she couldn't follow "…five miles from here. Not an accident. A heart attack." The officer kept talking. "The death was fast," and there were more words beyond her comprehension.

Later Terra replayed the downed boxelder with the hollow where its heartwood had been. How the insects ate it all. How the woodpeckers flocked. How the limbs lost leaves. They knew it was dying. How had she not known his heart would stop? How could he not have known? Where were the fucking signs? Why was she so angry with him?

Someone asked again if they could call a neighbor. She must have said "Okay." Someone drove next door to the Olsen's. Someone stayed, a heavy hand on Terra's shoulder. A boulder of a hand, Terra thought, as though the hand were responsible for knocking her dumb. Nothing seemed to stick in her head after that point. It was only that day she replayed as she slept or walked without direction.

Emile on Goat's Back Ridge Farm

Emile wasn't one to miss a funeral. Weddings and funerals always steamed somebody. But this thing was called "a celebration of life." She'd never heard of that one before. Rumor had it, no body. And so, she saw no purpose in going to the thing. Barflies thought her ghastly for saying behind the bartop a proper death needed a proper box. What were people going to look at without one? Like the person just up and moved to the cities is what it seemed like without a body. Sure, she understood those soldiers flown back from Iraq, Afghanistan, Syria, (was America in Syria? She couldn't remember) but remains probably couldn't be looked at by everyone unless you had an expert mortician sewing on limbs and faces. There were still coffins. You could imagine a person, the person, inside. Although coffins always did look smaller than the person. Something about being horizontal instead of vertical making a person. Well. A person.

She was holding court at the Junction Bar again; she was nearly thirty, it wasn't like she was a baby anymore. As she filled beers, Pauly said, "Oh hell Emile, would you just fall off your high horse and go to it."

A stretch of sun lit the countertops and Emile glanced out to the stream just twenty feet from the front door. Simon regularly kayaked and came in for a chat and a cold nip. She'd liked that one.

Then Jason said, "Heard the ex and daughters will be there," he smiled as he held his empty glass out to her knowing she'd take the bait.

"That's rough," she said, and she honestly felt sad for Terra the second wife, the younger wife, the barren wife (not that Emile'd ever say that in public unless side-whipped by three, maybe four, white Russians). But then she'd slogged through the first crap of widowhood with her mother after her dad died. A hole of a time for a long while.

She'd only seen Terra a coupla times at the bar. Terra was one of those Emile liked and she didn't like many women. She sometimes felt for those bar widows. Not that Terra had been a real one of those. Simon came now and then but wasn't an every week drinker like Jason or some of the other farmers, young and old, who were never going to figure out how to do home lives. Course, it gets lonely sitting in a cab all day or talking to cow teats.

"You know I'm not one to miss a scene," she said and slid a cold mug of Miller to Jason.

"Didn't think so." He sucked in some foam.

"Sad, sad thing. Just saw Simon out on his bike," Pauly sipped his beer, "Seemed like he couldn't just set still."

"Just like every farmer," she said.

Simon was a person Emile'd miss. He looked right into your eyes when he talked and asked about your life. So, she'd go even without him there. Bring Terra a casserole or pan of bars, though she probably wasn't eating just like Emile's mother couldn't eat for weeks after Dad died.

On her way to Goat's Back Ridge, Emile had the windows down even with the dust from the back roads. Her hair flipped as the wind bullied through, swinging the air freshener from the mirror. Papers slipped free from the folder where her boyfriend should have sat. Instead, he was out checking affordable farmsteads. She wasn't sure if this was the next step in their relationship or his easy out.

She'd stuffed a bottle of Jameson in her oversized purse in case she got close enough to Terra. As the pick-up hauled up the drive, she could see that drinking with Terra would be unlikely. Cars and trucks sat on the grass like goose turds. Some even parked beside the downed boxelder that needed more cutting. Crap wood. Otherwise Emile'd offer taking some.

She stopped beside a baby blue Prius just in case they needed help towing out of the tall grass (more for the show of a country girl towing out a city guy). Tiny shit of a car, couldn't be anyone she knew around the Hollows. She wiped dust from the rearview mirror, licked grit from her lips, applied lipstick and combed through the tangles. She grabbed the bars from under all the papers. *Not bad looking for a funeral*, she thought, as she straightened the sundress, jean jacket, and cowboy boots before hiking up the long drive.

As she assumed, people were disorganized, chatting without purpose inside the opened garage and outside the house. *See*, she thought, *with a body there's focus*. She moved through a mix of clean-heeled, silky-haired city slickers standing just outside the opened cavern of the garage before she found her kind. LaVonne, a fixture in the Clayfields' region, and even in the nearby town of Hollows, one-armed her and took the bars like she bought the farm.

"So good to see you, Emile. Just saw your mom today lookin' sooo good."

LaVonne cracked the Tupperware lid, "Cookie bars that's sooo thoughtful. I'll put them right next to Florence's favorite turtle bars. Right after I cut them up."

"Actually, I was thinking of giving them to Terra to freeze."

LaVonne pinched her face, she reminded Emile of a badger.

"Oh, I wouldn't bother her. She's sitting with her folks right now, poor thing."

"Whatever."

"Now tell me again Emile, where is Jed?"

Emile bristled, but explained the property which had LaVonne nodding along like she was pretending to understand. Emile let LaVonne whisk away her bars to the long folding table draped in several tablecloths. Emile'd catch hell if her mother heard she was sassing the bossy old broad.

Buried in all types of casseroles and crock pots, the table stretched along one corner of the garage. LaVonne and a couple other busybody oldsters sliced and organized food. They'd all be noticing that Jed wasn't here. It's what they did: eyed-up attachments and the unattached. And she hated that it mattered to her after she'd told Jed it didn't. Glancing at her phone she saw his photos of the property, and she remembered the old adage, "Why buy the cow if you get the milk for free." She couldn't believe old Jed was like that; he just needed time to get over his divorce. Still, she sent him a frenetic little text about coming to Terra's.

She looked up and waved, recognizing her aunt. She'd look for her cousin Esther's dessert somewhere in the long spread of cream-topped Jell-Os. She fingered her phone again but made herself drop it inside her purse.

The boys had to be around, and they were always good for a drink. She spotted Etzel at the end of a table in the garage, a cup of coffee stationed in his hands instead of his usual glass of Bud Light. Emile strode in through the opened garage doors and immediately the temperature cooled from the concrete floor and small windows. She weaved through folding tables with locals stuffing faces. She skirted around Geirolf and Gin Olsen with their daughter Lupine and old man Etzel. She ignored Jason and Lani, winking at Pauly and Meg before she came to the empty chair beside Etzel. His granddaughter, Lupine, concentrated on her meal on his other side.

"You want me to spice that up for ya?" She leaned into his good ear. Trying to avoid bringing in his family.

"Emile. Now we have some good people." He began singing, "Emile, my fair famile…"

She put her finger to her lips. The chair creaked as she sat beside him, bag between her feet. She couldn't let the hens of this flock see as she cracked the bottle open under her skirt and dribbled some into Etzel's and her cups. Thank God for tablecloths.

"Don't see you enough at the bar anymore," she said in his ear again.

He thumbed toward his daughter Gin, "Got me in lock-down." He grinned and took a long sip.

"Now this is what I call a gathering," she said holding the cup high.

"Here's to Simon," Etzel solemnly ticked his into hers. It made her look for Terra. She scanned the garage for the wild haired woman.

"She's sitting with her sisters out back behind the garage," Etzel whispered, which came out like a loud honk and

Lupine turned to smile at Emile but then was caught in a conversation with Pauly about his farm. Emile had no interest in farms.

A glass clinked somewhere else, and Emile thought others were toasting Simon. Clink. It kept insisting until people at the tables stopped their coffees, their bars, their mouths. All swiveled to look at the clinker.

"Now that's gotta be one of Simon's brood," Etzel half-yelled, catching some pained looks.

The woman's clear wide face. The thick red hair. Not beautiful. Stunning. The woman hugged her cabled sweater to her, which seemed excessive for late spring. Another similarly tall, sweater-clad woman came up beside the first. LaVonne shoved a portable microphone at them. No wonder Terra sat surrounded by her own family.

"Thank you everyone for coming here to honor and remember our dad. My name is Solveig if we haven't met. It's been a shock for us and I'm sure for the whole town. I know my sister Astrid and I always loved coming out to Goat's Back to visit. Dad always picked up a fresh bag of the Hollows' Creamery cheese curds. Even though he and Terra made goat cheese, he always bought us a bag right at eleven when the newest batch was turned out."

This got a laugh from all the Clayfields' farmers and the Hollows' townies, which made up most of the audience inside the big garage. Emile doubted Simon's girls had more than three bags of curds for the amount of time they came out this way. She noticed most of the outsiders weren't eating at the folding tables. Many stood along the edges of the garage or just outside the opened doors.

"Our mom, Laura, Astrid, and I are all wearing the sweaters from our family flock in Iceland. Mom knitted us all one to remember that time. When I think of my dad, I will always remember him as that strong father in Iceland who carried me and Astrid on his shoulders and chopped wood to heat our cottage...."

Emile couldn't believe this shit. Where were these loving daughters the fifteen years that Simon and Terra were milking on the Goat's Back? She couldn't remember Simon or anyone in town talking about these two. Here they were like great pillars of salt sucking everything out of Terra's land. Sure, Emile thought, every coin could be flipped but she knew Simon well enough and liked him. It was clear they missed their dad (Emile could understand estranged relationships). But this Icy speech was a farce. She checked the group for Terra again, relieved she didn't catch her. Then she scanned to see the look in people's eyes. No one looked back. Everyone was too goddamn Midwestern: passive aggressive and polite. Emile keyed into the daughter's last statement.

"Which is why we brought our dad's sweater to cremate with our family picture. We ask you to join us and poor Terra out back for our ceremonial fire," she looked around the garage seeking out Terra.

Emile thought the daughter was miming this false pity for her stepmother.

"Fuck this," Emile hotly whispered to Etzel, not caring that LaVonne would tell her mother. And she'd ream Emile, try to stitch her back together as a Lutheran lady, which never worked. And screw Jed for not being here too.

She grabbed her Tupperware of uneaten bars that sat on the table behind Simon's daughters and said, "I brought these for Terra." Emile waltzed out of the chilled garage to the warm hill where Terra sat with her family.

Lupine Milking

Lupine with Etzel and Gin

Lupine loved milking, no matter the cow or doe. But it was an adjustment going from the cow's fist-sized four to the delicate, two-teated does. Pulling could wreck a goat's teat or udder, she knew. It was her newest homeschool assignment, and she'd watched enough YouTube videos to make Grandpa Etzel laugh.

Her hand easily held the smaller pillars. No cream in goat's milk, and she liked that consistency. It tasted grassier than a cow's. She squirted milk into the pail. Does nibbled sweet hay above her in Terra's shed; Terra's land used to belong to Lupine's grandpa twenty-odd years ago. She wanted to sit with Terra in her grandpa's old house and tell his stories, but Terra wasn't ever out anymore. Like she'd died herself. Lupine milked Terra's goats every morning and would continue to milk until she was told to stop or the does required drying. She hadn't expected to milk this long, but she'd not experienced Terra's grief.

One would think Gin, her mother, had suggested she milk her neighbor's goats. She wasn't that kind of mother. Lupine wasn't an average sixteen-year-old.

The first morning Terra was hauled into their house. Eyes like a deer mid-road. Mute. It was the policewoman who'd said Simon was dead to Gin and Lupine. Geirolf was already out with the cows. The cop said the Olsen's were the closest house to Terra's. She hoped they'd put Terra up until her family drove up from Chicago. Lupine and Gin put her to bed in Lupine's pale room with a brandy and tea mixture. Terra slept and cried alone in the room.

As soon as Terra was plopped on their doorstep, Lupine knew those does' bags were straining. She kicked on over and muddled through it. While Terra cried, Lupine milked and fed the goats. By midafternoon, Terra's mother and sisters blew in from out of town and carried her home—all perfume and bright clothing. Not at all who she had pictured to be part of Terra's rural life.

Lupine figured she'd continue to milk the does and study up. No one said a thing. It was good to get away from her family farm. Terra was nowhere. Maybe she was inside her house. Maybe she was with those sisters. She knew Gin liked the house quiet, which puzzled her. Why didn't her parents want her in school, but not want her at home? She knew it had something to do with her big brothers' trouble in school, them leaving the farm. But that was all kept hush hush.

Lupine finished the last doe, dipping her teats in an astringent mixture to lessen the chance of mastitis like the cows. Then she let her out to roam with the others. She noticed Terra out on the deck chairs as she brought back covered pails of milk. Lupine waved to her, and Terra seemed to nod, so Lupine walked toward her. She noticed the sweatpants, the huge arm-pit stained shirt, the greasy locks of unbrushed hair.

"Didn't want the milk to go to waste," Lupine said holding out the two large buckets.

Terra shook her head like she didn't care.

"Just finished with Surly," Lupine said, "she's been giving me problems, but I think we've got it now," she grinned at Terra whose face soured.

"Hope you don't mind I'm using your milk," Lupine hurried on, trying to change Terra's face.

"No," Terra finally said, "That's not it. I just got really tired. Think I'm going to go back to bed," she said and pushed herself up like a much older woman. Like Etzel. Terra disappeared back inside her shuttered house. Lupine wished she could follow her but knew better than to try that today.

She loaded up the milk in the four-wheeler. Goat's Back Ridge spanned a bluffside. Nothing about the twenty acres was flat. The farmhouse was nestled against one side. The goats and sheep climbed up the wooded bluff behind it, steadily working at the sumac, buckthorn, and grapevines that grew everywhere. They left the sugar maples and black walnuts that Simon and Terra had carefully wrapped and fenced, which made the hill grassy between trees. A place to sit in the hottest summer if one could avoid the social does. Lupine drove the four-wheeler down past the weedy gardens and gravel drive. Milk slapped against the covered pails and she slowed. A haze of humidity hung above her as she turned east onto the road toward her farm.

Time to try another round of cheese at home. She'd botched the first. Gotten the stink-eye for her war in the kitchen. What a mystery, Geirolf's cookbooks. She just couldn't mix a spot of milk into cheese. She'd try again. She bumped along on the four-wheeler on her way back home where Grandpa Etzel righted himself.

He slept in the little back room which used to be Gin's office. Lupine and Gin had carried all the labeled boxes to her parents' room where they'd pushed them beneath the bed. The computer and Gin's walnut desk moved upstairs, which they sweated and inched up the narrow farmhouse stairway. Her parents' bedroom was tight with all the furniture. All Gin's papers had been boxed and shoved beneath the bed. Her face tightened at the sight. They were making room for Old Etzel's dying. Lupine wondered if Gin hurt.

When he'd first arrived, Etzel had woken at five like the rest of them—the internal farm-alarm. He'd been sleeping longer—sometimes eight, sometimes nine. A regular bed-head. Lupine had no one to talk with 'till midday. He always needed some throat warming for his "speaking cords," though his singing chords were a-okay. Give him some instant Folgers with powdered cream, "hot as a hooker's sweet spot" and he wouldn't stop talking.

She didn't know which was dirtier, the coffee or Grandpa Etzel. He was from the time of margarine, T.V. dinners, and Spam. Apparently, it didn't matter which side you were on in World War II—nobody learned to cook. Lupine had snuck fresh, hot goat's milk into his coffee. A teaspoon at a time to loosen the old man's tongue. Help her through her long days. It surprised her he didn't notice. She spooned in a little more each day until it wasn't even powdered creamer. What would happen, she thought, if she switched to real coffee beans? It was a takedown like the Oleo Wars in Wisconsin's 1960s unrest that her grandpa used to joke about.

Lupine drove right up to the side door, knowing full well it'd piss Gin off to see her haul in more milk. The Hernandez's rusted pick-up, Hiran's Neon, and Sam's truck were still parked outside the milk parlor. They must be finishing the morning milking. The silver milk truck picking up another load for the Creamery. Calves could wait 'til she chatted with Grandpa Etzel. She pulled the cooler jugs off her four-wheeler and dragged them to the door.

As she lugged in the coolers, she peeked down the hall at Grandpa Etzel's room. His room and the bathroom were ajar. He must be readying himself for the kitchen. She smiled, set the coolers on the kitchen floor, and went to the bathroom door.

Knocking softly, she asked, "Grandpa Etzel? Can I help you?"

He opened the bathroom door for her. The nose-pinch of cologne and mold. She took up his razor and shaving cream, lathered his cheeks and throat. She hunted for the fine gray whiskers, licking them away with the edge of the razor. His skin moved and she held smooth his wrinkles so she could shave without slicing.

"Lilly, oh Lilly. If there's a hilly, let willy nilly up it," he sang as she struggled beneath his chin.

"You're losing your rhyme, Old Man."

"Rita, there's nuthin' sweeter…," he broke through the musky air making Lupine laugh and nick his jaw.

"Here, let's get some paper on that."

She pressed a petal of tissue into the blood where it colored and opened like a small rose. She poured the aftershave into his palms and brought them up to his cheeks with her own. She wet the comb and drew through the couple dozen hairs like they'd been sketched and weren't grown from Old Etzel's glowing head.

He refused other bathroom help, only allowing her to button up his red and black plaid shirt in his bedroom. She sat between his feet in front of his rocker, laced his indoor shoes.

They moved into the empty kitchen where she readied his coffee. She hid the goat's milk behind her hand. After his first cup, he started talking. By his second he wouldn't stop.

"When I was one year older than you, I left my *mutti* and *bruder* in *Oldendorf*. I didn't know it'd be forever. Well, I didn't know it was Wisconsin I was headed when the English shipped us to the U.S. Someone somewhere whispered, 'It's like the home country. They got a lot of us there. Twenty thousand of us in Fort McCoy and other branches.'"

Etzel took a big sip of coffee and swiped beneath his glasses. Lupine was at the stove managing his bacon. He kept reverting back and back like no more memories could be made.

"Why Wisconsin?"

He cleared his throat, "Think us German POWs were all over, really. But Wisconsin needed field hands. Factory work too. A friend of mine worked at a canning plant in Hartford, could earn a packet of cigarettes. Heard some guys got hard but good work at a tree nursery. Fed 'em a big breakfast before they dug around tree roots and wrapped 'em. Sure was glad I was put to work on a farm."

The bacon sizzled and she flipped it with a fork. Grease speckled the burners. With a rag, she sopped up a pool of coffee.

"What about real Nazis? They weren't out on farms or in factories, were they?" She'd never said Nazi to him before and she kept her back to him. He sighed heavily. His chair creaked as he leaned back. She wiped the Formica counters and swiped at the sink, giving him time. She turned. He watched her.

"Ach, Lou. I don't know where the true believers were. Not with us. Nope, not with us babies," he sipped and stared out past her. She let him. Checked the bacon. Checked his coffee.

He sighed again, "Don't know where the Nazis went. Heard though they'd kill ya if ya worked with the Americans." He sat up and looked at her, "Don't want ta talk Nazi. I was on a farm most days with a couple others. Old Norske woman. Sons off to war. Husband? Not sure. Really, I don't think she was all that old. Seemed like my *mutti*, though. Good with food. Baked us strawberry rhubarb crisp, apple pie, squash. She just wanted someone to feed."

Lupine forked the bacon from the pan and slid it onto a plate and then in front of him.

"Perfect story timing, eh? Just the length of crisping bacon."

"Don't think you finished it," she said.

Lupine cracked two eggs in the bacon grease. They turned white. Their edges crisped in the fat. Not a pinch of salt needed. She was careful not to break either yolk. It was the only meal she could cook—Grandpa Etzel's bacon and eggs. He'd trained her, but she guessed her love for him helped. His *mutti* fried him eggs and bacon every morning. He knew the colors of the eggs, a warm brown somedays or speckled just a shade darker than his mother's fingers. Smoked bacon from their hog.

"Old Norske got my tongue layin' flat by singing with her records." He crunched a thumb-sized slice. She attended the eggs with a spatula. She grabbed a jar of pickled, red cabbage from the fridge. She'd add it last, try to limit the bleeding into the eggs.

"Once, 'bout a handful of months into it, think we were detasseling corn, guard who used to come at first, asked me to go get his gun that he left on the porch."

"Guess that's trust," she forked out a portion of the cabbage and dropped it inside the pan.

He laughed, "Yup, he trusted me. Knew I had no wheres to run. Everyone knew us by then. Don't think many places round here had too many guards on us by the end of the war."

"What made you stay?"

He coughed, "Couldn't find my *mutti* or *bruder*. And those cows. Wow. Thirty cows this Norske woman had. Thirty milk cows. Knew I was meant to be a dairy man."

She flipped the eggs onto a plate with a side of hot, red cabbage that she'd spooned into the bacon grease as well.

"No one makes eggs like you Lou. Not even my Ginny Lou Hoo."

This pricked Lupine's eyes as she saw Gin walk into the kitchen, a tight smear of lips. It was hard telling what set her off.

"Gin makes a mean scalloped potato. There's not a potato that looked me in the eye and let me peel it."

Lupine tried to make a Grandpa Etzel joke to lighten her mother's mood. It really was true Lupine couldn't peel potatoes. Her hands a mess when the orbs slipped and she peeled her palm. The joke came out wrong and flat like everything she said to her mother.

"I guess I'm not hungry," Gin said as she walked out of the room.

"Ahh Ginny, how'd ya get so skinny," sang Old Etzel to Gin's narrow back.

He went back to stabbing a bit of egg with an edge of bacon and some strands of cabbage, ignorant of his daughter's anger. Perhaps he knew, but then Lupine couldn't think how to approach her grandpa or her mother. How could she crack a wall shaped brick-by-brick, year-by-year? Lupine knew her grandpa was halfway out the door by looking at her mother's back.

SUMMER

Hay Moon

Cheese Daze

Esther and Katie

Every day sixteen-year-old Esther watched for him out of the small window from the bagging area at the Hollows' Creamery. A partial wall separated them from the rest of the store. Chilled and lightly-salted, white cheese curds spilled in front of her and Katie on the stainless steel counter. Their little metal food scales on the countertop where they weighed and vacuum sealed 16 ounce plastic bags for sale. The cheddar curd eaten before being formed and aged in 40-pound blocks. A million pounds of milk driven in daily from the county farms made into fresh, squeaky curds. Their big, bullet-shaped trucks sprayed down and disinfected in a large garage on the side of the building. All the other cheeses were shipped in from nearby creameries. It had become a bang-up business. Fried curds could be found in every surrounding bar and restaurant.

Esther and Katie took turns eyeing the cuties who swaggered through the double doors in the retail section. Most customers were old ladies. Or pudgy parents with kidlets who grabbed all the squares of sample cheeses without using the toothpicks. Sometimes they had young couples, but mostly oldies. It was that kind of store. As the crowds grew over the years, the old brick building expanded as did the tchotchkes. It wasn't a bumping spot for cuties, though neither was the Hollows.

Katie and Esther were set back about ten feet from the checkout counter and soft serve ice cream. They had to keep an eye on the two registers in front of them—help the cashiers when necessary. On busier days they emerged from behind their window to mix malts or swirl a coffee-flavored ice cream cone.

Mostly they bagged curds and talked about boys or friend make-overs. Recently Katie became more philosophical and wanted to talk out a better plan for their "cheesy," cheese day festival.

"I mean it's like you could walk into any small-town event and be listening to bad country singers. Like the UFO days could be anyplace USA with their jumping house. Does every freaking small-town have a different animal-shaped bouncy house? I mean where do you people come up with all this hot air?"

Esther thought now may be the time to disengage from the friendship. Katie who always used to be interested in the regular things like hair was going nerdy on her. Not at all focused on her school crush, Hiran. He hardly ever crossed the threshold of the fat, brick building awash with foam, cheese head bonnets, scented goat-milk soaps, and silly grilling aprons. The kitsch remotely related to good Wisconsin cheese. Maybe Hiran was lactose intolerant. That's why he never came in for the soft serve and malted drinks most football boys craved. Or maybe that was just Asians who had trouble with dairy. She couldn't remember where he was from now, or she meant his father.

But when Esther looked up from the white globules of cheese there was Hiran Biswa with a red grocery basket in hand. Outside of school he'd allowed his hair to grow. She stared at the curls on his brown forehead. She squealed and elbowed Katie who peered up before stuffing more curds inside the bag. Esther poked her side again, unhappy with Katie's response to the boy.

Perhaps sensing eyes on him, Hiran looked their way and Esther quickly hid her hairnet covered head. She wished they weren't wearing the required fluorescent tie-dyed T-shirt and plastic gloves. Looking up through her lashes, she saw him wave in their direction. But she couldn't be certain it was at them he waved. She watched him lift a carved cow cutting board, then a foam cheese-inspired cowboy hat, before he moved out of her sight in front of the large glass coolers where rows of Wisconsin cheeses were shelved.

Esther had this fantasy: she'd bake Hiran a strawberry rhubarb pie with the fruits picked from her garden. He'd swoon over the buttery crust with crushed almonds. The sweet, the sour. The vanilla ice cream painting pink rivers across his plate and down his chin. She'd gotten really good at crusts like her mother, though she'd taken to substituting butter for the lard. Richer flavor. She didn't do bars or cookies like the other girls. All those sophomore girls stirring great hunks of flour and sugar for high school speech demonstrations.

She interrupted Katie, "What if I baked Hiran a pie? Do you think he'd die or what?"

Katie stopped.

Esther continued, "I mean I'm sure he knows good food. I'm sure his people, grandma I mean, cooks all day long for a meal. I mean that's what I hear."

"His mom's from here." Katie filled a small plastic sack with fresh curd. It sat on the scale. She weighed it and hermetically sealed it.

Esther stopped filling her bag, "Ya, I know."

Katie filled another, "He's hardly foreign."

"I wasn't saying that." Esther watched Katie's movements, not filling anything of her own.

She wondered where Katie was coming off. She was the one who led them through the fantasy of him being a superstar athlete for like the Green Bay Packers. Like Davante Adams or Ty Montgomery, though of course they knew he wasn't black. Katie. Superior, politically correct Katie, when it suited her, making Esther feel small just 'cause Katie was born in Seattle. Well. Why didn't Katie go packing, move back in with her mother if she was so cultured. Freaking yogurt cup was what she was.

"So, this is my plan: I'm going to list all the local shindigs within a 30-mile radius. Or what do you think? Would 50 miles be too far?"

Esther wasn't going to play Katie's game after the last snap. She stared at the curds she was stuffing, weighing, and then sealing. They clumped like warm plastic.

"Oh, come on, Esther. I'm sorry I wasn't supportive of your pre-feminist dream of nailing your love-boat with a pie."

Esther sniffed and a large tear wrecked a whole glove-full of squeaky, fresh curds.

"Oh, Esther. I'm sorry that was mean. I forget you're a softie. I really am sorry."

Katie hugged her; their gloves lifted high off their backs. Sanitation drilled into them. Their hairnets meeting in a kiss of a flimsy material. They separated and went back to stuffing.

Esther kept her eyes hidden but looked for Hiran's tall body, those new curls. Up he came and sat his basket on the counter some feet from their glass window. He smiled at them, and this time Esther knew it was for them. There was verve to her next handful of curds as she stared at his wide shoulders and long arms. She wished she could see what his basket contained, what the old woman was ringing into her register. This kind of sighting made her day. She let the good feeling spread to Katie's ideas about traveling around to small-town events.

"OK. I say 45-mile radius," Katie continued barking at her, "We go and take notes."

Esther puffed out her cheeks.

"Hey, maybe you can enter some bake-off or taste test or something," said Katie.

Then she went on about getting some local boys to caravan with them. Katie knew how to hook Esther. Boys and baking. So here went the summer.

The Ex

Emile and Jed

Emile blasted home, happy and a little full. The heat and company from the bar pink in her cheeks. All week Jed had flipped through online property pictures. She'd let him imagine this or that vegetable for his imaginary gardens. Let him have dirt in his fingers. She was busy planning horse trails. This had to be their next chapter. He never talked so much about futures. Because of that she figured they were destined.

She climbed up the long staircase up to their apartment and opened the door to stifling heat. The air conditioning must have gone out again. Jed's huge, freckled back wrestled with the unit, and all Emile's happiness evaporated into the dense heat of their living room.

She was going to tell him how old Etzel came down on the back of his granddaughter's four-wheeler. How he'd gone on and on about the tornado that laid his barn and set his wife moving. The pilings still visible among Terra's maple saplings. The old homestead hers. Emile wanted to talk about connections: how everyone was everybody to someone in this place, even Terra, what with the old bones of Etzel's place.

But Jed's back looked tense. She watched the muscles bunch and release as he finally pulled the enormous conditioner out of place.

"Always did hate that old thing," she joked.

Jed was in no joking mood. His face pained, raining sweat. He did this at times: shut down. No conversation for a day or two when before he'd been jovial and planning out the gardens. She had a mind to scream at him, 'Is this why she divorced you…this silence? Cause it can't work for me either.'

She opened the door as he carried the unit out and grunted down the outside stairs. She trailed down after him, figuring he'd need help lifting it into the pick-up. He silently hefted it up on his own. He said barely a word to her before closing the door and backing out. Did his eyes even glance her way in the mirror? She couldn't tell. Had he gotten too close to her? Was that it, she wondered as he drove away to the recycling center?

She trudged back up the stairs, a pool of sweat on her back. She looked at the ugly apartment door, wanting to hit it. Inside wasn't much better, the heat unbearable in the tight space. She'd tried to spruce the drab walls with fresh paint and pictures of her family barn, the green pastures. She'd liked all the black and white specks on the hillside. But now all her decorations, the ceramic horses she collected, looked like she'd tried too hard. This space was a dump. The beige carpet stained even after she'd cleaned it. This was the first adult place outside living with some girlfriends, and she'd felt proud of it until now. How could she ever fit herself into a divorced man's life? Jed was not ready for her.

She heard his heavy feet on the stairs. He took them so slow, perhaps looking out after each step. When he opened the door, his big round face looked sad.

"I'm sorry, Emile. I didn't mean to just run out like that," he said.

And it was all she could do to not run over to him and kiss his cheeks and those drooping eyes. She wouldn't let herself fly at him, though. She couldn't smoother him like she'd done before. They'd talked about giving him time to recover after the divorce. Always the divorce coming between them. Pinching Emile's happiness.

She put all her love for him in dinner. Chopping up garlic and herbs for burgers, basting the patties with oil, buttering buns and then toasting them. She sliced potatoes for homemade chips and shook garlic, paprika, and cumin over them. They drank cold Leine's on the crammed-in little deck. The bottles growing in the center of the table.

She was telling Jed about Etzel's life in Germany. How he milked only five cows as a kid. Couldn't afford more. When she looked up at Jed's face, she could tell he wasn't really listening to her, focusing on something else beyond her.

She just knew the sadness wasn't from her. She knew she could irritate Jed and he'd sigh. She knew she never made him sad. The Leine's made her forget she was supposed to give him more time.

"Spit it out," she said finally.

He sipped more. Looked out past the Creamery into the surrounding fields. Set his empty bottle down.

He'd seen his ex-wife, he said, which wasn't surprising since she lived right outside town with another man. It bunched Emile's undies that he was still so affected by her.

She almost told him to stop his telling. The ex was pregnant, he said, his great head down.

She almost kissed him then, yelling huzzah the old witch is dead. No way now for those two to rekindle their flame. But his mouth looked ready to break from his face. Never had she seen a sober man so sad (Lord take all the drunken ones sobbing into their beer foam). Quietly she swore to herself she wouldn't get pregnant for years until he let that woman go for good.

She went to him and pulled his face to her chest, running her nails through his thick hair.

"Don't you go silent on me Jed," she said, and he nodded his face into her side, leaving drops of sweat or tears. Emile couldn't quite tell.

The Bonfire

Lupine

Her brother, Anders, threw a party for his college friends, most who'd never set foot on a farm. They wouldn't know the back end of a cow 'til it kicked. That afternoon it'd looked like an REI fair with all the colored, nylon tents. Geirolf muttered in Norwegian while he ran the second milking of the day. She couldn't tell what he'd said, but his pinched brows meant it wasn't good. But then he was always pinched these days.

Anders no longer talked much with her since his return in May. Used to be they'd feed the calves together. Catching up with his friends, she guessed.

He'd used the pile of buckthorn and sumac behind the barn for a bonfire, close to the ten-foot corn stalks, rows that stretched to the bluffs. She watched the smoke grow heavier from her second story window and guessed they were burning wood pallets. Smelled like it. No longer the fresh green but chemical in the air. She climbed down the oak beside her window to get a closer view of all the mess. The wide limbs, familiar and where she usually sat. But tonight was about escaping her room which felt warm and too small when she could hear all those voices outside.

The barn made a secretive spot. Dark forms laughed and passed bottles then laughed harder. Some pairs kissed on the square bales her brother had set out. The night was still, and the smoke stood up in the air like a mast.

Most of the kids were out of towners, though she thought she could make out the thick body of the Peterson boy. And was that Hiran? Manny? She looked for Anders but couldn't find him among all the bodies. People she thought she knew, then they turned, and it was just the look of them in the shadows that tricked her into thinking they were familiar.

Years back, she, Anders, and Henrick stacked cedar and white pine limbs they'd trimmed on their land. They used a long-handled saw to cut the lowest branches, most with needles that trembled and dropped with the first cut. Sap swelled and ran its amber path down the silver and brown trunks. Their arms were covered with it. Needles knitted in their hair. Wet wood was piled with the dry they'd collected in a huge, haphazard teepee. Anders squirted the pile with kerosene. The eruption so sudden and hot it burned off her eyebrows, eyelashes, and bangs. She'd shrieked and fell underneath Anders's weight as he smothered his own shirt into her burning face. The heft of him was such a comfort even with the heat. She didn't cry.

For months after, Anders and Henrick called her hedgehog while the hairs grew back spiky and stiff. If she could find Anders now, she'd razz him about almost setting her on fire before she turned thirteen. With the flickering light she caught him with some girl, faces locked lip on lip. Beer cans nearly sideways. She knew better to interrupt him and gazed back into the flames.

She could have stayed happy seeing the fire climb and the shadowy figures beside. Then a guy wobbled into her.

"Hey, didn't see you there," he slurred, zipping up his shorts. "Are you Anne?"

"Nope."

"Who are you then, I can't see too well now that I'm away from the fire."

Her eyes had adjusted to the dark. The moon was out. She could see the boy's chin length hair and sharp jaw. He wasn't much taller than she was, though his chest and shoulders were wide like many of the wrestlers in this area.

"Lupine," she said and stuck out her hand, feeling immediately like a little girl.

The boy grasped her palm and opened it to his mouth, touching his tongue to the middle. It reminded her of the goat kids over at Terra's place where she'd been milking mornings—an animal act. It shook her. Not enough to let go. She prided herself on being a farm girl. And this was her brother's college friend. An outsider. Anders wasn't beside her.

She wanted to see where he would lead. The possibility of danger interested her. She liked the necessary labor of feeding calves, milking goats, but it was solitary work. Without public school she felt even more alone when Anders left. This wasn't her brother. She knew this absolutely and knew he wanted something from her. For once, she wanted to be seen.

"Lupine, I like it," he said into her hand. "Hey Lupine, did you see all this corn. It's like a black hole."

"Where are you from?" she asked knowing he couldn't be from the Midwest.

"Boston, and look what I brought with me."

He pulled out a flask. Interested by his intensity and that she'd only stolen sips of warm PBR from her brother's stash, she took the warm metal. His lips were wet with the stuff. She imagined she was pressing against his mouth as she swigged. She threw her head back, and the liquor burned her throat.

"Whoa, that was a mean drink."

She coughed, "You didn't say your name."

"Gus. So Lupine, do you want to go to the fire or explore the corn?"

She could have told him she explored the corn all the time in full sun, but she felt the liquor ignite her cheeks.

The corn was something different at night. If animals used it as cover during the day, all sorts of nocturnal critters were doing the same thing at night. She'd rather not run into a coyote or badger. But the danger excited her. This night when no one seemed to know her. Instead of telling him it was a dumb idea she asked for another drink. It burned less than the first.

"I'll follow you," he said.

His heat was closer and hotter than anyone she'd known. It was hard to tell if it was the alcohol or Gus who had her heart racing. She looked for a wider row. All symmetrical except for one or two long openings. She turned back to see the fire grow and leap higher—wondered if Anders' had added wood. She smiled. Gus, thinking she smiled at him, grinned and grabbed her. He probed her mouth with his tongue. His mouth was slick and hot and tasted slightly like the flask and something muskier. It made her lose her breath. She wasn't quite sure she liked it and pushed back on his chest. He held her and grinned into her face with a doggedness she'd never seen in a man. Not that any man had ever looked at her. His spit was still on her lips. She didn't know quite how to wipe it off without him seeing. She shoved at him again and then turned into the corn, finding a slightly larger row so they could move more freely.

Leaves still flicked against her pajama pants. Webs caught her cheeks and hair. She wished she'd made him go first, irritated at herself for not speaking up. Then his hand went to her shoulders just below her neck. It traced down. She stopped. With his other hand, he squeezed her hip.

"You wanna stop here?" he asked.

She did, even though she thought it was silly to be inside such a narrow space. She would have led him to the haymow in the upper barn where the air was sweet. But she was curious now after his kiss. She stood still and let him turn her. He kissed her eyes, ears, and left wet streaks down her neck, making her legs tremble. What was she doing? She wasn't sure how to use her hands at all, laying them like blocks of wood on his shoulders as he moved down her, kissing the whole way.

She let him lift her shirt and tug down her pajama pants. She stood in her underwear and long hair while he kept kissing. Every place he didn't touch felt cold and very naked. She should be embarrassed. When she thought of other people, she felt colder, like they were turning from her one by one. But she liked the kissing: how it coiled inside her—a snake ready to strike.

When he said she was lovely, she couldn't quite believe him since the stalks blocked the moon. Still, it was a nice offering, and she allowed him to pull at her panties. He threw off his own shirt and shorts and boxers. She could only half see his skin glowing in the fractured moonlight. He wanted her hands on him. His chest. His hips. She could tell as he took her hands in his—moved them to each place. His body hot in comparison to hers.

It didn't seem odd to her since she'd witnessed so many animals breed, though there was hardly such preparation.

Really, she never followed the squeamishness of her mother, Gin, who'd seemed frightened of tampons and Lupine's bleeding.

It was awkward in that small space. He tried lifting her to his hips. But he felt like sandpaper, though he seemed satiny in her hand. The leaves and stalks were knives against their skin. He wanted her to turn around and kneel, but she wouldn't. That was too far. She wouldn't have her first time without someone's face beside hers, and she liked the kissing. The pushing she could do without except for that coil in her belly.

Kissing her mouth, he stood her back on the uneven dirt and she felt relief to have her bare feet in the soil even though it was cold. Her head spun from the drinking. Or him. She wasn't sure. He took her hand and pressed it back on him, pulling her hand back and forth until she understood what he wanted her to do. She felt detached from her body and his then. The darkness helped her and so did the thought of the bonfire that her brother had made.

As Gus helped her dress, she hid her face behind her hair even though she knew he couldn't really see. He put his mouth to her hair-covered ear and said, "Thank you. You're beautiful," which made her feel both pleasure and the need to cry.

They tripped their way to the fire. She laughed as he fed her more alcohol. It helped her with any tinge of shame. They toppled over one another on the hay bales. His arm slung across her shoulders, hand squeezing a breast.

The fire lit up Anders's face across the way. She shrugged Gus's hand off. With her fingers she combed her hair over her face, hiding from Anders. But he'd already seen them.

He was beside her fast. Even with the firelight his face looked dark. She knew she was in trouble.

"Shit, Lupine. You're supposed to be in bed."

"Hey man," mumbled Gus and pulled her onto his lap.

"Fuck you, Gus. This is my kid sister."

Anders hauled Lupine to her feet. Up to the house he dragged her.

"Hey, I can walk," she said. But he didn't respond. Maybe he didn't hear, she thought. And she said again, "Hey, let me walk, will ya?"

They were unsteady on the stairs. When he shushed her, she could smell smoke and stale alcohol on his breath. He stunk and she guessed she did too. She could feel his fingers digging into her upper arms. Still, she thought he might talk with her like he used to nights before he left for school.

Instead, he growled as he shoved her inside her room, "Stay away."

"Why?" She stood grounded in her bedroom doorway.

He tried pushing her inside again then harshly whispered, "Gin needs to have a talk with you is why. This isn't up to me."

"She doesn't talk." She wanted him to come in and sit on the old rocker. Legs hanging over one side.

"That's not my problem."

"You're the only one besides Grandpa Etzel who talked."

His face wobbled close in front of her round and glowing, "Listen, Lupine, I'm drunk. Now is not the time to have a little fuck-chat with you. I'll talk to you tomorrow."

He snuck back out to the fire, his friends, and the alcohol. She wondered what exactly she was supposed to stay away from: Her brother? Men? Drink? What really had she done wrong? The ceiling swirled in front of her. It took time to release the images of her brother and Gus.

Over the past year, she'd emailed her brother then joined Facebook just so she could see him post selfies that had nothing to do with her, farming, or family. It hurt to see his superimposed smile, arm around a stranger whose face was just as large and fuzzy from alcohol. She missed him.

Anders never did talk about the bonfire even though she waited on the straw bales beside the charred remains of pallets. The nails glowed in the afternoon sun as she waited for him to come sit beside her. She heard the calves bellow. And then watched all the colorful tents stuffed inside packs. Ander's friends, all strangers to her, packing up their cars. A parade of out-of-state license plates. Maybe she saw Gus climbing into a Volvo with another girl, Lupine wasn't sure and anyway he wasn't looking for her. She sat and watched the corn bend and sway. The cows tromped back inside for evening milking. And Anders never came for her.

Terra's Half-Dream

Simon's arms were bronzed, exposed to the elbow. His plaid shirt rolled up, which caught Terra. The provocation of sinewy forearms and fine fingers. The work they could do. He was onstage speaking about something. Even at the time, she hardly grasped a word. Maybe it was permaculture, wool versus cotton, or geothermal. It really didn't matter. He seemed different from those strutting young men, full of their chests and words. It was like comparing a rooster to a ram. She thought about unbuttoning Simon's shirt throughout his talk. She never did catch the theme. She was young then. She found him afterward with goading from her friend.

When she sidled up to him among his cluster of middle-somethings, she felt pleased with her tight, soft jeans, long wild hair, lithe frame from hauling wood for the kiln. She thought she knew hard work. She'd chopped kindling, formed clay slabs. She knew she was striking and young. She couldn't remember what she said.

He looked at her with clear eyes, mulled her statement, and replied as though he'd weighed every word. This was before she knew he was like this with everyone. Offering his whole self. Inside she'd melted. Everything she'd wanted in life changed to him. He was Paul Bunyan. That kind of big. He took up the air when he entered a room.

"You're not a farmer, I take it," he'd said.

"Me? Nope, I'm a ceramic artist."

"Ah sure, the hands. I see it now."

And he'd taken her hands in his own callused ones. To look at the creases? She wasn't sure. It wasn't supposed to be sexual. Yet the flare went through her shoulders and followed down into her belly. She felt the fire in her hair, believing it stood on end. Admiring him, she imagined biting his lower lip right at the freckle.

The rooster startled her out of her half-sleep. Mr. Punches pulling in the sun. She flipped over to rest her thigh on his chest. He wasn't there. Simon would never be there again. She'd dreamed him again. Found herself in the lie that he was still alive. This memory-dream trick was one of the worst discoveries since Simon's death. She hated the errors of a half-asleep brain. If she could, she'd have gone back to sleep. Dream of rainbows and ice cream and pony shit. What a kick in the gut. Like reliving those first moments after his death. The feeling he was absolutely gone, she was alone.

She had to get out of their room. Out of their house. She ran through the yard barefoot, in dirty pajamas. The air thick with fog, the grass thick with dew. Warm days and summer-warmed soil coupled with cool nights, and caused a dreamscape. Maybe everything was a joke, maybe her waking life wasn't true and her dream-life true. Simon and she just met. She could do it all over. This time with slight changes. If she could just feel his hands on hers…. She sank into the old hammock hung between two straight walnuts. The trees edged all plants out with their long drooping limbs. The hammock was soaked, but Terra couldn't care. She felt desperate to sleep. The sheep *baa*'d in some corner, but she couldn't hold her lids open.

When she woke next, the dream webs stuck behind her eyes weren't of Simon. They were of black. Nothing. A long thin girl emerged from the fog like some spirit. The Olsen girl, Terra remembered.

The girl approached Terra, "Hey, sounds like the goats need milking." She set down a bucket of grain and indicated uphill to the calling does, "Figured I'd milk through the summer. Don't know when you want them dried off."

Terra said nothing she only nodded. She shut her eyes. Just too tired. The girl kept standing nearby, Terra could feel her eyes on her. If Lupine said she was sorry for her loss, Terra didn't know if she could hold herself together if she heard that again. She wanted all people to go.

Until she heard the girl rattle up the hill with her grain bucket, she kept her eyes closed. Lupine was milking Terra and Simon's goats. Terra didn't know what happened to the milk. She could pour them over those damn Icelandic sweater ashes and mold them into a little bone man for all Terra cared. If she saw Simon's doe, Surly, she knew she might puke. She got a small thrill about thinking that Surly might kick Lupine or anybody that wasn't Simon. Anyone else who dared touch her.

She knew she needed the girl and felt ashamed. Terra had watched or heard her ride in every morning on the four-wheeler. She wondered if Geirolf was cutting her hay, or maybe it was Jason, maybe Paul, the men Simon used to chat up at the bar. Whoever it was she was glad they didn't bother to ask. Just did it because it needed doing. And she was tired to the bone.

Sometimes when that long girl methodically carried up grain buckets and hay Terra thought she might be able to work again. As though the girl were pulling her from bed by taking over her chores. Someday when she could think again, she'd be embarrassed.

The warm morning smell of fresh milk. The ring of first milk inside the steel bucket. Thinking about milk made her stomach lurch. All food made her sick, especially anything Simon used to cook or eat. Terra inhabited somewhere out of time. Out of space until she was physically pulled out by her sisters. Lupine long gone.

"Come on, girly. Time to get up."

They both lifted her body from the damp netting. She'd forgotten they were coming. Not a thing was marked on her calendar. Nothing ever would be.

"Come on sweetheart, let's get you in a hot bath."

"You run the water. I'll start some tea," Freja directed.

Terra had nothing to add. She couldn't talk about her day, the past weeks, or how she felt. They already knew anyway. She was obvious as the fog. She felt she was the fog, wrapping its silvery tongue around the black tree branches. Spitting flecks of wet into the wind.

"When was your last bath, baby?"

"Oh…I couldn't…say."

And Freja began to cry when Terra was the one dry and broken.

"Terra, it hurts to see you like this. You have to still live, honey. I really think you should live with me or…, or even Mom. Even if she's a creeping Charlie."

The reference to their pet name for their mother made Terra smile, inching her back into her former life where naming her mother after an invasive weed was normal.

"I can't leave," said Terra.

She truly couldn't. Simon would be utterly lost to her. On Goat's Back Ridge Farm, she could imagine his feet in those torn high tops. She could picture that thick, speckled hair topping over a doe's spine as he milked. Simon was still here. Though it hurt her, she had to be here too.

55

FALL

Harvest Moon

Jason Harvesting

The fleet of Case tractors worked the Clayfields' hills, cutting corn and soybeans. Row after row of golden brown. Jason loved this time of year, the necessity of the plants. You had to work between the rains. The tractor's revealing lights changed night into a purplish haze of harvest. He'd helped with Goat's Back Ridge earlier even though the corn was small and hardly worth the time. Figured it'd make fall more bearable for Terra. It sure seemed lonely up there on her little hill.

He turned the massive machine into another row. When he'd been up for days without more than four hours sleep, he thought of nothing more than woven fields. There were moments when he dreamed other things for himself like diving deep into the oceans, studying coral and the swimming creatures. The push and thresh of the combine reminded him of water and the white noise of thrashing waves, although he'd never really imagined he'd be anything other than a farmer. He worked and loved the land and the Midwestern people who inhabited the land (when he had time for them). If he'd wanted, he could have explored deep sea diving. Lord knows he'd worked and worked and gained. At first the gaining had surprised him, not the labor of course. He'd toiled since his memory became memory, and maybe even before. He had nothing but dirty, hard work to define himself. And a pole shed parked with millions. At forty-one, he didn't want to redefine himself. He had gotten past his father's face.

This season was different. His cell phone was in his shirt pocket, clicked to high volume. The call couldn't be missed. Lani made him promise he'd pick up before he'd left the house this morning.

The storage tank was full of grain. Pulling beside a cab and trailer mid-field, Jason positioned the auger over the truck bed. Corn rained down. The young guy in the other cab jumped free and watched the storm of falling corn. Jason joined him.

"Hey man," the fellow said scanning the field and open sky, "Good day to be out." He took a can of chew from his jacket pocket, flicked open the tin and inserted a white packet inside his cheek. He offered one to Jason.

Jason shook his head and adjusted his hat. "Yup, perfect day." He pulled off his gloves, thwacked them against dusty Carhartt pants. Grime lined the cracks in his hands and wrists.

"Wanna grab a beer later at the Junction Bar? Coupla dudes are going after dark. Think Emile's working too. She always gives ya one on the house."

"Nah, thanks man. My old lady's gonna have a baby any day now." He slid the gloves back on. Corn kept raining, a low sound now that the metal bottom was covered.

"Gotta be a sober driver for that one," the guy laughed.

"Don't I know it. Don't wanna wreck my life for one night out."

The sky was brilliant. Jason loved this time of year when a clear day came round. He was out in it all day. Most of the night.

"Well sometime you oughta join us at the Junk' Bar. There's this dude who comes in. Crazy, interesting dude."

"Yeah?"

Jason noticed this guy had dirt caught around his mouth and eyes, in the wrinkles. Still looked young.

"Pretty average Joe type. Don't know that I ever caught his name. Anyway, he flies an ultra-light every day after work. And the man has some wild stories."

"Huh. I think I've heard of the guy. What's his name… Jerry something…" Jason leaned against the boxy, red frame of his combine. Letting this guy take his mind away from Lani.

"Yeah, yeah that's it, Jerry Achteburg. So, he can bring like one person with him, and I know a dude who went up and shot a 12-point buck with a .22 magnum one week out of season."

"What'd they do to track it then?"

"Well, this dude was ready for hunting and had a GPS app on his phone. After their crazy ride tracking the deer, they marked where it lay and drove four-wheelers in around midnight. Dude said he brought the meat to the food shelf. Kept the mount."

"I 'spose."

Jason didn't hunt much. Hunting season's right around his busiest time. Deer season came and he was too tired to sit on his ass in a hunting blind.

"Sounded like a crazy flight and ride in. I guess that Jerry dude always carries a hip flask on him. Don't know if I've ever seen him sober."

"Huh. Not sure I'd want to be up forty, fifty feet with a drunk, flying."

"Jerry's wild, but he's a good pilot, so this dude says. Anyway, you should come to the Junk' Bar. It's quite the place." He smiled with his straight teeth moving the chunk of chaw.

Kid couldn't be more than twenty-two, Jason thought.

"Yeah, I've been there a few times over the years. Jason didn't want to embarrass the kid who was figuring out how to become a man by spending most of his wages on beer. Listening to old drunks.

"Well," the kid said. "Looks like I got a full load, so best get on the road."

"Don't think I caught your name," Jason pushed off his rig, grabbed the kid's tan hand.

"Danny, man."

"Good shootin' the shit with ya, Danny. My name's—"

"Yup, already know who you are."

"Sure, sure.

"Good luck with the new one if I don't see ya before."

Jason probably had talked with the guy. Afterall, Jason was his boss. There were so many trucks and tractors rumbling between fields. Jason couldn't remember all the guys he hired for the season especially when all he saw were hat-covered faces through cab windows.

He climbed back inside the cab, checked his phone for missed calls and dove the combine head back inside twelve rows of corn. The strange pilot interested him. He'd been nearly dry these past nine months alongside Lani. He liked the idea of flying over all the fields he'd planted and managed. A change of perspective might just be the thing. Though a pilot with a hip-flask was a risk. He liked the idea of seeing stalks from a higher point rather than looking at them inside out.

The kid had freedom to fly outta this place after work. He felt for his phone again. What a crazy time to have a baby. Harvest-time. One of his busiest seasons. Now, winter would have been a good time to den-in.

When Lani told him the potential due date, he'd stopped. As though she'd planned the pregnancy to stop his work. He knew it was a crazy thought. He'd rubbed her back and felt nothing, no cracking open of his heart, no joy, just annoyance. He knew it wrong and selfish. Couldn't stop himself. How in the hell could this happen again?

In the cab, he spun up the volume of Tool and then back down to low again. He had to catch the phone call if it came. He smacked his cheeks with his hand like it was sleep that nagged him. Maybe he should use chew just to keep him up. He tried to think about girls, about fishing for muskie, which he hadn't had time to catch in years. He thought about cracking a cold can of PBR after work, but took a swig of warm, gas station coffee.

"Jason, man this is going to be a shit ball kinda day," he laughed at himself, caught in his past.

When Lani'd been pregnant with their first, he used to come back from spraying fields with ammonia or Round Up and strip in their mudroom. The clothes that he'd wear the next morning stinking and dead on the floor. A hot shower and then he was in bed with her where he'd slip his hands over her tight belly. She'd taken to sniffing his fingers, checking that no residual chemicals were there even though he wore rubber gloves and had always taken care. He couldn't get irritated with her because he thought her worry showed she'd be a good mother. And then her skin was silky like she'd misted herself. He'd rub Nathan, figuring out his head, his feet, his small spine.

The first time Nathan kicked him, Jason jumped. Lani laughed at him. Her belly moved with her laughter, a taut drum. He'd called Nathan their Karate Kid. Later Nathan flipped and she became a watermelon.

It'd been his idea to grab dinner at the Junction Bar. He'd wanted to drink. They both knew it. The beer chilled and perfect for his hot palms. He'd worked all day in the sun. The sun soaked inside the black pavement and the humidity waved off it. His hot throat needed soothing, and he'd clicked his dry tongue in a joke to convince her. It was a time when she laughed regularly.

It was late and still light. The longest day not that far behind them. They sat out at the picnic tables eating cheeseburgers and fried curds. A pitcher of Miller. A pitcher of water. Emile walked up all curve and sass to take over the night shift.

"Is that tap water?" she'd asked pointing at Lani's glass that she'd steadily been emptying.

"I'd assume," snapped Lani.

He knew Lani and Emile had been best friends in high school, but some past infraction came between them. Over what, he couldn't say, maybe it some rift between their families. These fallouts happened. Were they second cousins? He couldn't remember. He wouldn't ask Lani why she didn't hang out with Emile anymore.

"You shouldn't be drinking that," Emile said.

Jason wished she'd just shut her mouth. Just leave them be. The sun setting in Lani's hair, her eyes wider, deeper with the pregnancy. Something he could swim in.

"What? Why not?" asked Lani.

"This water's full of nitrates. You gotta have bottled here."

Then Emile opened the thick door, hauled out the young bartender. Bitched her out in front of them and had her bring out a bottled water. Jason dumped the pitcher on the ground where it soaked into the grass. Lani set down her burger, her face pinched and white like all she could see was Nathan dissolving inside her.

"It's just a little water," he'd said. "I'm sure the baby isn't hurt."

She refused to say anything or eat, staring beyond him into the trash trees that hid the river from view.

"How many farmers' wives had babies here before they knew about run-off, before nitrates?" he'd said.

Now driving the combine, he knew Lani blamed herself. She felt she should have known. She'd prided herself on reading all the baby books, eating kale and spinach. And he felt responsible too. It was highly unlikely the water killed Nathan. Still. Still, he couldn't drive past the Junction Bar without cringing.

This time round he'd be better. He wouldn't leave the room. He'd hold her hand all the way through if she wanted. Massage her shoulders. Her feet. He'd ask her to marry him. He'd be a better version of himself. Maybe he wouldn't work as hard. Take a day off sometimes. Hold the baby. Rock the baby. He checked his phone for messages just in case she'd messaged him. Lani moved slower like last time, but she cried all the time too, which scared him.

More hours put in this season since he may have to quit soon. He turned up the music again and felt for the phone, terrified she might call. He didn't want to be responsible for her breakage.

Rotation after rotation of corn folded beneath him. The dust covering the cab. His nose ran. He snuffled through autumn. Leftover prickle of corn. Breathing part of his country, this land. Even in its irritation, he enjoyed the invasion of the crops he'd planted, kept, mowed down. If the land wasn't his—never completely owned by a person—he still felt it inside him. He knew the land better than most. His acreage grew every year. It's what he knew. What he'd always known.

He turned again into another twelve rows, leaving ruin behind. The front of the combine looked like a prehistoric, horned creature diving inside the corn. The bugs and chaff flying off its great back.

Etzel Dreaming

He was in the north woods again as a young man, his body strong and unbowed by time.

Standing up to his knees in cold water, he snagged a stench. Musk like he couldn't believe. He thought it was a black bear come to steal his catch. Got him nervous. He froze mid-stream. "Aber was sonst? As if that's gonna help," he thought.

A flag of color. He saw it was a man. He tensed for a fight. He hadn't seen anyone in days.

"What you catchin?" the stranger asked.

"Think I got a brown on. Little guy."

The stranger watched Etzel reel in a cigar-sized brown. Etzel wet his hand, cupped the fish, and pulled the hook free before releasing it. He felt the stranger eying him, aware of the slick stones underfoot.

"You fish?" Etzel asked.

"Nah, out hunting bear with a couple friends. Gotta get 'em when they in full winter fat, . He pressed one dense finger against a nostril and blew. Then attended the other. Etzel broke a worm in half, threaded it onto the hook then cast.

"You ever hunt bear?" the stranger asked.

"Nope," said Etzel.

"Got a gun on you?"

Etzel stopped jigging and stared where the line slit stream. His toes and shins numb. His brain felt cold too.

"Grandpa. Grandpa Etzel," Lupine was knocking lightly on his door. He was in a fat chair facing the window. The corn tossed in the wind. It got him to wake up like this, his youth behind his eyelids. It had been as present as those small capillaries. As he came back to his old body, he realized his life had already been lived. The only thing that gave him hope was Lupine. Her brightness. Her loudness was so much of what he thought connected them. She was more of a daughter to him than silent Gin. Lupine was his all.

"Lou, Lou. My dearest Lou, I'll skip for you before the cows come home," he bobbed his gray head and made like he'd dance if his legs were stronger.

"No need to get up, Grandpa. Just thought I'd get my dose of Etzel stories for the day."

"*Ach du lieber*," he grabbed his heart. "You want a story from this old man? How about a Deutsch song instead?"

She looked at him and he knew he should dig down into the threads of his previous life, but he didn't know if he could. Things got so tangled and turned around: was it he or his *kleiner bruder* that kept all those eggs piled in the cast iron tub for a joke? Did his *mutti* or *vater* crack an egg over coffee grounds for morning coffee? It must have been his *mutti*, for he could only vaguely see his *vater* now if he tried, he'd died so long before. And then as he explored such questions it became nearly impossible to come back to this room in his daughter's house, his granddaughter looking at him with those round eyes of hers.

Lupine sat opposite him still waiting for his story and he explained how one could catch a big fish out of a little stream. Mama fish gleaming with belly fat that one must throw back to populate. He told her how to guide the hook from the mother's jaw. Brookies, the loveliest and tastiest—hardest to return. He called himself a long-term fisherman. He felt the luck come back to him one brilliant scale at a time as thought he might return to the riverbanks with Lupine next spring.

How to Leave a City

Helen

She should screw Evan's old man. Give up the son. It might mean a farm. The old man would leave his wife. Those oldsters always did. He would write in Helen as his wife walked out. Then she wouldn't be in this concrete purgatory pulling a Sisyphus with a wannabe artist, puking four different types of crackers into a friend's puce-colored pot. The color was enough of a kick. Thankfully the *friend* was already folding jeans and shirts at Gap. She at least could puke and rage in peace. She imagined what she'd say to Evan as she released more bile, "You know that flu I've had for a week? Ta da, the bug is yours."

In hindsight, the IUD woulda been the way to go. It'd seemed overpriced at the time. Look what all that organic well-being got her. She'd even been charting her cycles. A blue plus sign complicated things. This was a place she'd never been before. She pulled herself from the lip of the toilet and scrubbed her teeth before bending and dry heaving.

"How's about you and me ditch the gallery and cut out a patch of your daddy's land with a bun cooking? Let's start that CSA in the middle of nowhere when all we've done the last five months is tango," that would go down like a shot of Prairie Vodka. Theirs hadn't really been much of a talking relationship. She realized now she'd really only liked him when he talked about the farm. When he was telling those pastoral childhood stories after sex and a few shots. She'd never met anyone who grew up on a dairy. Who actually milked for a living?

"Worst hangover ever," she joked to her blotchy face in the mirror, ready as she'd ever be for her day. She tried to line her eyes, which made them look worse. Haggard like she'd never been before. And she guessed this might be her new life. How in the hell could she make this work? She didn't even have her own bed.

With her empty belly, she needed breakfast. She propped open the fridge with her foot and stared at the six pack of Miller, mustard, and leaking meat, trying to make something edible appear. The cupboards no better.

She threw on her jacket already bracing for the wind that barreled through the buildings, something about being by Lake Michigan. Cold as hell mid-winter; hotter than hell mid-July. If she could just get to Evan's daddy, lick her lips a little after some over-the-table chat. Unbutton his shirt a little in his cornfield. That old Wisconsin farmer probably had a beer and cheese belly. She was down with that. Knew she could do it to get outta this windy city.

Hoofing it several blocks from the apartment to the closest store, she turned inside a little local co-op. She'd always wondered about the religiousness of it; wondered if she could make a go with green things. It had a long aisle of various crackers and sea salted chips: rice crackers, almond, teriyaki…. She needed buttery, warm creations for morning, crisp, sea salted gluten-free for lunch and grahams with a touch of honey that could carry her through a night of hurried tables.

The co-op smelled green—a place she'd come for a spring fix when there was only snow upon snow upon concrete.

After grabbing three boxes of crackers, she trolled the meat section with all the grass-fed, hog-happy meats. She threw in sausages, hot dogs, summer sausage. Her mind with all those big-hearted piggies but salivating all the same. With one swoop of childbearing hunger, she lost a week's worth of tips and her vegetarianism.

"Are you a member-owner?" asked the cashier whose hand painted tag read Nia.

"Nope. Helen was wishing she'd gone to Whole Foods where they weren't so nosey, pretending to be hometown, homespun, and farm cooked when it took hours of bumper-to-bumper traffic to see a strip of green longer than a torso.

"We're part of the Co-op nation and take 10% off a number of items to show how much we love our member-owners. If you're a member of any of the surrounding co-ops like Green World, The Root…"

"Nope," Helen threw the dogs, meats, and crackers on the conveyer belt.

"Did you get a chance to check out our fresh produce today? We have several local farms who provide heirloom…."

"Nope."

"Kale is a great way to give your little peanut the necessary amounts of vitamin K."

"The fuck you say?"

"I just noticed you're planning on eating some nitrates here," she flicked her braceleted wrists at the pork. "I thought you may want to ingest some leafy greens along with all this sodium. Nitrates aren't good for wee ones."

Helen stuck out her pierced tongue while her insides quaked, threatening to break. The pile of bright cracker boxes and sausages reminded her of those stupid Christmas cards her mother still sent, too colorful. The big-eyed cashier smiled at her with her tongue out. Made her feel dumb, and she wished she could get a drink. She just wanted her hands in the dirt. Then everything would be better. She walked out to the busy sidewalk.

Down the street at a hole-in-the-wall market were shelves of Cheetos and Funyuns. The guy looked like someone who might offer you a cigarette in the eye which was exactly the type of guy she needed today, or she might just cry.

Once outside the cracked market door, she was ready to nail Evan. She'd walk inside his carefully carved metrosexual life and nail his cock inside one of those elaborate gold frames, Renaissance-style. Farm daddy on the back burner.

Cursing and chomping on chips, she took the L to Merchandise Mart near dozens of galleries. The empty train car had been used after a night of too many rum and cokes. She smelled the flavor in the poorly mopped piss and puke. Another reason to leave. The concrete killed her. All she wanted was some soft green to lay her eyes. There was no reason to stay in Chicago. Except it's what she knew. Knowing could be as comfortable as a pasture.

Instinctively, she reached for her abdomen. She didn't love it, but it was hers. She didn't love its father, just the possibility of him. She hated him just the same for giving up his inheritance of land. For a whiff of fresh soil each morning, she'd lay that old man right over his John Deere tractor.

At her stop, the street air wasn't much better. Twelve-foot windows were too large to kick in. Not that she was crazy enough to really smash a window.

Now that she was here in front of Evan's gallery, she realized she didn't know what she wanted: alimony, partnership, or half the cash for an abortion. She knew he wouldn't take her back to his family farm.

She stopped in front, her hand on the knob. But she knew she wanted to freak out Evan's boss. Let Queen Gerard drain as white as his skinny jeans he'd worn the night she'd humiliated herself in front of all the snorting, white collared artists. So, she'd bottomed her plastic wine glass too many times at an opening. She bet the artists were snorting cocaine off one another's foreheads. Flippin' Renaissance, rich kids. Evan ate it up as much as she stuffed her dreams with seed saving and chicken-crap-compost, making that grass on the other side of the ethereal fence emerald.

Emboldened she opened the heavy glass door. A blonde with thick black frames, asymmetrical bob, and layers of black material looked her way. It was like the beauty pageant turned inside out. The blonde didn't ask if she could help. Grimly she walked toward Helen. Then smiled. It was as obvious as bad hair that Helen wasn't there to buy a painting.

"You suck eggs," Helen hissed as she passed.

"Excuse me?"

Helen ignored her.

"What does that even mean?"

Helen walked past enormous collages, metal sculptures, towers of white plates and teacups. She turned behind a large, half-wall.

"Hey, you can't go back there," the blonde followed her.

Helen stomped around a table with coffee pot and array of hand-thrown mugs. Inside a portioned office sat Evan at his laptop. Gerard beside him. Gerard and Evan turned, both waiting for her to say something. Gerard smiled in his smug little way, with his tight-ass pants. Her belly throttled like a ship on a tidal wave. A handful of Cheetos from the straw bag on her shoulder found their way into her hand. She mashed them into her mouth. The two men stood. Not exactly what she was thinking when she arrived. She couldn't remember what she'd been thinking before she arrived.

"What're you doing here?" Evan asked.

She chewed harder as if the salt could calm the little slug inside her. His face said he was embarrassed to see her here. She'd invaded a space where she didn't belong.

"Hey," several processed orange bits flew out of her mouth.

She was going to be sick. She had to make it back out to the street. The blonde followed, comforting or pushing her out, Helen wasn't sure. She couldn't make it through the grand door before blowing chunks across the mosaic entry.

"Gerard's god-awful pants made me sick," she coughed before pushing out onto the street.

The only sweet thing was the shape of the blonde's full lips as she left. No profanity could produce that look. Helen was liking her little alien even if she didn't know where to go next.

Lupine's Change

At sixteen, her body was in flux. Flesh mounded in one place, flattened in another. Sometimes a swollen nub in a tit or a peeked ache in her belly. And then the flick of acne on her cheek bones, hard, red freckles. Dreams ransacked her bed. She had to unwind sheets from calves, pick up pillows from the floor. Hair given another life, like Medusa. When she brushed, she armed the counter with detanglers, dry conditioners, big picks.

As a small child, she woke crying from pain in her lengthening body. Anders used to rub her knees, ankles, and elbows. The growing had scared her. She dreamed of Norwegian trolls from her father's stories pulling her apart like string cheese.

She checked her underwear daily for the second month in a row. No period. She realized something grew inside her. The toilet yawned like a great mouth that could suck her down to the septic, dirty parts first. Gin's part-time Catholicism had her whispering Hail Mary's as she counted back to her last menstruation.

"This isn't good," she thought, "I'm on the pot, saying Mary's name for my sin." She wondered if it was another sin to be half naked revering Mary above.

Minutes later as she brushed her teeth, she mumbled to herself, "Here I am brushing my teeth, pregnant."

Throughout the day she said, "I'm feeding calves, pregnant. I'm riding a skid steer, pregnant." It made her laugh so much that Hiran, Luke, Manny, and Mathias all asked "what's so funny?" She thought to herself, "I'm talking to Hiran, Luke, Manny, and Mathias while pregnant," though she said, "Nothing."

The DNA was already mapped. The fetus perhaps the size of a grub. She imagined it curved into itself like the June bug larvae she found last spring while planting carrots. Thoughts of this made the pregnancy a restoration. It was from a warmer time. It was a beginning. She liked comparing the fertility of her womb to soil when frost covered the gardens. Scarlet nantes carrots, sultan's crescent beans, rattlesnake snap, forellenschluss lettuces, all on catalogues she hoarded beneath her bed. She pictured her baby on a cascading bean vine, stretching its limbs out from the small center. She wouldn't tell Gin yet. She'd keep it hers for a little while longer.

The next week she loved it. She hugged it all day. She said to herself, "This is craziness," and tried to talk herself into telling someone. But then the conversation would go with Gin quickly saying:

"Well, that's gonna cost you."

"Yup, I know. It was an accident," and immediately regret it.

"What are you going to do?"

"Keep it?" she'd say with an extended question mark.

"Not here."

And that would be that.

Saturday, she felt sick—lay in bed all day. Sunday morning, she missed church. By afternoon, her abdomen was tight and ached. She woke from a nap dreaming of an ocean. Her legs covered with blood.

In the bathroom, she threw her soaked panties and pajama bottoms in the trash. The hot shower soothed her. Blood on the washcloth. She pressed it to her vagina to seal a wound that couldn't be stopped.

She toweled off. A rip inside. She sat on the toilet. Blood and new-made flesh. "So easily made," she thought and didn't know who to tell.

As easily as the new cells proliferated her womb, they left it.

WINTER

Cold Moon

Helen Leaving

She stuffed her T-shirts in the corner of the duffle, making room for her sleeping bag and pillow. Everything ragged and second hand. She felt calm and clean leaving the square foot life. Her note giving little away other than a quick bye and good riddance. She was sure only her money would be missed, but it'd been hard living in a one bedroom with her co-worker, especially now.

Hairbrush, toothbrush, soap—all stuffed in a plastic bag and shoved into the duffle.

She wasn't coming back and the only lurch in her belly was the baby and Evan's reaction. He'd asked her if she was sure it was his, and then acted as if it were all her fault. She was prepared for this and not prepared for this. She'd thought maybe he was different, not as hard as the rest of Chicago. He'd grown up on a dairy in the middle of nowhere.

She grabbed a small handful of jewelry and a fat envelope of pictures from a drawer in the kitchen where her co-worker had let her keep some of her minimal things. In the cupboards were her stash of crackers, and she took out a handful before adding the boxes to her bag.

She wasn't going to bend Evan's dad over a tractor; that was on her crazy day she knew. Hell, she felt too sick for that kind of fun. She never wanted to see a penis again, really, for the good it'd done her. She'd become necessary to his family, and then spring the baby on them. Evan had talked her ear off about his dad asking him to help him with the harvest. "Evan had artistic talent. Evan was going places." Fuck Evan. He was going places? Helen would too!

She'd memorized Evan's address but looked at the envelope again. Evan had all his mother's cards taped to his concrete walls. Artwork from renowned artists. In a way, it was both charming and adolescent that his mother wrote to him and he not only kept the cards, but displayed them. It gave Helen hope.

Heaving the bag over her shoulder, she simultaneously shoved a stocking cap low on her head. If she was going to keep it together, she had to get outta this city.

Unable to keep her bag with her on the bus, she'd pulled out the envelope of photographs and tucked Evan's address inside. Forehead on the window glass, she hoped to dissuade talkers. It didn't stop a small woman who slid in beside her from asking where she was headed.

"A family farm," she said pretending like it was her own that she'd worked on as a kid. One of those fresh-faced teens who knew how to labor.

"Where abouts?"

The woman wanted to place Helen, make connections between her own family farm and Helen's imagined one.

"Where I grew up it was rural, rural," the woman was saying. "Not at all like Chicago," she turned to inspect Helen, "I was visiting my granddaughter and her new husband. He's Somali. Just imagine his stories, right?!"

She put her hand on Helen's arm, trying to engage her but Helen leaned closer to the window, fearful of the intimacy a stranger was presenting. She hoped her gut would settle.

She looked out at all the cars inching beside them. No horizon to be seen.

Helen imagined being born into Evan's life and the painted simplicity of it: a Grant Wood in her mind. She pretended her mother was a singing teacher who wrote letters, that her father was a quiet farmer who gave up writing. Evan always mentioned how he would never tie himself to the farm, like it was a noose that tied his father to farming and not an umbilical cord.

Helen pushed her cheek to the window. The woman kept talking as Helen watched the traffic pick up speed. She remembered her foster mother writing her postcards after she left, and now she realized she wasn't supposed to get them. She'd been sure the woman had stopped because another child had come that she'd loved more than Helen, but it must have been the social worker who knew it wasn't ethical. You couldn't keep up such connections. It soothed her a little, remembering, and she could feel her anger at Evan drain.

Somewhere before Eau Claire, Helen woke to the prattling woman beside her. It was dark outside. Helen couldn't possibly see anything, but she felt it: openness. She gathered the woman was talking about some kind of communal farm to live, she called the Poor Farm. It perked Helen's interest and in over six hours of travel, she turned from the window and spoke.

"What do you mean by Poor Farm?"

The woman didn't seem at all startled to have her hours long soliloquy finally answered. "It was a big house just out of town. I think it's a rental now," she brought her fingers to her lips to ponder it, "Folks who couldn't pay taxes or food worked the surrounding land for a room and food. Still a little cemetery out there in the woods. That place always scared the devil outta me. My father always said if I didn't work hard enough, he'd send me to the Poor House." She added, "My father wasn't a very nice man."

"Neither was mine," said Helen.

The woman waited for Helen to add more. Helen waved her hand, "I don't even know if he's dead or in the city."

The woman swiveled in her seat, "I thought you said you were visiting the family farm. I thought your dad was a dairy farmer."

"Well, no," Helen explained, "not exactly."

It was a friend of a friend she said holding her belly since she thought she might be sick again from want of food or the fact she was traveling hundreds of miles to approach strangers about work, she didn't know.

The woman studied her. Helen realized through all the wrinkles and ambling talk the woman had keen eyes. She was reading Helen, and it made Helen uncomfortable.

"Why not work for me?" she said, "You're skinny but I can see you're strong enough or could become strong. I only have one milk cow, but I sure could use help with my land now that my Lars is gone."

Helen only took a moment before saying she couldn't, though she'd love the opportunity. There was no way she'd get mixed up with granddaughters or others who might push her out. With Evan's folks, she might have a legitimate place. Her plan was to become necessary first, then explain. They couldn't kick her out once she started showing. She needed to start thinking about the kid, though it scared her even when it was no bigger than her pinkie.

The Farm

Paul with Helen

Paul tinkered on the riding lawn mower—changing the oil, charging the battery. Without animals in the winter, he was either in the pole shed or browsing seed catalogues 'til Meg returned from school. Abruptly, the volume of Ted Nugent lowered. Paul swung his gaze over the hood of the mower and pushed to standing. At first, he thought the woman beside the stereo was Meg, but she was too narrow. She watched Paul strain to figure her out. He hated being caught.

"You have work for me?"

She wore Sorels and a colorful coat. She didn't belong in Paul's pole shed.

"None that I can think of." He swiped his hands across his jeans.

"I thought you were a farmer?"

First, he wondered if he was a farmer. Cows long sold. Chickens dead. Then he supposed she might rob them. But she said she didn't own a car and seemed determined to stay. There was something so sad in her face, he couldn't imagine what could have done that to a kid already. He asked her in for coffee. As they walked out to the house, he could see she hadn't lied about the car. It was like she dropped off some hippie hot air balloon. Who was this girl, and why was she really here?

He yanked off work boots, and she slid past. Again, he suspected she might steal the new flat screen but those thin legs and face. There was no way this girl would hurt them. She needed something but he was sure it wasn't stuff. She left tracks across the kitchen floor before nesting the coffee pot under the faucet. Paul dragged a damp towel across her footprints while she watched. His knees creaked as he bent and straightened.

"I used to drink rum in my coffee." She watched his face.

"Every morning?"

He sat down at the little linoleum-topped table. Let her wait on him then.

"Yup. Finally, my first hour teacher caught on, so my family sent me into foster care."

"How old are you?"

She poured water into the coffee maker and opened cupboards.

"Twenty-two. Carpenter by trade, but I've gotten into Ag. I waitress to make the big money," she laughed and it tasted bitter.

He got up to help her. Opened the can of Folgers and spooned grounds into a filter.

"Oh, I was hoping you had whole bean. I suppose you have cream, though."

"Yup," he replied guiltily, not realizing why he felt sorry to disappoint this girl. He pulled the creamer out of the fridge while she continued to move around his kitchen. She took out two mugs that his son Evan had thrown, flipped them over, traced his name in the clay, and gripped both in either hand.

"Nice handles."

She smiled and her nose ring and teeth glinted. They sat across from one another.

The girl, Helen, painted pictures in spilled coffee on the tabletop. He warmed his aching hands with his mug and wondered again what she was here for even though she kept talking about farming, about CSAs, about small farms, how city kids had lost touch with the soil.

They heard the back door shut and someone struggle out of her boots.

"What a strange time for coffee," Meg said.

He took that she meant the situation was strange: an old farmer sitting across from a strange girl. Meg hovered in the entry.

"Would you like a cup?" Helen leapt up as if this were her home, as if the coffee were hers to share.

"Helen, meet my wife, Megan."

Meg smiled tightly, "Why yes, Helen, I'll take a cup, and why are you here?"

"I'm helping Paul," Helen removed a cup and filled it with coffee and cream, not even asking how Meg took it.

"Oh," Meg gave him a glacial glance. "How did you hear of us?"

Helen handed Meg the full mug, sat, took a gulp of coffee. She swallowed, grinned then replied, "I followed the signs."

He wasn't keen on her inside joke and looked away when Helen tried to find his eyes. But after an hour of talk, Meg asked if Helen liked cookie bars.

"Bars?" Helen asked.

"Sure, you gotta try my peanut butter and chocolate chip bars. You'll love 'em; soft in the middle, crunchy around the edges. Meg began pulling out measuring spoons, ingredients.

Helen jumped up to help her, and Meg began doling out cooking tips. She was ever the teacher, Paul thought.

He sipped another cup of coffee, and then edged outside again when neither woman wavered their focus from the cookie bar creation. The girl overeager in a way that made him nervous.

Helen stayed. Meg just had to invite her to dinner and overnight. He tidied Evan's old room. He heard Meg clank around the kitchen creating a meal. He lifted a framed picture off Evan's desk. All four family members stood before a field of hay bales. It was the last they worked together on the farm. Sam had been a senior while Evan was just in seventh grade. Meg wore a blue kerchief. He and the boys' white foreheads glared against red faces. He squirreled it away in his bedroom. It wasn't a picture for outsiders.

Over dinner, Meg said, "Pauly used to write poems for me when we were in undergrad," she looked at Helen and then Paul. "You should write a memoir."

"About what exactly? he asked.

"Use your imagination."

Meg looked over to Helen like she was on her team. Helen chewed. Soon Meg was singing one of her school songs then teaching Helen the lyrics. She was talking like she never did with just Paul. He supposed she was happy for the diversion from this winter.

Once upstairs, Meg rubbed cream into her neck. He listened to Helen pace in the guestroom. Helen fiddled with objects on the shelves. It unsettled him. He was happy to have removed the family picture.

Bathing the Baby

Jason

The baby kicked around in its miniature tub. To Jason, it seemed his infant son had just come awake. He'd become a thinking, aware being. When the baby kicked, it knew it kicked. He was finally aware those milk-thickened legs were his own. The baby didn't startle himself anymore. His eyes too were changing. The dark blue that seemed to bleed into its surrounding white had shifted in dimension like the iris was drawing the color back into itself to better see this world. Now, Baby Ned looked at Jason, and Jason thought he recognized him as his father. Well, maybe not father, but the other tall being in Ned's life. The baby wasn't just focused on the contrast between Jason's pure-white forehead and black hair, or so Lani had joked. He had the urge to hike up his nonexistent hat, but his hands were full of splashing baby.

He cupped one hand beneath Ned's head to keep him above the water, trying not to let the small fish of his son slip away as he slathered him in soap.

"Oh wow," Lani said as she walked into their kitchen, "that's a lot of soap for a little guy."

Bubbles leaked out over the edge. The baby kicked and watched Jason's face. A puddle appeared on the kitchen floor where the tub sat. She pushed bath towels beneath to sop up the water.

"He's a slippery guy. Aren't ya, Ned?"

Jason liked talking to the baby now that he gurgled at him like he was taking part in the conversation.

"Here, let me help you," she grabbed a bowl and filled it with warm water.

"Hey Baby Boo, let's rinse out your hair," she poured the bowl over his head.

The baby squawked in surprise. She wiped his eyes with a cloth, and used it behind his chin and ears where the milk caught.

"You won't remember that one on your wedding day. I promise," Jason said cradling the baby's head, one hand beneath the small back. His knees were wet even with the towels.

She elbowed him and wiped the baby's eyes again, "So when's this wedding?"

"Up to you, dear," he made like he was kissing her, his hands full.

He readjusted himself on the floor, his knees and arm muscles fatigued from holding the squirming baby above water. If he'd been in charge of the bath, he'd already be done.

"Hmm. We'll see," she said and then focused on Ned's feet, "Hey Boo, let's get those toes. It's an important day for your mama, big guy. So, no crying," she sang as she scrubbed.

He liked it when she sang. Happy people sang. The baby liked it too and opened his mouth, watching his mother as her hair tumbled down over his face.

"Yeah, don't piss on the pastor," said Jason. "That's the biggest word of advice I can give to you."

"Jason!" she smacked him with her wet hand. "Don't make him naughty like you yet!"

She smacked him again on a wide shoulder. He couldn't react more than flinch and twist his face in mock fear. She laughed at him and feigned another hit. Then she pulled her hair back into a messy bun and snuck her smaller hands beneath Jason's. Taking over.

"Can you grab me a towel?" she asked as she scooped the baby up from his bath.

He grabbed a soft yellow one from the counter. A long white dress was slung over a chair. She must have been hiding it from him since this was the first he'd seen it, "You can't be serious. You're having Ned wear that white thing today?"

It was lacey. It was ribboned. It was made of delicate material.

"Yes," she said with no sign of movement from her mouth. "It was my grandad's. All the uncles, aunts, and cousins have worn that *thing* for their baptisms, and so will Neddy."

He fingered the cloth and then held it up to get a good look before casting it back over the chair.

"It's a white, lacy dress, Lani. Does that make any sense to clothe a person who poops bright yellow every half hour in a white dress? I mean this thing is old. What if he stains it? Come on. Ned's a boy.

He only added the last bit after he'd made a more solid case, knowing she may go off the deep end on him. It'd been known to happen whenever he mentioned gender. He couldn't help himself.

"Ned's a baby. I knew you'd say something like that, but my grandma specifically asked if he'd wear the dress today. Ned's going to wear it. He'll just have it on during the service, which is like maybe an hour, so I doubt he'll poop, or pee, or spit up like you say. Then I'll take it off."

"You better hope not since your grandma wants to keep wrapping her great-grandkids in it."

Once Grandma was involved, he knew he'd lost. He owed her grandma a big wedding already, and he couldn't be squeamish about a baptismal dress. Lani said she'd agree to be married in a year, after she'd lost the baby weight. There'd be a year of awkward baby events where her grandmother would be giving him mean stares.

Carefully, he lifted the full tub and walked it slowly to the bathroom, spilling water the whole way. He dumped it into the bathtub and heard her yell out to him.

"Just so you know, my cousin Esther and her friend Katie are playing a saxophone duet."

He came out of the bathroom with another towel and swiped down the hallway back toward the kitchen and where she rubbed lotion on the baby.

"What? Do people really do that at baptisms?"

He grabbed the soaked towels on the floor. She fastened the baby's diaper as he wriggled on the towel.

"They do at this baptism. I thought it'd be beautiful remembrance of Nathan," she squeezed the struggling baby to her chest.

"Here, let me take him."

His mother had said Lani's sadness was just hormones after having the baby, extra estrogen or something. "She'd get over it." He wondered if it was something bigger.

They strapped the baby inside his car seat and she zipped up the fleece cover. The baby looked like an enormous, fleecy egg. As she stood, her stiff hair brushed against him. The smell stung his nose. It was to combat the static cling of the season, she said.

He didn't like being inside a church for the same reason he didn't like being inside a house. Most days he tried not being inside anything but a tractor cab. He sat still inside the country church pew. The little Lutheran church was almost too small for both sides of the family.

His leg jittered like it might take off. Lani squeezed his thigh to stop. He froze. Then she squeezed again. She held him like the end of a helium balloon, he thought. And then imagined his big body full of helium, floating over the congregation, smashing through modest stained-glass windows. He coughed, and she squeezed his elbow.

He wasn't looking forward to the saxophones, knowing they'd make her cry. When the girls adjusted their stands and looked at each other silently counting, he stiffened. It was like she got spit in the eye from their first notes. There was a squeak right at the moment when he tried to get into their song. His knee jumped, and she held it. He asked to hold Ned whose white bonnet was getting wet.

He kept thinking, "Dear God, I've done nothing for you, but please God, give Ned a good life. And please God, help her to stop crying."

They did the stand up sing, sit down pray, stand up praise he remembered from last Christmas. The simplicity of the Lutheran songs and prayers lulled him back to his childhood when he'd attend this same church with his grandparents. It was a farmer's church.

The young pastor asked them to come forward. He felt for Lani's hand, leading her out of the pew. Perhaps the pastor used creek water. No, he thought, it'd be high in nitrates, and it wasn't the time of year for fresh water.

The wet palm on Ned's head was like theirs during the baby's morning bath. The pastor carried him down the aisles so old women could touch him. Some flashed their iPhones. It seemed like he was part of someone else's life. His baby was small and white, floating in the way the pastor draped the baptismal dress over her arm. It seemed the baby emerged beside her of his own will, and not within the wall of her arm. A father should know, he thought. But then there was his own childhood looking back at him.

He whispered to himself and to God in the small carved sanctuary, "God please make me a good father."

When it was over, the church basement filled with spicey chili and calico bean soups. Horrible little cupcakes lay at one end. Delicate filled Danishes were cased in paper boats. He was sure they were created by Esther and grabbed two.

People touched his face and hands and arms. Patted the baby's round, bald head. They told him there was striking resemblance in the jaw, cheekbones, eyes. And he joked about his balding. He felt fatherhood possible when so many people willed it.

Pep Band

Esther with Katie

The whole town had come to cheer on their boys, maybe the whole county. Cheering overwhelmed the hometown pep band, which Esther felt for sure irritated their conductor Mr. Sundberg, who they all called Mr. S. She watched his face grow tight, his eyebrows inching closer—two gray caterpillars.

"How long before he blows," yelled Katie, 'cause you couldn't whisper in that space.

"I give him through 'Louie Louie,' and then I bet the electric bass gets revved too high,"

Esther shouted back before she inserted her alto sax mouthpiece between her lips. Her tongue licked a large crack in her reed, but she wouldn't change it now. Her case was under the bleachers. She was at least five rows above the gym floor, crushed in place by her bandmates. She'd just fake notes to the fight song, since it didn't seem to matter if she sang through anyhow. As it was, she sat second chair.

The two boys on the mat struggled against one another in a war she never understood. Wrestling was the way here in the Hollows because of all the farmers, the physical nature of farming, she guessed. And then there was Coach Frank. He was only the second wrestling coach since 1950. A fellow could get a reputation for that many years. He'd raised her parents and grandparents, she heard her parents say. Her dad one of those wiry, running forms in the high school hallway. Spitting and starving himself before weigh-in, though some things changed in the Hollows since the seventies. Her parents eyed her little brother for mat smearing. If you could manage Holsteins and hogs, you ought to be wrestling pretty boys from prettier towns. Their boys were that good.

She fudged fingerings through the song then yelled to Katie, the first chair alto sax, "Do you think Hiran Biswa's going to state this year?"

Hiran was the only reason she signed up for pep band wrestling events and made Katie sign up. Now basketball made far more sense to her. There was a ball. There was a basket. You put the ball in the basket. Obviously, Esther cared little for sports. Really, her interests lay elsewhere. She wouldn't tell Katie, but she suspected her friend knew that she just liked looking at boys doing things. Katie, well, she might just vomit on Esther's shoes if she heard it.

"Hasn't he gone every year?"

"Do you think the pep band will ride the same bus as the wrestlers this year?"

Esther knew she sounded lame. She already knew what going to state looked like since a whole team of Hollows kids drove south every year. The entire high school marched their wrestlers through the halls while the band played on. Police cars led the coach bus full of wrestlers to highway 12. Elementary school kids waved. Pep band kids boarded a school bus after they finished the very important and very studious day of school (like anyone could concentrate on state day).

Katie rolled her eyes at her like she'd read all Esther's convoluted thoughts and disapproved. Her look made

Esther fidget for a piece of gum. It was an outright breach of pep band law. But her reed was broken, and she doubted sugar-free Trident spit would junk-up her instrument. She bowed her head and snuck a piece of gum.

"Esther," Mr. S mouthed.

Mouthed instructions instead of yelled ones were a sign of trouble, but Esther didn't see him. Not until every kid in pep turned to stare at her did Esther realize her fault. Still, she didn't move. Then Katie gave her an elbow jab to the ribs.

She stepped between five rows of instruments to reach the gym floor where Mr. S stood. By the time she reached him, she'd fallen over the trumpets and flutists and stuck her already broken reed in snotty Stella's eye. All for one measly piece of bubblegum, she thought. Her body trembled as much as her face. She knew she'd just made a couple of enemies in her procession down. She wasn't used to being front and center. Her body, all Wisconsin-grown curves, wasn't built for it.

A look at Mr. S's face made her think he intended to swat her. She cringed at the thought of the entire community watching her bottom be reddened. A small prayer floated into her head about being a better daughter and saxophonist if God would just help her through this difficult night.

Mr. S didn't smack her, that'd be too 1950s, so Esther told God and Jesus and the Holy Ghost she would attend church with her grandmother this Sunday and the next and all the Sundays from here onto her eternity.

Maybe Mr. S. did have a soul inside his musty Hawaiian shirt. Maybe he knew deep down that Esther wasn't a problem student, never would be because he sent her to the bathroom to spit out her gum. He also gave her another hour practice sheet to be signed by both her parents.

She spent several minutes inside the women's bathroom stall, her jean-clad bottom on the pot. She listened to the muffled cheers and could barely make out the pep band notes of Twist and Shout. Her goals were not only of dating Hiran, though she liked that smoggy dreamland. She had other dreams too. Her crush on Hiran made sense to other teens, not to Katie of course, but Katie was no Hollows' teen. Esther wasn't comfortable being different like Katie. Esther wasn't beautiful. She wasn't that smart. She thought about just staying inside the stall for the evening. But she'd reasoned with God. To screw it up this early might get her into a bigger pile. Not to say she believed in God like her grandmother believed in God. Esther just as firmly believed in karma, which she also knew would get her a tongue-full from Katie. Esther never said anything about her beliefs.

She tried to wash the shame from her cheeks, only succeeding in smearing her mascara. More time was spent correcting her eyes with a wad of wet toilet paper. Finally, she returned to the stands.

After a once-over, Mr. S. must've figured she'd been crying and had nothing more to say than, "You'll stand with me and play."

She nearly sobbed into the gold neck of her saxophone. Play up front away from Katie. Play up front away from all the other sound-blocking bodies. She stopped and made herself turn this into a positive like her grandmother always made her do: Hiran may just notice her as he walked out to meet his competitor. Cheeks beyond repair, red as Olin Christianson's Corvette. She lifted her saxophone to her lips and made an unapologetic, nasty screech of her existence.

Marie's on Main

Paul with Helen

At Marie's on Main, pickle jars lined shelves.

"Grandma Marie makes them," Paul said when he saw Helen looking at the backlit jars. "Best darn pickles I ever ate. Sells pickled asparagus, which is even better. Pickled vegetables too."

He picked out three jars for her, which sat on the table between their weak coffees, sugars, and Sweet-N-Low packets. A hunched old woman whisked over, coffee pots in each hand.

"Need a warm-up, dears?"

Helen covered her thick cup. Paul pushed his forward to the waitress.

"Good morning, Marie. How's Vern doing these days?"

"Oh Pauly, so good to see you here. Sorry, my eyes aren't what they used to be. My kids keep at me for that blasted cataract surgery." She leaned in with speed and caught his cheek with a wet kiss. "Vern's such a good boy to his old mama. He's actually over in the back booth with Geirolf and some of his milking buddies."

"I'll have to catch those boys before I leave you a big tip."

She laughed and picked up one of his hands, kissing the back, "I'm guessing a nice boy like you washed his paws before breakfast. Now is this one of yours? She looked at Helen.

"Sorry, Marie this is Helen. Helen, Marie."

They shook hands. Marie waited for more information.

"She's, uh, helping us out at the farm."

He poured sugar and cream into his coffee, picked up a spoon and mixed.

"Well, happy to meet you dear. Enjoy your breakfast kiddos," her shining white shoes waltzed her off to other coffee cups and chattier clients.

They only had to shoot the shit for a couple minutes. Stare out the window to the highway where commuters zoomed onto bigger places before another waitress, twenty years younger with Marie's face, held their breakfast high above her shoulder on a tray.

"Is it brighter in here because of you, or did you just wash those windows?" he asked her.

She coughed out a laugh from smoke-damaged lungs, "Oh Pauly, you old dog. Megs better tie you up when she's gone," she set the full platters in front of them. "Marie had us paint the place. We used the same color as, thirty-odd years ago, of course. You shoulda seen the difference between the two colors. See we had smoking in here 'til the smoking ban. Guess it was 2010. You know Vern and Barry may have left a spot in the men's room. You should check it out. Anyways, yous need anything else? Ketchup, hot sauce, sliced pickles?"

"Nope, we're good here," he said.

When the waitress was back in the kitchen he said, "Sorry, didn't want to get into more of a conversation with that one, we'd be here 'til noon."

Helen shrugged and forked in some of her omelet. Still chewing, she held up a little plastic creamer, "Why do you suppose places like this," she waved around at all the blue hairs and baseball caps in wooden booths, "in the heart of dairy country, don't use fresh cream?"

He hemmed and worked his ham with his molars. He just wanted to eat breakfast.

She pointed her fork tines at her omelet, "I bet they used American cheese, you know the dregs, probably stuff that falls on the floor from all other cuttings, and you can see the Creamery out the window."

He nodded and sipped.

"Why not use fresh cheddar?" She shoved in a large bite.

He could go into the costs of their breakfasts. How a five buck meal would become ten. Then who'd be buying? Not old farmers. Not him. But he didn't speak.

Helen settled after asking Marie for a 'cup of the real stuff,' holding one of the tiny creamers. Marie was the right one to ask with her old-time sensibilities. She even brought over one of her homemade cinnamon rolls for them to split. Warmed with local butter slipping off the top.

After leaving a healthy Midwestern tip, coins and all, he made his way to Vern and Geirolf. Helen went to the restroom. Three large Latino fellows across from them. Platters fresh white. Knives and forks neatly crossed in the center. Geirolf sopped up gravy with brown bread, and Vern had a full cup of caramel-colored coffee. Crushed creamers and sugar packets spread round his plate. They listened to the fellow in the battered Farmall hat, chatting enough for everyone.

Vern looked up from nursing his mug, "Howdy Paul. Where've you got yourself to these days?"

Vern stuck out his thick hand and shook Paul's.

"Haven't seen you at the old watering hole much either, Vern."

"Nah, my old lady don't approve of me sittin' on my pork chops anymore."

"Same story here," said Paul and leaned over the table to shake Geirolf's mitt.

"Good to see you, Geirolf. How's the milking business these days?"

"Ja, can't complain, Paul. Up to two hundred head, milking hundred eighty. Prices lean. But corn was gut last yar and hoping for gut, early spring. Not too hard a winter dese days. Hired dese men few yars back, now," Geirolf motioned to each as he said their names, "Manny, Mathias, and Luke, this is Paul."

Paul shook each man's hand. No need to exert pressure. They all had the callused palms of farmers.

"Jason just left," Vern cut in, "He was talking about friends of his who are in a bind with Canada no longer buying their milk."

"Ja, dat's a bad deal for some of dose small farms," Geirolf said, and everyone nodded.

Paul felt relieved for once not to be worried about the flux of the market, changing distributors.

"So, how's it feel to sleep in these days?" Vern asked.

"Ja, what do you do wit your day? Knit wit Megs?"

"Can't sleep in. Too many years up before five," Paul replied.

"Who's this?" Vern asked like he knew what Paul had been doing.

All five men watched Helen move forward and stick out her strong hand.

"Hel. I'm helping Paul go organic."

Paul flinched as he was sure the others did before gawking at him for more. He felt like Helen knew she was toying with him and all the rest of the old timers in town. He wished she'd just shut her mouth, or that he hadn't brought her into town at all. God knows how everyone would talk.

"You're planting crops this year?" asked Vern, eyeing Paul.

"Vegetables," Helen said.

Their heads snapped to her.

"Huh," said Vern.

They were thoughtful for a moment.

"Sounds like you should be at his neighbor's place," Vern thumbed toward Geirolf.

"You know Terra?" Geirolf asked Paul.

Paul nodded. He remembered the strange spectacle of Simon's ex-wife and daughters burning sweaters out back without Terra. How Megs made him stay. He didn't want to be associated with those ways.

"Isn't your kid still milking up there? Vern asked Geirolf.

"Was, ya," Geirolf's jaw set like he might have more to add.

Paul couldn't wait for another round of questions.

"Tell Marie, good chow as usual," said Paul and shook hands all around before leaving with Helen and three pickle jars. He felt Vern, Geirolf, and the three big Latino men's eyes burn through his Kevlar coat. Helen burned him too, but he wasn't yet sure of her damage to him.

LATE WINTER

Hunger Moon

Of Trees and Cornfields

Lupine

It wasn't until winter, when her brother was long gone, that she realized female sexuality was ugly to him, or at least her sexuality. That it wasn't natural for her like the cows, goats, chickens, or cats on the farm. Rather her sexuality was a treasure other people held.

When the fields were silent under snow, she buckled on her grandpa Etzel's wooden skis. They smelled of pine tar. She tucked a rag in at the toes then skied to the windbreak, identifying trees by bark and shape. Oak, ash, hickory, elm....

She rested on a sugar maple stump with *A Guide to Wisconsin Trees,* and took out a hard roll with sharp cheddar and salami. Her grandpa made the wide stump years ago. Maybe he made boards of the heartwood. The maple still hadn't rotted through. Strong, tight grain for floors, though she loved hickory best.

She wished she could come back as a tree, or begin as one. Watch the changing land. Maybe she could come back as one of the hundred-year-old walnuts in front of her grandpa's house where Terra now lived. Those trees had seen the house go up and a tornado take down the barn. Her grandpa had watched the clouds spin into a woman's face, he'd said, and then they'd formed a funnel. Said he'd thought of his wife who'd gone south that year and never returned. Thought she'd take him out with her own breath.

Lupine researched storms from the eighties online to get a sense of her missing grandmother since there were no images of the woman. Lupine found photos of the funnel clouds. She found the face her grandpa had talked about. It spooked her that the gauzy woman's forehead might be the same as her grandmother's features. Lupine just couldn't understand that ferocious kind of love. She understood crops. She understood trees.

She rubbed the maple grooves with her gloves and finished the last hunk of cheese, then broke from the trail to the bluffside. Years after a rotation of corn could be tricky going without enough snow cover, especially if the roller hadn't broken down the chopped corn stalks. Plenty of snow this year. A good sign for spring. She glided for stretches, her tips free.

She unfastened her skis and leaned them against a tree, switched ski boots with the heavy fur lined ones tied to her pack. She tugged her cuffs over her boots. Hiked up the bluffside using sumac and spindly ash trees as leverage. Dead underbrush made climbing easier, but the rubber soles were slick in the cold. She tried to avoid buckthorn. She'd told Gin she was looking for deer damage on young hardwoods as her homeschool project today. She was grateful for the freedom of homeschooling. Most days she felt fine being alone. She guessed homeschooling was her dad's idea: his way of connecting her to the farm. No way Anders or Henrick would come back.

Gin didn't hold to state standards, so Lupine stayed out of the house most days. Terra didn't need Lupine milking anymore; back to milking them herself. Lupine felt the absence of those summer and fall mornings with all those does.

The young deciduous woods used to be full of white pine, oak, and maple. Trees logged years ago. She wondered why people had chosen to lumber the hillsides. It couldn't have been easy to remove large trees. But the bluff top was her main interest. She wanted to look out—see her two parallel tracks across the cornfields. Maybe she'd see deer foraging or a flock of turkeys. Most likely she'd see nothing. The fields asleep for months under the winter pack and frost. A forlorn picture when compared to the leafed trees, crowned soybeans and tasseled corn of last summer. One could lose themselves in the cornfields, though her dad's fields ran into the bluffside. She wondered if she'd lost herself last summer.

Lupine pulled herself up to the meadow. Except for a handful of squat apple trees and a large cottonwood, it was open. She sat and looked out and remembered the green sunlight beneath the corn leaves. How she'd walk through the slender aisles of corn even though Gin said they could cut.

She spun through her thoughts again on the bluff overlooking the snow-covered field where she and Gus had been. And she knew her baby had never really been a baby. It grew into something wrong. She knew it was silly to grieve an idea, but she did. The parallel tracks disappeared with the coming winds.

Seed Catalogues

Paul with Helen

The seed catalogues came. Glossy pictures of purple beans, rattlesnake snap, striped yellow and green tomatoes, tiger cantaloupes cut in half like sunshine opened at the kitchen table. The possibilities for the new year endless. Gardens tilled, composted, and planted in Helen and Paul's minds. They flipped through the seed catalogues with full coffee mugs. Meg already at school singing with the country children. He watched Helen as she circled plants with her fingers and wondered how much she really knew about organic standards, planting plans, and vegetables. She was a city kid who clearly read a lot, but he wondered how much "on the land" experience she had. He'd overheard Meg dig for details, but beyond the foster parents and rum in her coffee, they knew little about her.

"I could label it as grown to organic standards." He said

He liked talking with another person in the morning, even if he didn't know her background. His day given weight. Light spilled across the table, brighter with the snow. Sun dogs faded in the east. Spring weeks away.

"Not yet. I mean, you used herbicides and pesticides last spring, right?"

Her hair had been braided in a complex ring around her head, an askew halo. When would a person have to get up to create such a spectacle, he wondered? It was fascinating to see how another put themselves together. A careful mother or foster mother must have taught her how to fold strands over strands, laid fingers on top of hers. It just didn't seem consistent with her story.

"I sprayed Round-Up. But its compounds break down so quickly, it's no longer in the soil."

"Round-Up, well that blows our idea. Can't sell anything as organic this year. Maybe you could call it natural. We could start out as a CSA."

Her nose ring flashed. Later in the garage, her rolled-up sleeves revealed small, black insignias on the inside of each wrist. Kids needed to write all their stories on their bodies. Post pictures. Text. Couldn't they just talk? And still he wondered what she was hiding.

Evan called right as Meg walked in from school. She shook off her coat and went upstairs to change. Paul guessed he was trying to catch Meg. He answered anyway. It'd been maybe a month since he last spoke to his youngest son, and he finally had something to say.

"We have a volunteer gardener staying on," he stalled waiting for Meg to come down, but she was taking her time. "Name of Helen, from out in your neck of the city."

Paul tried picturing his son's small, concrete apartment. Not that he could exactly remember it. But then he heard honking in the background and realized Evan was on the street somewhere in that windy city. With a cell phone one couldn't place a person anymore. He tried to picture the lake, maybe his son was walking with a view of the lake. Nah, he thought, he must be in between buildings and stopped picturing his son anywhere, because he just couldn't picture Chicago.

"Helen," Evan swallowed on the other end. "Is she staying at the house?"

Paul hadn't expected to be able to read him and was excited for him to come home. "Yup, Mom put her up in your old room." Paul paused. Though he already guessed, he asked, "You know Helen then?"

"Know Hel? I guess you could say we've gotten on these past few months. Give me Ma, will ya Dad?"

"Sure, sure. Take care then."

Meg grabbed the phone. Paul watched Helen as she listened. He wondered why she hadn't mentioned Evan. They must have been close enough for him to have given her their address. How else had she ended up here? It took some of her sheen. She did not just end up at their farm looking for work. There was something else at stake, and he wasn't sure what. Maybe he'd misunderstood exactly what she was stealing.

"Well, it sounds like Evan's coming home this weekend," Meg said.

He could see her planning some kind of outing. Helen stood up from the wingback, her fingers fluttering to her ears, her hair.

"Oh," she said.

Helen sat back down. She was something to his son he was sure of that at least. He wanted it to be good. Let them be, he thought. He'd never asked his sons questions before, never second-guessed them either. He wouldn't start now, but there Helen was in his chair. Strange girl, calming her hands on the seam of her shirt. She caught him watching her. He looked at the woodstove (so much for an early spring). The tiny window of glowing embers.

"We'll have to move you into Sam's room since Evan will want his bed," said Meg already taking out a broom and dustpan like Evan may arrive any minute. Paul could feel her energy. He just hoped she could let things be.

"No trouble, Meg," Helen picked up a rug from in front of her chair, and it wasn't clear if she meant Meg shouldn't trouble herself with the sweeping. Helen shook the rug right there on the floor, even though Paul knew to take it outside. The dust puffed out into the air. Dust motes danced on the mantle and couch.

"I don't mind sharing a room with Evan," Helen said as Meg skirted the broom around Helen.

"Oh," Meg stopped. "Well," she swung her gaze toward Paul, and he went to the woodstove and poked embers, avoiding Meg and Helen. He nosed a log inside. Meg regained herself, picked up the broom and dustpan.

"I guess. So, you know Evan?"

"Yup," Helen grimaced and replaced the rug.

Paul rushed outside to carry in more firewood. Out of range, he drove the maul into a slab of elm. He propped up the halves one at a time and struck into them again with the axe. His movements had gotten slower, and he massaged his hands after several strokes. Fat flakes fell on his leather gloves, and it felt like every other year when winter just wouldn't end. But it was also good to be in the cold, out of the house. After enough armloads of wood were laid in the bin, he dithered around with his old boat motor. No need to be inside that house.

It snowed through the night, the next morning, and continued the following evening. Tree limbs reminded him of the frosted pictures Meg had made with the kids when they were small. Helen and Meg shoveled. Paul ran the plow up and down the drive then over at Terra's place. Evan couldn't get out of the city, and Meg couldn't get to work. The three stoked the fire. Paul and Helen split wood. They all went to bed early; Helen always first. Tired like Paul had never seen a young person before. It got him thinking, but he would never say aloud what he thought.

Nights in bed, Meg asked again and again, "Why didn't Evan tell us about Helen? He didn't know and flipped over instead of answering.

After the third full day of snow, Helen said she'd take the truck to town for movies. He'd have gone instead, but it was a relief to have the house back to themselves. He missed Meg's quiet and his afternoon naps in the chair. He missed the soft sounds of their living. They'd shown their best selves, talked for her sake. Fed and fed that girl. She'd be gone for a couple hours. He admired Meg as she wiped down the table, stooped to pick up food bits, stood again. He nested his hands on full hips and pulled her back to him. Her spine against his chest, he nuzzled her neck. Escaped tendrils of her hair brushed his face. She swatted him with the wet cloth. He kissed her ear.

"It's good to have you to myself."

"That's your fault," she said. "Does she want the farm?"

What a question he thought. But he wondered too. Then he heard boots scuff the front mat. An outer door creaked open. A snow-covered form clomped inside.

"Evan, you're here." Meg rushed the door and clasped Evan's bulk. Paul stood back as she helped Evan shed his coat and stomped snow from his boots. Even though he'd been in the city for the past few years, Evan at least knew how to dress for the weather.

"Hey Ma," he kissed her cheek, "Caught the only bus leaving Chicago." He stripped off the balaclava that wrapped his reddened face, "Is there cheese in the fridge?"

"For sure," she took his gloves, coat, and hung them up.

Evan tugged his boots off and set them on the rug. People in the Midwest revealed their bodies slowly in winter. During a party it took ten minutes to know who just walked in your door.

"So, where's Hel?"

Paul worried that Evan would disappoint Meg with his concern about the girl. Paul felt the need to talk more, make it cheerful. Make it a father-son moment of connection. And he felt everything he said was on the surface of what he really wanted to know.

"Went to town for movies."

"I'm surprised you let her go alone, Dad."

"We're surprised you're home. How did the bus manage in the snow?"

He grabbed for Evan even though it felt awkward. He wasn't naturally a hugger. Evan felt slimmer. He didn't lean into Paul, which wasn't a surprise. Long time since his boys wrapped their arms around Paul's neck. Evan moved to the kitchen away from his parents. He peered in the refrigerator.

"Helluva long ride."

He cut thick slices of strong cheese for each of them. Meg placed beers and bread on the counter. They cut side-by-side. Paul liked watching working hands. Evan's were dry and strong from all his ceramic work. Evan turned one of the beers, reading the label.

"Never too early to celebrate," said Paul, happy to see Evan seemed to approve his beer choices.

Evan cracked off the top and took a swig. "Hmmm, hoppy," he gave Paul the bottle.

Evan turned to Meg, "Try it."

"No, I don't care for hoppy beers. I like Leine's Honey Weiss." She sipped her own beer. "We could tour the Leine Lodge while you're home."

"Nah, that's okay. I mean," Evan took another drink of beer, "I bet they aren't having tours with this much snow."

The door groaned open again. Helen bolted into the kitchen. She slammed into Evan's stomach while he stood with an opened beer and a slice of cheese.

"Nice to see you too," he groaned.

"Lucky I have gloves on, asshole."

They watched as Evan set his bottle on the counter, slipped the hunk of cheese in his mouth, and yanked her upstairs.

"I'm going to unpack," he yelled down.

They looked at one other as Evan's bedroom door shut. They said nothing as the two yelled and thumped overhead. The unmistakable whine of the bed made Paul cough and gulp more beer. Meg smacked hers down. She moved toward the stairs, but Paul grabbed her waist.

"Let's not embarrass ourselves," he said.

Two beers later, Meg shook a pan of popcorn over the stove and stirred caramel sauce. He was at the cutting board, chopping pecans. It reminded him of a life before. Evan and Helen didn't return when they drizzled the popcorn with syrup, nor while it was in the oven. They didn't return during the movie or when they sliced broccoli for soup. Meg stuffed three Cornish hens and slipped them into the oven, saying Helen could have soup; she wouldn't fuss with veggies tonight. The two still didn't come down. They finally returned after the table was set and the hens were cooling on the counter. Neither seemed embarrassed.

"I'm coming home after I finish this semester to help Hel on the farm."

What had felt like a beer buzz to Paul, faded. His tongue locked. He tried to shush Meg as she fought to respond. She'd set out dreams for the boys in those books she'd read them at night. The dreams never involved farming. She wanted them to leave behind a hard life. But then he couldn't help the glow when Evan said he'd help with spring planting.

Weekend dragged into Monday. Meg and Paul grew used to awkward disappearances. They'd taken to leaving the house whenever Evan and Helen toppled over one another to climb upstairs, an excuse slipping Evan's lips. Helen made none—never appeared ashamed. The snow kept dropping. It was easy enough to make excuses for another bout of shoveling. Whenever Evan and Helen moved toward the pole shed, Meg and Paul went inside. Whenever the young couple walked inside, the old went out. It was a game of avoidance.

In the upstairs bathroom, Paul opened the door on them. Their white bodies shone through the shower door. Before clicking the bathroom door closed, he noticed more tattoos splayed over her back. They didn't notice him. He pictured her half-naked, the tattoo artist's needle—her blood repeatedly dabbed free from the intricate designs. The thoughts choked him with bile and desire.

By Tuesday, Evan mentioned staying for good. Meg was beside herself at the thought of all that money spent and no degree. She whispered harshly after they were awakened by another frenzy. Evan had to go back. This time Paul pounded on the walls. He was sick of it: The lack of sleep;

the raw sex in their house while they slept, or ate, or shat. It felt like the breath-catching tropics—a barren whiteness outside. The two stopped, or at least quieted for the night.

Evan rose early the next morning, while Helen still slept. Plows rumbled past. Meg showered for work. Paul scrambled eggs. It was just him and his son.

"Make us another pot of coffee, Evan."

Evan's blond hair stuck out in tufts. Paul was reminded of Evan as a toddler—how he'd wake with him when he'd get up to milk cows. And Paul loved him again.

"Evan, you need to go back to school. We all have spent so much on this degree."

Paul bowed over the eggs mixing with a fork. Evan said nothing.

"You have one semester left."

Evan concentrated on pouring water from the pot into the reservoir and didn't speak. Paul carried the plates to the table and sat down, nudged the eggs around on the plate.

"I won't allow you to quit, not now," Paul said.

He looked toward his son's straight back in front the coffee pot. He watched him until Evan turned and looked back at him. Nothing more said, but Evan nodded. He sat across from Paul, forking eggs into his mouth.

Evan left before dinner with some high school friends. Meg cooked a pot of vegetable soup, rye, and apple strudel with cinnamon whipped cream. Paul searched for his pipe in the brightly lit pole shed, finding it between his records. Evan had snuck him a packet. Smoke crawled down his throat, nudged out his confusion. He couldn't understand how Helen and Meg could spend the afternoon cooking together. Hot as hell in that kitchen, the women stirring and cutting. He couldn't understand them. It had been a day of elbowing Evan out of the nest again. Few words and no hint of his next visit. Was he the only one who missed him, he wondered?

Cooking covered the smoke embedded in his coat. The washer and dryer rumbled from below, even the machines took over his house. Helen and Meg sprawled across the sofa, yarn between them. He went to bed and avoided the living room. Two hours later, Meg followed upstairs. She switched on the side light to read before bed.

"I thought you didn't like her," he said. He'd never understand women, their whims.

She hummed and kept reading, ignoring him like most nights together now.

"Do you want to turn the tables on Helen?, Paul pulled her to his chest and thumbed her nipple.

"Oh, there's been enough sex for this house," she whispered and turned the page without a hint of arousal.

The lamplight warmed her throat and the soft flesh around her eyes. A painting of someone he knew. And he wanted to explain how it wasn't just the sex itself, but the closeness of their bodies that he needed. Laying in a king-sized bed with their books couldn't cut it. As he leaned on his forearm watching her breast rise and fall, he imagined his life in his cold pole shed, smoking. He felt worse than when he sold his last prize heifer without Meg or his sons there. He felt alone when Meg was right there beside him.

EARLY SPRING

Sap Moon

Hiran Milking

Every morning before school Hiran was up milking 180 head on Geirolf's farm. Every morning he pulled on his coveralls in the concrete hallway before the milking barn. He pushed on rubber boots so manure wouldn't splash his Nikes. Some guys entered school reeking of shit, left dried worms of it beneath the first hour desks. Poor, prissy Ms. Gilberg teaching junior English with a roomful of rednecks. Hiran didn't want to add to her pain. He couldn't help it if his hair sucked up the manure. The nature of his work. Mainly, he thought, he enjoyed the calm cows. He liked that he was part of something big. When he was at the Hollow's Creamery buying curds, it was milk from the cows in this county. Sure, the Olsen's milk was mixed with thousands of other Holsteins, but the cows Hiran milked were part of the mixture.

This morning like others, Sam, the lone white dude, burst in through the milk house door as Hiran methodically washed his hands, collected udder wash, teat dip, and other necessities on the milk cart.

"The three amigos," snickered Sam as he ushered in Manny, Mathias, and Luke Hernandez. Sam always riffed on some racial joke to show his openness. Really, he was an awkward kid who couldn't make a friend if he produced quarters instead of farts. Hiran ignored Sam. Let his rotten sentences hang in the air while he walked away.

Hiran entered the great barn, the massive black-and-whites jostled for their pens. Numbers 1–15 waited for silage inside the metal bars. He washed number one, the veins wobbly on her distended udder. At first it had unnerved him handling the thick teats and full pink bags of milk like genitalia. He'd thought how funny it was that so many ruddy men dealt with the most intimate bits of labor, birth, and afterbirth. In the movies men fainted, but farmers had steel constitutions.

The rubber-coated, metal machine already sucked at the air. He inserted the washed teats and foaming white quickly spun through the clear tubes overhead. Red automated numbers ticking off the poundage. He moved onto the next udder, wiped and inserted. Luke poured buckets of sweet silage in front of the wide, wet noses while Manny worked the back ends, talking about their sisters, cousins, aunts in Mexico where Hiran assumed they sent their money otherwise they would be out of Mrs. Pearson's rickety house. Manny's face looked wider beneath his Farmall hat. Must be all old Mrs. Pearson's snickerdoodles, Hiran thought. They spoke English while they were close to Hiran, which he appreciated. They slipped into Spanish as they moved down the line, which was even better, like a song he could listen to but not decode.

Manny cleared manure from the last stalls. He shoveled then sprayed the black gold from the concrete and down the center trench behind the beasts. Dark swirled behind. White above. Energy in. Energy out.

Geirolf Olsen hustled in after breakfast. He checked on the working gears, Hiran guessed. The man's thick thumbs stuck inside his belt loops. A whittled toothpick was stuck between his lips. One had to admire the man's work ethic.

Never missed a morning. He worked alongside them—his craggy, tall frame from the fjords. Cheekbones like cedar boards and hair of even stiffer stuff. All but Sam foreign in their own ways. Norwegian driving its way into a sentence with Spanish, so they spoke "Mexwegian" according to backassed Sam.

Then the long, developing daughter slid in with her silly rain boots. Geirolf had her working to feed the calves with Luke. Maybe it was the men that were made silly by her long legs and moon-eyes. Manny was on her already. Hiran could hear him say he brought more of the paper-wrapped enchiladas.

"Made them last night for Mrs. P.," Manny said.

Luke came over and poked her back, "Where's my Norwegian word, I already gave you a whole sentence, lady Lupine."

"I already told you," she said, "I don't speak much Norske, you'll have to ask Dad,"

They all rolled their eyes at her like anyone would talk to Geirolf. Like Geirolf talked.

"But I can give you some backward German. I'm learning it from Grandpa Etzel."

"Oh no, you can't be messin' about with your grandpa's language. We wanna learn Norske," said Manny, scooping shit and goading her.

"He got you some Tamarind Jaritoes in the car if you give him some pretty phrases," said Luke.

Hiran never looked at Lupine. He hadn't the time for girls, especially pretty ones. This pleased his pharmacist father whose dream it was for Hiran to become a doctor. His father, Nikilchandra, knew everyone. And he knew all their ailments.

Hiran moved onto the next udder, washed, dipped, and vacuumed. He ignored the others. He ignored Sam, who came in with his arm raised like heil Hitler, how the others just turned from him to continue their flirting. Hiran did his job. He had plans. He didn't need a fuss.

The Olsen dairy, he knew, was well-run. It was clean, the animals kept healthy. Not all in this county were well-kept. Knechts were expanding their herd. Excavators dug for weeks. Construction crews erected more steel quarters. Five years back some of the part-time employees sent rumors round about calves and cows standing in foot-high sewage. The rumor never made it to more attentive ears because everyone in town knew the news would be bad for every dairy in the county especially for the town creamery. Such squalor wasn't retold. Now the Knecht's fluorescent, open-barn lights never went out. The cows docile and ruminating in their pens. He imagined them rotting from the hooves up. Dairies could contain ugly business but mostly it was honest work based on sun, cycles, seasons. And unless you were part of the Knecht crowd, dairy-men had second jobs. Geirolf's was driving milk truck.

After 25 pounds, Hiran moved the vacuums to the next cow. He helped shovel in between. Sweet, strong manure. Luke and Lupine fed calves. Milk churned overhead, immediately cooled and stored in an enormous steel tank in the clean hallway. The cows chewed. Manny and Mathias laughed. Hiran was methodic.

Two hours later, he stripped off his boots and coveralls when Lupine strode into the hallway.

"What a day!" Lupine yelled out to him.

Hiran wasn't sure if she meant that already the day was a "helluva" morning or great. He figured great when he saw her smile.

"Yup."

"You could turn your life around on a morning like this."

Did she mean his life? He had no idea what she was saying.

"Uh, I guess."

He slung up his backpack and was out the metal door before she could say more. Most days he caught a ride with the three on their way to their Freedom Gas coffee break. He ran instead, the pack knocking his spine, his sweat thankfully smelling like Irish Spring soap from his morning shower. The dairy was just on the edge of town. Perhaps a three-mile run. He welcomed the meditative smack of his sneakers, the full thwack of AP books hitting his back. He needed the thump of his own heart in his ears.

The Waking Life
Terra

Sassy and Curry nickered, waking her. Their udders were full after being penned from their kids overnight. Milking duties had fallen from twenty-four to two does over the past year, hardly cost effective but time effective. She'd only had energy to have two of the easiest milkers bred. A first crop of alfalfa seemed unlikely. Last year Geirolf and Jason planted, cut, and baled for Terra. Geirolf's gangly girl milked the freshened Nubians and Toggenburg does 'til winter. People made allowances for new loss. Terra was inside the after-grief that productive folk aren't fond of.

You can only sit on your duff waiting for the dead for a year, she thought, then flipped the quilt back. Books piled on both marked, wooden side tables: *Organic Gardening in Wisconsin, Memory of Trees,* and *Stalking the Wild Asparagus.* She grabbed a T-shirt and jeans from an untidy pile. Slumping downstairs, she wondered if all the choices Simon and she made together were clear-eyed and independently beneficial.

Terra spooned out two tablespoons of coffee beans into the hand grinder imagining herself a small, satin monkey on a bike rolling peaceful coffee from Guatemala to Wisconsin. Maybe it was Sumatra. She hadn't taken any notice just needing caffeine and buying Simon's brand. Yet another instance of Terra following Simon's lead.

"Everywhere by bike," she'd questioned when he'd first bought it.

"Yup."

"Except when you drove it home in the gray goose," she'd poked.

"You just have to stir the pot."

Terra missed those back-and-forths. She sighed and looked out at where the old Ford Ranger or gray goose sat under the white pine. It looked dead, but she figured the truck would outlive her even if she tried to kill it.

The blue flame from the ignited stovetop purposefully flicked the full kettle just as she felt the purpose of morning milking. It was the lazy afternoons that confused her. They shouldn't be lazy had she kept on top of the crops, the gardens, the goats.

Once the pot whistled, she poured hot water through a single drip into a clay mug. Coffee first then chores. If she was waking at five, she was sure as shit getting coffee down her gullet before tugging teats. Lord help her if she felt the urge to go completely local. No coffee. No chocolate. No olives.

After her wake-up cup, she was up and down the hill with two loads of grain, cracked corn, and a mix of alfalfa and timothy. She'd sprinkled the grains with Molly's Herbal Wormer. She'd also added dried seaweed to silken her herd's coats. It was Monday so she routinely spiked their breakfasts. The only indication of a change in the week.

Two mesh bags hung off the fence posts where she stuffed the first lot of hay. Grain buckets stayed outside the fence so Sassy could be enticed out. Terra opened the barn to a whining fugue. Two large pens held six does each. Two more bags needed hay. Then she pressed inside the kids' pen and filled the last. Four white noses dove into the hay. She checked beneath their wagging, upright tails: noted their clean bottoms, a sign they were healthy. They'd be reunited with their mamas once milking was finished.

She caught the collars of the largest cinnamon-colored does, Sassy and Curry. Grain was coming and relief, so they allowed Terra to lead them out of the barn and inside the milking shed. She discretely grabbed one of the grain buckets on their way. Early on she and Simon had learned unpenned goats meant chaos during breakfast. The ladies knocked them over a handful of times before Simon built pens, and Terra devised a morning routine for the least amount of jostling. She still felt a physical ache in her gut when she thought of his hands on the boards. Coarse, freckled hands with clean, round nails. Dead hands. That time of her life, dead. She would keep on keeping on, and she would forget, and there would be no one else that could fully remember their time together on Goat's Back Ridge Farm.

Nubians were big girls and the Toggenburgs weren't far behind: between 120–135 pounds. They weren't Jerseys and they sure weren't the Holstein ogres Terra saw at the fair last August. Some neighbor friend thought it'd be good for her to get out into the sunny hullabaloo of a county fair—catch the bovine lactation plantation. Terra heard the trick was to rub a bit of wax at the tip of the teats, so milk wouldn't drip all over the judge's shoes. Each cow led in by a 4H kid was three feet taller and wider than Terra remembered as a child. After the cow parade, a whole line of Holsteins pranced in front of the milking parlor just feet from the ring. Massive, veiny udders the size of Terra's torso nearly had her off dairy entirely. She'd surprised herself: still milking a year after the accident.

Once inside the shed, Sassy and Curry danced on the clean concrete floors then leapt onto the platforms of the two milking stanchions. The head catch was open. Sassy nosed the tray in front of her, ears sweeping left and right. Terra quickly sprinkled grain out with a touch of molasses (Sassy had a sweet tooth) and clasped the catch around her neck. It was wide enough for a goat to move her head comfortably back and forth but wouldn't allow her to back out. Terra stroked her cream nose up to a black mark saying, "What a lovely lady. You must have gotten your beauty sleep last night, you're such a silky girl." Sassy murmured back. Terra smoothed their coats and breathed in their grassy, humid smells like a mother sips in the breath of milk-fed infants. Eating their aliveness, their resolve to live. Terra moved to Curry and added grain to her tray, rubbing her black ears. She fastened the catch around Curry's neck.

Normally this was Terra's only conversation, but she was forty today and a zippy dooh dah of a day. She counted: A call from her positive sister. One. A call from her negative sister. One point five. A call from her mother. Two point five. Maybe her friends: Emily, Liza, Molly, Clarissa. Six point five calls. A record communication day if all called.

She clicked on classical WPR, washed and dried her hands, plucked a fresh rag from a basket and wet it with soap, water, and a drop of lavender (for herself or the goats, she wasn't sure). Calm and clean. Then she pulled out a strip cup and a stainless steel pan from drawers beside the makeshift sink and carried them back to her milk stool. She wiped Sassy's teats and udder then Curry's. She flushed any dirty milk from them by squeezing four squirts into the strip cup, which helped twofold by telling her the does had no abnormalities or blood clumps in their milk. During her whole routine, Terra murmured things like, "Good girls. Lovely rich milk. Beautiful ladies." Her mind on her own body. It, like a book. No, a wooden beam, no longer the living, emotional person she had been but an object—a tool to be cared for, not loved. Should she take a yoga class in town, a lover? Her sisters kept at her to get out of the sticks, "It's been nearly a year. You need to move on." But she didn't want to move on. Her grandmother never moved on and she had been only fifty. Terra understood now. She never moved on because she couldn't let herself forget. And all the buildings had Simon's prints, and they were Terra's. Thank God they'd married the year before, or his daughters might have the land. All the physical and emotional labor would live only in her mind.

After nestling the pan beneath Sassy, she began by trapping the teat between thumb and forefinger with both hands and squeezing down. It was pleasant work with a compliant doe, the first spray of milk whistling against the steel bottom. Sassy moving on to her alfalfa, cracking stems. Lavender, warm milk, hay, and beast rising in Terra's nose. In five minutes, the pail was full. About a half-gallon or less, Terra eyeballed. Immediately she covered the pail and set it inside the fridge then moved on with a fresh pail to milk Curry who was younger and less willing. Terra knew she should be milking twenty more ladies, but she couldn't bear to hire help. She couldn't share her space every morning with someone else. It had taken a year to milk alone without Simon's eighties songs. When he was alive and bellowing out "Raspberry Beret" at quarter to six, she'd wanted to drive a clod of manure in his maw. Now, well, now was now, she thought.

Once done, Terra led the ladies back to their barnyard and released the four kids to their mothers. She threw scratch grains to two dozen chickens and one enormous rooster, filled grain buckets for an Icelandic ewe and ram. She filled waters. She left the milk for later and finally walked back inside for more coffee.

A loud unsteady knock sounded on her kitchen door. It was 6:30 a.m. She shoveled in more eggs. Another knock. She poured steaming goat's milk into her coffee. The knocking continued. She went to the door. There leaned the long frame of the Olsen girl. What was her name? Rosemary? Sage?

"Great morning, Terra," she crowed.

The girl seemed unaware or uncaring about the time, but then this was the way of most farm folk—assuming all people were up and working by five. She was a homeschooled kid who was at once comfortable in thought and uncomfortable in society. *Must be six-foot*, thought Terra as she looked up into her round face (and Terra was no petunia). Lupine, that was her name. She'd helped her milk last summer. She appeared more like her namesake this summer, slim and tall. Terra hardly spoke with Lupine that summer. Terra had spent summer lying in bed or in the hammock—tired like she'd never been before. Grief grabbed days. At least Terra had begun grabbing some back.

"Good morning, Lupine. I see you're up with the sun."

Lupine didn't catch the knock or ignored it.

"I was going to visit earlier, but I knew you'd be milking—didn't want to interrupt. Gin says I get a bee in my bonnet," Lupine smiled, and it nearly shook Terra from her pity party.

Terra thought it was lucky for Gin she'd not enrolled her daughter in public school.

"Well come on in and tell me about this bee." Terra waved her inside her light-filled kitchen.

"You drink coffee?" Terra asked, moving to the stove.

"Tea, if you please," the girl replied as she pulled back a stool by the butcher block island. "I'd like you to be my mentor," she continued in an earnest bellow, "I want to learn how to make cheese. Milk every day for you. Learn about micro farms."

Terra placed another full kettle of water on the stove, "Don't you have enough chores on your parents' farm?" She set several covered, glass jars with loose tea in front of Lupine and a spoon.

"Yes and no. I mean Dad's hired a lot of guys on to milk. I help with some of the calves I guess, but you know Dad."

Terra nodded. Dad was a perfectionist and occasional bully. She revised bully to patriarch: old-time, Norwegian patriarch. She crossed behind where Lupine was perched and opened the big bay window that looked back to her beasts of burden.

As Terra heard it, Lupine's grandfather, the previous owner of Terra's farmhouse, took a chainsaw and carved an impromptu bay where there was only a spy hole. She suspected drinking was involved. There were a lot of stories about Etzel. He'd filled ashtrays of ticks at the Junction Bar during morel season. Pick, squeeze, swig, then a saucy song, Terra imagined. It was probably good Lupine's mother married the Norwegian, though not nearly as interesting. Unless hard, quiet Puritans could be interesting. Clearly Lupine took after the Ulbrichts in spirit. Terra turned and watched the girl scoop some raspberry leaf and nettle into the netted spoon.

She didn't want Lupine to fill the milking shed with her voice, her long body. She wasn't sure she could share her does. The kettle whistled and Terra filled Lupine's cup.

"Okay," Terra muttered, then frowned. Her voice betrayed her, as though her body knew better.

Lupine flipped over her stool and nearly knocked her mug, seizing Terra inside a bear hug.

"I only have two freshened does," Terra whooshed out.

"Oh, that's easily fixed," said Lupine into Terra's crown as though she were the mentor, the adult.

It had been a month since Terra had been touched by a human. It broke her. Once Terra began crying, she didn't know if she could stop. Shamed and angry at herself, she couldn't speak to say this wasn't how things were done. Lupine held her harder. Perhaps she didn't realize, Terra thought.

Lupine did know, using the same tone as Terra did with her goats, "Yes, let go. It's good to cry," which made Terra sob harder.

How could someone so young understand grief better than most adults she'd seen at the local library or grocery. People who said they were sorry last year, or wrote they were thinking or praying or whatever it was they said then avoided her. People didn't like to see grown folks cry or talk about sadness as if it were catching. Finally, Terra let go. She sobbed and Lupine held her.

After she put herself back together and her heart and lungs slogged on and Lupine had carried wads of toilet paper to blot her face, they sat on either side of the island. Terra felt poppies burst open on her neck and face, her eyes full of burdocks. She rubbed them. Lupine curved over her spoon. A Klimt litho in her kitchen. Click click click, the spoon hit the cup's belly. Tap tap tap, the spoon finished on the rim before she set it dripping on the counter. Terra had a passing thought about how Lupine might know grief because she had her own sadness. And then the thought was gone.

"It's nearly April," Lupine said. "What is it…five months gestation for goats?"

"Brings us almost to September if all goes well," Terra said. "We'd be milking into the cold season."

"Cold's in my genealogy."

"Have you milked in a cold, cement shed before?"

"No, but I'm willing. It's not like I'm a necessary cog in Dad's machine."

It was the only moment she had seen the girl not try to blow sunshine out her bum, but she lacked the energy to respond.

"The girls won't have the spring green grass. Different feed; different flavors," Terra said.

"Yeah, but different can be golden."

A ring broke their conversation. Surprisingly, Lupine responded with social grace, exiting after Terra said looking at her phone, "It's my sister."

"We're on our way," shouted both sisters over the car stereo.

"You shouldn't," said Terra, meaning don't come.

One would overdrink, scare them with her brash happiness and puke in the sink. The other wouldn't drink enough and sulk about her unfit husband and her bad choices, though she'd call it bad luck. Terra preferred their youngest brother. He'd never gave figs over birthdays. He might be in Indonesia again, "escaping love" their mother would think. Terra knew it was them he fled. Them and first world indignities.

"Happy Birthday Terra! We're bringing your friend Jack," her sisters shouted like teens escaping overprotective mothers. It was their families they fled and they the mother-hens—suffocated by toddler, husband, and work needs. They had fought for careers, partners, pregnancies.

"We'll be there around three. I'm bringing some cave-aged cheddar," sang Freja. "And Dar picked raspberries."

Well, thought Terra, *not everything could be bad.*

The Junction Bar

Emile

The Junction Bar was set back from the road—front door open stream-side. Customers came from between junk river trees or from the farms in the hills above. Most days the lot, if it could be called that, was full. If a stranger sat down, Emile loaded them up with tchotchkes. A young stranger fiddled with an orange hunting multi-tool equipped with toothpick, whistle, and flashlight. Emile had also given him a hot pink Koozie cover and baseball cap. He hadn't refused, which meant something to her after a long week of local, old men.

The stench of last night's manure still stunk up the air even though Emile had doused everything with three parts water to one part bleach. Now it smelled like bleached shit and this outsider's cologne, which was warm and inviting for a change. Her circle of cleaning had narrowed around him. With the slow draw of early spring evening, she'd had one other customer. The farmers out tending their fields, fresh off winter.

"Anyone says managing a bar in the sticks is easy better sit down and call a cab." Emile swiped a suds-filled rag under his beer mug. Invading his space again as he'd invaded hers.

"Now when that old hag went and shot her man a coupla dozen times then came in here for a drink *that* was bad for business. All those police questioning my customers. Who wants to drink a beer when cops are like flies?"

"Why'd she come here?" the stranger asked. He boasted one of those gelled, faux Mohawk haircuts. He was young, so she continued with him even if he was from the cities.

"You mean you haven't heard?" she put her damp hands on her hips pleased with how they flared, the rest of her frame strong from all the riding and chores. She wasn't yet cushioned by too many whiskey sours, though regulars could see the softness was coming on. She threw her body into the story, sick of her Jed's cemented feet. Sick of living together for months in his apartment without one slip into the next step. Here was fresh DNA that could be added to the homogeneous gene pool. It was one pheromone talking to another, baby.

"So, this old bat a coupla houses down the road comes in while I'm working, and I've got a whole bar full of farmers right after harvest eating burgers, drinking bloodies, having a fine time after a hard day and evening." Emile took a sip of her drink, watched how the stranger was taking it before starting again.

"She sits at the bar, says how she just mopped up a big mess of blood and would I make her a rum and Coke. I sorta know her, you know: she comes in with her skinny husband and drinks like a fish. Man, can she put them back. If she wasn't so mean, she'd drink the guys under the table, but nobody wants to get near her. And her husband asking for pickled pigs' feet, gizzards, eggs. Never knew folks still ate that crap. He'd be nibbling at those stinky things while she's drinking. I never seen her stumble. Anyhow, I know they ain't farmers, so it ain't cow's blood and it really ain't the birthing season. I'm thinking maybe she's hunting."

"Was she full of blood?"

"Nope. Scary girl had every stringy, gray hair slicked back in that little bun of hers. Mennonite-like, maybe Amish."

"She was just sitting there drinking?" The guy slid his empty mug forward. With a stitch of irritation on her brow at his interruption, Emile filled it with Spotted Cow.

"I love this stuff," the guy tapped the now-golden glass. Foam buried his upper lip. He sucked it. Emile frowned. He was starting to rub her wrong, like a city slicker.

"Sorry," he mumbled and looked into her eyes again.

She leaned forward across the bar, her scooped shirt too low, "So I ask her, 'what blood?' It's just what she's wanting: she goes into this rant about him smacking her for burning dinner, which I still don't believe. She takes out the .22, and he doesn't think she'll shoot him—just laughs."

"Whoa. Do they have kids?"

"Yeah, like my age. I think their son was a coupla years ahead of me in school. They've been married decades, right? Probably lost their virginity to each other. Grown kids. Grandkids. Her man laughs cause it's gonna take a helluva long time to kill someone with a .22. And she shoots him. He swears. And she shoots him again. And again. She reloads and keeps shooting. Twenty times she shot that poor, sorry guy."

"Bet he never saw that coming," he took a large swig of beer, "She just unloads all this on you?"

"Yeah. I ask if he's dead. She says, 'Does a bear shit in the woods?' like it's some joke. She's sittin' in the bar while her man's full of holes, two houses down the road."

"Well, I guess he learned how to whistle," the city slicker laughed, but Emile didn't join him. He took a slug from his beer, reengaged, "What did you do?"

"I was freaking out, but trying not to show it. I mean I've got a murderer in my bar just how-do-you-do-drinking. She says, 'Just cleaned up the mess and needed to wet the whistle.' Scary old bat." Emile took a sip of her Coke with just a splash of rum, readying herself for the finale. "I wait a bit cause I'm afraid she's watching me and I can't tell any of the guys."

"You must have been pissing your pants." He tapped his glass again. As she was refilling, Emile thought how this guy probably balled up his dirty socks and shoved them down the sides of couch cushions. She'd already had a crumb of a boyfriend who did that until she couldn't bring herself to screw him without thinking about dirty socks. Jed never did that. Jed never interrupted her during a good story. She slid the glass in front of the stranger with a huff and hiked her shirt up into a more appropriate neckline. Rude men: no boobies.

"I had to sneak into the bathroom and call the cops before she finished her drink. She's pleading insanity, but she's just a snake."

"There's a professor, adjunct really, who's being tried for murder. She cut up her boyfriend, shoved him inside a Christmas box, and offloaded the taped box to another boyfriend in Arkansas."

"Yeah, I heard that. Not far from here," she snapped.

He'd missed the point. She wasn't interested in murderesses. She poured a mug for an old regular.

"Good to see you, Pauly."

"It's like you breed husband killers in these pastures," the city slicker waved his hand around the near-empty bar as if to bring about a henhouse of murderesses.

"Nah," said Emile. "It's just country feminism."

She moved to chat up Paul who had just taken his usual stool beside the old Juke box.

Emile and Paul lugged the sloshed city slicker out the door and into a cab headed to the motel closer to town. Emile hadn't been outside since afternoon. She squinted into the leaving light. For a moment she thought about sitting out on the painted picnic tables with a brew, putting her feet up, chewin' the fat with Pauly. But pick-up after pick-up turned onto the gravel drive from the road and parked.

"Well, I better skedaddle. Megs will wonder if I had more than two," Paul laughed then lowered his voice, "Don't mind what I was saying before about that girl at our place." His eyes caught hers with an animal look, "But if you know anyone needs help. Let me know." He laughed, rubbed his short beard, himself again, "Looks like the next generation's taking over."

"Looks like Jason's done planting," Emile said and patted Paul's shoulder.

"Should be a wild one. See ya." He climbed inside his own rig and rambled home. She watched as he curved out of sight, figuring how to help him out of his bind.

The younger men sidled up to the bar thirsty and thrilled to be free from their tractor cabs. She only recognized Jason. The rest were not her regular stool warmers. Jason was the owner's cousin and was like many of the solicitous cousins, uncles, and friends who pushed the line.

"If it isn't the prettiest bartender in the county." Jason swatted at her bottom as he strode through the door.

She skirted him, "Or the dirtiest farmers. Watch out. You'll leave mud on my cheeks."

The group of filthy men moved to a high top where they barely fit. They were like her cat who worked out his power by sleeping on the highest thing in each room, the fridge, the stereo, shelves. Let them pretend.

"What'll you have?" She leaned on one of the younger guys' chairs. No need for a notepad. Nice thick pelt on his head, she noticed. The others in baseball caps making it hard for her to scope.

"Two pitchers of Miller and three baskets of cheese curds," said Jason, the spokesman for his crew.

The door swung open, and three women sidled up to the bar. All five sets of eyes followed their legs, their asses, their curves. Emile smirked. What a surprise handful for her night. She recognized Terra once the women sat and twirled their stools around, eyeing the place.

None of the other women were familiar. She hadn't seen Terra since last summer after Simon's funeral. Then she'd barely spoken with her just dumped the bars in her lap and said something, she couldn't remember now. She'd wondered about Terra off and on, but mainly had forgotten about her, which gave her a small rush of guilt. Not the emotional type she countered and forgave herself.

"Be right with you ladies," she called out, and sorted through her good stories just in case she had some talkers. It wasn't often she had a full bar of women. With this mix, she knew the next few hours could be a hot mess. She filled pitchers and dunked frozen curds into grease before concocting drinks for the women.

"Are you three sisters?" Emile asked as she shook the metal container with a round of Moscow Mules while the women told her the ingredients. In a country bar, bloodies were the most common mixers. She could throw together a mean bloody, but lady drinks weren't her forte.

"How could you tell?" said the one with short black curls as she smashed the cheeks of her sisters into her own.

"Freja," She whisked her black lacquered nails over the back of Emile's hand, "Now squeeze in fresh lime juice, lots in mine, Emile."

Emile took out another lime from the small fridge, began slicing it on a square, wood cutting board. She liked the quickness of her hands, preferred it to her quiet afternoon and cleaning.

"Too bad there aren't copper mugs," complained the other sister whose large glasses made her small face smaller.

No way were they from around here with their lean brown bodies and black hair. *Bunch of Italians on her turf*, Emile thought as she shoved four tall glasses in front of the women and poked in colorful straws. But she also loved having the women at the bar, their heels cupped over the rungs. Their smell, the chance for a good jaw.

"So? Do I pass."

"Nice work, barkeep," Freja said.

Emile ran back to the kitchen and sifted browned curds into parchment covered baskets. By the time she set them at the high top, the paper was clear with grease. The men were laughing and she figured it was something lewd about the ladies.

"Need another pitcher, fellas?" As Emile walked back to the bar, she watched the women. Terra was the only one not smiling. Her thick braid slivered with white, not real obvious except to another woman. *She should throw some color on that*, thought Emile, *she's not that old.*

Jason's eyes followed Emile back to the table as she carried two full pitchers of Miller. She topped of the guy's plastic cups. She'd had a night a while back with Jason and wasn't up for another even if he was a millionaire bachelor farmer by forty. He'd worked buying small plots while harvesting and planting other folk's crops. Purchased ratty old combines and tractors and fixed them up in his daddy's machine shop. Then he took more harvesting jobs. Hired friends and cousins for cheap. Admirable guy in some ways. Never home. Emile had to admit Jason wasn't at the Junction Bar as much these days.

She didn't need a farmer in her life. She'd spent every morning before school milking cows. Fall, her daddy hardly ever came home except to drop into bed for a handful of hours before going back to his fields. He didn't travel. Ever. He missed her brother's west coast graduation because of the calves and died before he ever left the state. Nope, no farmers, especially one with a girlfriend and a baby. If she were nosey, she'd nudge him about a ring for poor Lani.

After the fourth round of pitchers and Moscow Mules, a static filled the air. Voices reached out louder than necessary. Emile put her all into keeping Freja off the bar. Not that Freja had tried mounting it, but Emile caught the signs: crazed eyes and unbridled passion for singing. As she kept her eyes on Freja, she couldn't help but ask Terra about her small farm.

"Goats are the poor man's milk cow," Terra was saying. "That's why Simon and I chose goats. Couldn't afford cows. Couldn't keep cows."

"You only have twelve goats, and you're making and selling cheese for a profit? That can't be right? I mean I thought we were a small family farm. Always had at least sixty head milking,"

Terra colored, "Nah. I downsized from twenty-four."

"So, you're milking twelve does by yourself every morning and night. How much milk you getting?" Emile leaned her elbows on the bar, close to Terra's empty glass. She pointed to it, asking. Terra shook her head.

Terra bent the pink straw down and dug in with her fingers for melted ice, "I've got two freshened."

"Two. You must be getting a thimble-full," Emile grabbed Terra's glass, rinsed it out and filled it with fresh ice and water. She pushed it in front of Terra and Terra nodded, sipping.

"Barely enough to make cheese to sell, maybe two pounds a day" Terra admitted.

Emile always felt a bar was a place where beer pushed through the dams of its patrons. A bartender knew more secrets, pain, or deals than anyone. The Hollows was a town without coffee shops or bakeries. The bars and churches divided the population of 3,000, though some folk could be perched on a bar stool one night and perched on a pew the following morning.

"I just don't have the energy for it now that Simon's gone."

"Get this girl another," Freja interjected.

And Emile remembered how folks talked about their raw, organic life. Unmarried for years. Weird old guy and younger lover. Their parties. How everyone in town knew they'd fail.

"Where do you sell?"

"Right now, I'm just selling to some restaurants in the cities. I dropped clients this year. I think they'd take me back if I got the gumption—they're co-ops and a fancy cheese store in Mad-town."

Emile was liking this chick, but the boys were waving their empty pitcher and she felt a wrinkle of self-annoyance at not being on top of empty glasses. She guessed they weren't hurting when Jason's flask flashed back into his pocket. She ignored it, brought back two more pitchers, and poured around. All the while she considered Terra and Paul's situations. As she walked back to the kitchen to clean the griddle, she thought about how Paul had whispered, "Gotta get her outta my hair….save my marriage. I'm sixty." She didn't have time to press Terra about taking on Paul's little friend. The sisters took over, insistent in their drunkenness.

As she came back from the kitchen, it was the splat of mustard on her forehead that made Emile realize she'd taken her eye off the bachelor ball. They'd stripped their barriers to the Midwestern world and become teens again equipped with plastic mustard and ketchup bottles.

"Jason, what the hell do you think you're doing?" she yelled.

He was too intent on squirting, hiding beneath the high top. All the women, except Terra and Emile, stood on the bar. A flick of red ketchup splattered their thighs. This was no night she pictured.

"Hey girls, get down. The bar can't take your weight," she shouted as she went in for the kill with a washrag. Screw with her bar on this spring-lit night? Not on her shift.

Too intent on killing each other with their crude ketchup guns, the men fell on the floor. She cringed at their dirty courage. The floor had only felt her feet and the right end of a broom. Three women shrieked in the background. As a drop of mustard fell from her lobe to her shirt, Emile thought, *so this is what divides us: the ability of men to shake off conscious society.*

She threw the cloth over Jason's head. The men noted, surrendering their bottles. All but Terra and Emile leapt on them. A tangle of shit-faced strangers. Emile nearly laughed at the mess until she heard Terra say, "Hey, you better look at this bar top."

Etzel Mid-Dream

After a fish dinner over his campfire, Etzel met Randy at a wreck of a bar. Dirt floors. Peanut shells cracked with every step. More people without front teeth than with 'em type a bar. Bear hunting would be a snap compared to surviving this place.

He bellied up and ordered when a thick stink grabbed him before a thicker arm and hand.

"I knew you'd come, Kraut. Meet Screwy Louie."

Randy swung him around to meet the lean face of his friend. "Hey, Etzel."

"Ja?" Louie grinned meanly. One eye froze while the other tracked around Etzel's face.

Louie caught him struggling with his fixed eye, "Doc said they run out a green, so I'm a rainbow, right?"

Tapping the eye with his dirty nail, he laughed, "Little glass fixture. Cost me more than my truck even without the right color. But I know how women are and I ain't havin' a pink, wet hole in my face. Course could use that somewhere else, huh?"

His laugh was sour, and he elbowed Etzel to follow him. Etzel did. These characters welcomed him more than scrubbed and rubbed down goodies back on the farm.

"Shot much?" Etzel asked.

"I can shoot at anything. Bear's only thing big enough for me to hit."

"Louie couldn't hit the broad side of a barn after that ole stick in his eye. But he's been working with me and Deborah. Sometimes he gets the target," Randy slugged his drink.

"Oh, I can hit things that matter."

Louie's arm went out to illustrate his joke and Etzel quickly avoided the jab. He pretended he had the urge to stand and drink.

"Ahh here's my Deborah," Randy slid his arm around a brick shithouse of a woman.

"Deb." She grabbed Etzel's hand and crushed it a bit before positing her weight on the stool beside him. Randy was on her massaging her neck and arms.

If Etzel were alone, he'd have mistaken Deb for a man. Except just then she pulled off her hat and red silk poured down her back. He'd never seen such hair. Randy twisted it round his hands like a bloody snake swallowing him whole. Etzel understood, might have fought to get his own hands inside.

"Never seen that color of hair," he said.

"Yeah, it's from my grammie, but sure as hell didn't get her body. This is all Daddy's," she squeezed her hips, laughing.

"Oh yes, it is Daddy's," said Randy, and grabbed more of her.

"So, how's a kraut like you end up here without getting shot?" she asked.

"Well, that's my own secret," Etzel sipped, "But I like to say a pick-up truck full of pickled pigs' feet and an old, Norwegian lady gave me America."

"Don't hurt none to have a rifle, eh?" Louie laughed but they ignored him.

"Norske, huh. Can you tell I got Berserker in my blood?" asked Deb as she sipped her drink.

"Should a' been named Lena," said Randy.

"And you'd be my Ole," she giggled into her drink and Randy had his hands on her again. Etzel sat on his stool and tried to look busy with his beer. Louie leered at his other side.

"He can't be an Ole. He's too much a randy ole goat," said Louie. He punched Etzel's arm, so he coughed on his ale. Soon the night got fuzzy.

Someone was shaking his shoulder. At first, he thought it was Lupine, come to save him from his earlier self. But then the voice came, soft and unsure and not at all like his granddaughter.

"Mr. Ulbricht." The nurse pulled him back into the small room and he was sorry to be awake.

"Just let me be," he growled in German so she certainly couldn't understand him.

He felt torn between remembering the horrible hunting party and this gaunt room where he now lived. He wished he would dream of his *mutti* and *bruder* when they all were young. For some reason he kept going back to the bears of the Northwoods, redheaded Deb, Randy, and one-eyed, screwy Louie.

"Have some soup, Mr. Ulbricht. It's good and hot. Come, Mr. Ulbricht, let's get you in your chair."

It was nowhere near to being his home, and he longed for Lupine and her stories. Where was Lupine and what about his poor Ginny? What had he done to his daughter to bring him here to the old folks' home?

Farm Affair

Paul with Helen

Helen apprenticed in the afternoons: mechanics, manure, farming figures, and natural soil supplements. Nights she cooked with Meg and knit before bed. Once gopher mounds showed, Paul announced it spring. And the flooding began. Runoff washed out the gravel drive and carried it along the country road in spring-made rivers. Neighbors found heaps of gravel in their yards once the water receded.

Quality Quarry backed in a massive truck. Helen and Paul were equipped with steel rakes. The truck maneuvered up the ruined drive without sinking its wheels and released pile after pile of limestone chunks as it crept forward. They raked gravel flat after the first pile was out. Paul's shirt stuck to his low back. The truck left for another load. They raked. They leveled sharp rocks that stuck upright. Dust covered his dark jeans and steel-toe boots. She worked in a huge T-shirt, her long-sleeved shirt already hung on a tree branch. He struggled out of his shirt and tied it around his head to stop sweat streaming into his eyes. The second batch came. They worked past lunch, stopping for gulps of water. Meg had parent-teacher conferences, so Helen and Paul worked up to dinner time. Pissing in the bushes. Blisters rose, popped, and bled into the weighty wood handles. Finally, the rakes became too much.

Rather than lift their arms to fix dinner, they stopped at Marie's on Main. Wet spines stuck to the truck seats. Sweat and grime covered bodies. At Marie's they ordered, then shuffled to the bathrooms to scrub.

Using damp paper towels, he sponged his neck and head which left paper clumps and spiked hair. Cleanup of his upper body exposed more filth. He fluffed his graying hair under the hand dryer.

Helen met him at counter with damp hair. Gray smeared her neck where she'd tried to wash. The supper crowd was just beginning its white-haired approach, so the waitresses were too busy to bug them.

"Looks like you missed a spot," he said with a grin, his back to the glass-encased morning buns and watched as she flapped her hands to her throat. She reminded him of a duck.

She asked, "Here?" She rubbed at her neck with a clean hand.

"And there. And there," he said.

She moved her hand to each spot rubbing the dirt deeper. She took her hand away and looked at the gray fingertips.

"Guess I'm going back in. Make sure to ask for Marie's special burger sauce."

She stalked back to the bathroom, annoyed by his fooling with her. He turned to look over the baked things, imagining the warmth of each on his tongue. Swallowed the rush of saliva.

On her second reentry to society, she was cleaner, but sopping.

"Never knew Marie had showers in the ladies' room," he poked and couldn't help laughing.

"More like a freaking fire hose," and then squinting her eyes at him, "You sound like a hyena," she said.

"Yeah, well you look like a hyena and not the head part of a hyena."

She clocked him in his arm. Their orders arrived in Styrofoam boxes.

As they drove out to look at a potential fishing hole for Sunday, they could barely hold back hunger. She handed him three fries at a time smothered in ketchup. The grit made it impossible to chew them at first, but after swigs of Coke and more fries, the grit worked itself free. She continued handing him bouquets of fries. Then stuffed three in her mouth. At the creek, they ate in silence. Cassettes toppled out of the glove compartment when Helen fished for napkins. She pushed one into the tape player.

"What's this, Old Man?" Helen asked.

Paul looked at her, "Steely Dan."

He opened the cab. She followed. Water lapped the banks making them sloppy. He slogged downstream where he'd seen a limestone face. A deep hole with dead tree roots looked perfect for skittish brookies. Debris made it difficult to see anything. By trout season, he imagined fat fish. Peering into the pool, she slipped and knocked into his hip. Instinctually, he grabbed her elbow. Pulled her upright. She twisted and clutched his forearm for balance. As she righted herself, she faced him. Her face glowed from the day's work. His fingers combed her gritty hair. He pushed her head toward his. Heads moved forward. Lips met. They slid tongues over one another's, tasting musky and wet like the muddy riverbanks.

Somewhere inside him a voice yelled to stop. She was too young. She wanted his farm, he knew it. But somehow, she desired him, he thought. He told himself, "I won't stop." He wouldn't think of Meg who couldn't want him. Or Evan who'd left. He skimmed his hands down her body, noticing the round belly. He unbuckled her belt. But she placed both palms over his and pushed him away.

"I'm all for free love, don't get me wrong. But, I don't believe Meg is, and I think when your head's on straight, neither are you."

He said nothing. She buckled her belt, watching him. Slowly she walked back to the truck. He stood beside the crick. He wouldn't have stopped, he thought again. Even though he loved the person he'd married, he'd have laid on this spongy ground with his son's lover. Water rushed to the Mississippi. Trout dug into crevices. Meg spoke with parents. She'd be coming home soon. Paul walked back to the truck and Helen. Steely Dan rang out as he opened the cab.

He yelled over it, "I'm sorry, Helen."

"No problem," she said, looking out the window.

On their way back to the farm, their bodies heated the cab to a great sweaty stench and he thought it was also her anger. Both were showered and in different rooms when Meg returned. Leftovers warmed on the stove for her. He rubbed his wife's shoulders and listened to the report. Helen knitted on the couch. After picking at her dinner, Meg trudged off to bed. He tailed her. He did not look at Helen's bare feet.

Meg's hair mushroomed about her face. Eyes already closed. He pulled back the quilt she'd stitched last summer and swiped her book from the side table pushing his body into hers as he reached across. He read what Meg had just consumed. Cleared himself of Helen, his son's girlfriend.

SPRING

Sprouting Grass Moon

The Tractor

Hiran

It took seconds to comprehend. He'd been bombing back to the farm in his dad's Dodge Neon. The low tree limb leaves just opening. No cab on the tractor in the steep ditch. The wheels. He recognized the tractor before the man. Old-time Massey Harris. Jason. He knew it was Jason's. Though he didn't know Jason, he knew what his father has said about Jason's girlfriend, Lani. Hiran realized he knew very little about the man splayed out in front of him on 425th Ave. Hiran's car stopped, parked now ten feet away. But he thought, *it is he who is stopped*. His fingers became wooden and unforgiving on the wheel. *He must reverse*, he thought. *Just reverse*. Let someone else deal with the tragedy of Jason.

He peered into the rearview mirror shifting into reverse. He couldn't move. A black jeep was parked on his tail. The man inside marine-style shave. His wrestling coach. The whole town's wrestling coach.

"God," he shouted, though he didn't pray.

Through the windshield he couldn't quite see Jason, though he could make out his shape. He did not want to see Jason. His inability to help was worse than his move to reverse. It is a moment he will replay for years to come. How he can't become doctor if he can't help an injured man.

But it is a spring day. A man laid out beside the street. The sidewise tractor like an enormous, overturned bug.

His coach came then and gripped the open window like he was gripping Hiran's arm or maybe Jason's.

"Call 911, kid. Tell him we're on 425th Ave., just off county W. Tractor accident. Tell them bring an ambulance."

The tractor had rolled down the ditch and stayed. A red spinning thing right beside a massive patch of asparagus. In a farm community, farm accidents still happened, but they were rare with all the safety improvements. Hiran hadn't lost anyone in school yet. The older men remembered. Sometimes on the news there'd be someone who fell into a corn silo—its poisoned embrace. He couldn't look anywhere. Out his windshield Coach Frank and Jason. Out the side— the spinning tractor wheels. Behind him—the black jeep like a hearse. He looked at his hands. He called.

Perhaps it was good to die in the arms of the old wrestling coach, one who'd sent so many farm boys to state. He was the surrogate father to thirty years of boys. Better than a boy holding your hand. Better than a stranger driving up. But Jason was most probably dead before Coach came.

Hiran spoke with the EMT on the phone. Then he sat. He couldn't talk himself out of the car. He couldn't even imagine how he could help the mangled man. His coach yelled. Coach turned to him and yelled. Hiran had to get out of the car. He felt for the lock button. Didn't push it. He found the door handle, opened his door, and stepped out like he was injured.

"You got towels or blankets, kid?"

Hiran shook his head, no.

"Give me your shirt."

Coach bare-chested, his shirt wrapped and soaked on the body. Then Hiran was bare. Young brown man. Old white man. Dead middle-aged man wrapped in their shirts. Coach kneeled beside Jason, one hand behind Jason's head the other on his hand.

Coach spoke first, "Stay with me, Jason. Stay with me. You're a fighter. I know. I've seen you fight."

Then Coach yelled, "Help is coming. Dammit, don't you leave."

He whispered in Jason's ear and Hiran couldn't hear him anymore. He couldn't look. And in a moment Hiran's whole future slid out of focus.

Morels

Hiran and Lupine

If Geirolf hired you, it meant you'd signed over a certain amount of your life for three years. Summer and Christmas. He made it clear without saying he would be working and so would everyone. Hiran didn't mind. He was always in at 5 a.m. But Sam was at him right after the accident asking what Jason looked like flayed. And Geirolf looked at him with somber eyes, asked if he needed a break. No. Nope. Hiran would work every morning like he had before.

Then Lupine began prowling before and after milking. She'd ask if he needed a ride to school. He wasn't comfortable riding shotgun in Geirolf's dualie pick-up with his only daughter. Not that Hiran cared much about locker room banter, but he knew she'd be the centerfold. The odd, homeschooled sister of two bad-boy football stars. Neither with farming plans. Too much work. Not enough pay. He didn't want to be seen in a truck with her. If he didn't feel so sorry for her, her smile may have melted him.

One morning she'd brought thermoses of stinking hot tea. Even Manny couldn't stomach it after adding several spoonfuls of fresh, raw milk (Geirolf would have burned if he knew Lupine had suggested it). She'd also said something about mixing nettles and rosehips, a tip from her neighbor.

Later the men wondered if she knew that you were supposed to remove the plant debris before serving tea.

It was that earnest awfulness that made Hiran agree to go on a wildflower walk with her one Sunday. Even though he knew it meant he'd miss mass. Even though his parents' wrath would come in silence, wholly in line with their Catholic guilt. For Hiran, a little silence seemed good. His mother kept asking if he wanted to talk with her or with some professional about his feelings.

Flowers were good. Flowers and ticks and buckthorn and grapevine. Things that wouldn't question him. As long as Lupine didn't ask him how he felt, the walk might do him good.

He wondered how a vibrant girl could come from old Geirolf. His wood and leather skin sprung from the woodblock print book of Norwegian trolls, Hiran's mother had read.

Lupine dressed in boots, baseball cap, and pack with Wisconsin guides to wildflowers. They took off toward the bluffs, walking along the wind block that split two emerging soybean fields. Once they reached the bluffs, she took off with him running behind. Shocking him, she crushed blooming trout lilies and a few fat trilliums as she leapt for some golden, bent-headed morels. The wildflower books a front. Here he'd thought she'd had a romantic, slow stroll in mind. He wondered if she simply wanted another person. He couldn't make her out and didn't feel the need to either. The quiet was okay with him.

She knew where to find morels and hit all the south-facing bluffsides and newly dead elms at her long lope. He was the one who pointed out the Dutchman's breeches, hepatica, blood root, wood anemone, wild geraniums and jack in the pulpits. Even when he spotted a lady slipper, she smiled moon-white, but kept trotting over stumps and moldering leaves, making him wish it were his mother with him. If they could just slow down. Maybe he was wrong about the talking. Maybe he did want to talk. Just not with his family.

The light bright in the woods without the green filters of full leaves. The sun only broken by the naked limbs just coming to life. Another one of her morel pronouncements was yelled back at him—oak leaves the size of mice ears.

"What a year," she shouted.

He fumbled through the buckthorn, his arms already a mess from a bramble patch he struck while tailing her. He'd never taken a spring-woods walk like this: off-trail, on land he no longer knew.

Against his better judgement, he suggested they make a morel supper. He had in mind cooking at her house with "normal" people. Walk back the way they came and eat soon. They'd been in the woods for hours.

Instead, she said, "Sounds great. I'd love to meet your folks."

His gut kicked like it was digesting itself, but he refused to alter plans. So, his mother wouldn't talk to them because they missed mass. His father would talk without break about zoning for the new community center set either on the downtown playground or to take over the old movie theatre. Both options had the whole town raging at each other in town meetings and over pages of the local paper. His father gave him nightly updates. It's how his father communicated with him these days: a paper in front of him, black glasses low on his lean nose. Hiran's sister and brother could walk out of the room for some sport, some assignment. As the oldest, he felt his father's approval. And guilt was there too—for he didn't want to become his father in this small part of the world.

But Lupine said she didn't like cooking around Gin. He figured if you couldn't call your mother 'mom' there probably was lime build-up in the piping. He didn't explain about the missed mass or where his parents thought his life was headed.

After hacking their way back to the farm, they caught a ride with the Hernandez cousins. He and Manny squished in the back seats. She was by Luke and Mathias in front. Her pack of mushrooms on her thighs. Before they all toppled out on his front walk, she plopped a paper sack on Luke's lap.

Hiran and Lupine left muddy boots and burrs plucked from their hair and jeans outside the front door. They headed back to the kitchen where soup simmered and his mother cut carrots. Without introduction, his mother watched as Lupine lifted brown paper bags from her pack. She folded down the paper sides. His mother, Kristin, ogled. Maybe he was off the hook for mass.

"Goodness, it's been years since I've tasted morels. Have I ever taken you morel hunting?" she asked Hiran's father, Nikilchandra, who came in from the living room.

"Nope, never."

"Really? Gosh, I thought that weekend we first came down to meet my parents…" She helped Lupine remove mushrooms from a sack then drop them into a metal bowl.

"Oh, that weekend," he laughed. His parents gazed at one another, sharing a before-life he didn't care to know about. His father kissed his mother's neck, brushing her hair.

"So, what do we cook them with?" Hiran asked, breaking his parents' moment. He opened up the fridge hoping to break his parents' awkward connection. He rustled through the vegetable drawer.

"I have some garden-leeks." His mother hurriedly moved him aside and dug inside their fridge.

"Great, if you have garlic that's even better," said Lupine.

She ran cold water over the morels and set them on the counter to soak.

"Always," said his mother, "wouldn't dream of a kitchen without those."

His mother opened a cupboard and took out a butter dish then reached for a head of garlic. She was proud of her cooking abilities, ticking off the full-course Bengali meals she'd made for his father without any direction from his Bengali grandmother. He'd heard it all before. His mother stood before Lupine, her white-blonde hair pulled into a sleek braid and Lupine's hair a mess. He could still see sticks poking through.

"So, Lupine," she began, "we haven't seen you around before. What do you do?"

Here it comes, thought Hiran. His mother's application process: who's your family, what are your interests, grades, college and job sights. She interviewed all his friends. Those who he brought over.

"Her dad is Geirolf. She doesn't play sports, she's homeschooled," he snapped.

His mother's eyes hurt him. He shouldn't have barked at her. He stared at the golden, gray curves of mushrooms, ignoring her expression.

"Oh," she turned back to Lupine. "I see. Your mom's Ginny?"

He thought Lupine's spine shifted; she became focused on turning morels over in the bowl of water with her fingertips.

"Yup," Lupine mouthed more than spoke.

He pulled out several different-sized knives. He had no idea what one used to cut morels. His mother already crushed the side of a large steel blade against a clove of garlic. Broke the papery seal and then peeled it off before slicing. Lupine remained silent as she continued with the soaking morels.

"You know she used to be a good friend of mine." His mother finished the first clove and began crushing another.

"Really?" Lupine stopped and looked at her, fingertips dripping water.

"Yeah. We were both going to leave forever, and do something big," she laughed, and looked meaningfully at Hiran's father, who was busy grinding their afternoon coffee, his back to them.

"I guess we lost touch over the years," she said, as another clove was chopped. She chose a leek, rinsed it under the faucet, peeled back the first layer to get at the mud, and began slicing.

"Yeah, that happens to people," said Lupine.

"Your grandpa is still making it to church, I see. Don't see your mom at mass, though."

"Gin is pretty caught up in the farm," Lupine said, straining water from the morels. "Do you have a knife and a cutting board I could use?"

He handed her the knives and slid a cutting board across the counter for her to use.

"Hiran, you can help Lupine cut mushrooms. I'll finish the leeks."

Leave it to his mother to direct things. His father stayed out of the picture as he did. It was surprising how Lupine was comfortable just inserting herself in his life. His mother didn't seem to have a problem with it. But he felt a problem brewing, though he didn't know exactly what.

Lupine even had a small stash of fiddlehead ferns for a dash of green. Hiran's mother sautéed the leeks and morels in butter. He was happy Lupine had refused to cook, leaving the meal up to his mother. He'd had an unfortunate sip of that tea she'd fixed and didn't want another of her concoctions.

"I think we have time to make crostini with some fresh sourdough. We could eat our morels, leeks, and fiddleheads on top. Who needs soup with treasures like these" his mother said as she put everyone in the kitchen to work with bread knives.

At dinner, Hiran's little sister Moumita said, "Those look like slugs." She pointed at the morels on her plate.

"Well, slugs love morels. Lots of crawlies, really. They have perfect hiding spots," said Lupine.

"Did you find slugs in these?" asked Moumita.

"Of course. And ants and caterpillars and spiders too," Lupine said with an open smile. Hiran and his mother grimaced.

"I am not touching this," Moumita said.

At the same moment Hiran's brother, Nitish, said, "Alrrright" and made lip-smacking noises.

Hiran couldn't stand dinners with these people. They drove him nuts. If he could just slip into his room. He couldn't believe Lupine seemed to be enjoying herself.

"Moooomm," Moumita shrieked.

It was then Nikilchandra who tried to dampen the tension by asking Lupine what she thought about the new superintendent. Hiran already knew the super had been suffering from migraines since he'd overheard his father say he wasn't surprised the guy was on brexpiprazole with all the headaches he was causing.

"She's homeschooled," said Hiran, which made Nikilchandra close his mouth after, "Ahh."

Lupine tried to smooth things over by saying, "Well, my brothers both went through the public school system."

Hiran looked around the table: Moumita's skinny arms crossed her thin chest, Nitish crammed morels into his open mouth, let it hang open so slivers of mushroom and bread slipped out. His mother was in her own savory world, and his father puzzled about his next topic. Lupine seemed the only sane person eating with relish.

All the awkwardness at the table should make for a one time stop, thought Hiran as he drove Lupine home in his mother's van.

"You've got a good family, Hiran," she said, "They're good people to be around."

He wondered if she was right. Maybe his eyes weren't seeing things straight anymore.

He said, "Ya, well, see you round."

She hopped out with her pack and the remaining morels.

Lupine said, "I'll probably catch you tomorrow morning after milking."

He guessed some people knew what they wanted.

Goat Breeding

Terra and Lupine

"Why don't you own goat bucks?" Lupine asked as she opened Terra's door before the sun snuck inside the windows.

"Morning, Lupine," said Terra.

Lupine took her usual seat and set an old thermos on the counter. A large one that had to have her peeing every 30 minutes. It looked like she was going on a camping trip.

She explained to Terra that she was trying out a new tea made with nettles and sumac. "I had too many leaves, so I added more water. Want a sip?"

"Thanks, but I'm waiting on my coffee," said Terra, and added more hot water to the drip filter.

"You going?" Lupine asked in a low voice.

Terra turned and looked at her, "To Jason's funeral, you mean?"

"Yeah," Lupine studied the thermos, scratched the outer shell with her nail, "Think everyone'll be there."

"Sad business, that," Terra sighed and turned back to her coffee, "I probably should."

Lupine coughed a bit, cleared the air, "About the bucks, though?" she poured her own hot water out into the thermos top and tried a sip. She pursed her mouth with the sour aftertaste.

"We had three," Terra was happy to talk about anything else than poor Jason, his kid, his girlfriend. It made her feel guilty to still feel like she couldn't get up some mornings. She exhaled it all out and thought about goats instead. She'd sold the bucks after Simon's heart attack. A friend helped. She'd wanted to sell the whole herd, but he convinced her she'd regret it. Instead, she'd offloaded the troublesome boys.

"Okay. You want to buy three?"

Lupine took another sip, grimaced again, and dumped the whole thermos down the sink. Terra put the kettle on for real tea.

"Nah."

Terra didn't know about beginning the workload again. She didn't think she could stomach it all on her own. The girl's interest was fervent at the moment, but Terra couldn't trust a teenager to milk indefinitely. And she sure as hell didn't know anyone else crazy enough to work for beans.

"Oh, okay."

"Not yet, I mean. I know someone in the Valley. I think she'd lend me a couple good bucks for a month or longer. Your dad doesn't have a bull on the property. Does he?"

"Nope, doesn't want to work with bulls. We got a good thing going with artificial insemination."

Lupine finally had a decent cup of tea steeping in front of her and Terra had her first cup of coffee with goat milk. Terra was easing into these mornings with Lupine. In the past she'd have been out the door already working, but then those were different times. She felt more like talking than she expected and it was the goofy memories and articles she remembered.

"Did he ever order semen from Toy Story? What did he sire like 100,000 calves? Did you snag any of that article?"

"Sure sure, Dad ate that up, but seriously, I have nothing to do with that end. Never have."

"I'll get on the horn and arrange things. Let's focus on making some cheese no matter how small the batch."

Lupine was ready to run, Terra could sense this. Not many clients, so not a lot of pressure. Lupine downed her tea, burning her throat no doubt. Ready to milk. Terra knew she was stepping into her new routine. It caught in her throat before she cleared her grief for that morning and allowed herself to move forward.

The Funeral

The small Lutheran church constructed 140 years ago on the western side of the Clayfields while the former Catholic Church held down the eastern section. Countless country congregations died out—the buildings converted into homes or antique stores, opened once a year for a pie social, or torn down. Nobody interested in heating the old timber through the winter or cleaning out all the Asian biting beetles. Young families moved to larger, newer churches with younger congregations and screens behind the altar. Or they didn't attend church at all, communing with nature, sports, literature, politics, web or any god or absence of God they felt made their lives longer.

This church was like so many country churches with a white spire reaching toward the clouds and God. The stained windows like everything else inside, modest. A working people's church. People with skin in the game.

On sunny mornings like this one, the stained glass colored the oak pews with prisms. The carved crosses were warm from it and the wooden altar and the ornate façade at the front all glowed. Light like a soothing hum from a great mother. Jesus in the mural looked skyward. Jesus a small note in the background with all that light. The pews were full, and people stood in the aisles where the red carpet had worn. The closed, simple casket (a surprise for some considering the wealth of the man). Money in this place tied up with land and equipment. And no one buried their money when it wouldn't fruit.

The Hollows' townspeople and the Clayfields' country people came. People littered the railings outside the church too, for not all could stand through the eulogies. They smoked their sadness instead, blowing it out with the wind. Emile weeping outside said, "Look, I think those old cottonwoods are crying."

Jed next to her nodded and sucked in more smoke while another man said, "Nope it's just dropping cotton."

"But it looks like fat tears," she insisted even though they all knew they weren't. Nature doesn't stop for a thing like this. The cows needed milking; the second crop of alfalfa needed cutting. The farmers knew you didn't lay down 'til you died.

And a meaner sort whispered just that to his buddy, "At least Jason gets to rest. Doesn't have to bring in the hay today before the rains." Even though he didn't fully believe dying was better than work cause work is bred into people here. Still, he'd be the one to come later that night with a bottle of whiskey, a bit in the bag himself. He'd pour shots over the mound of Jason. Drinking buddies to the end.

Inside the church, the young pastor had open palms and an open face looking upward like the mural behind her. She wept, silently. Thankfully. Her first funeral for a young person. She had the highest hopes for her new community. She said it was hard to reconcile such a meaningless death of one with such promise. A young son left (and an unmarried common-law-wife many think). Jason's fiancé choked and bawled into the downy hair of their son.

"Such events in our lives are difficult to grasp. It is okay to be angry, to question your choices, and your loved ones' choices. It is good for us to talk with someone, to know someone is there listening above, though God will not change our lives for us, our dreams, our futures. It is God who is there always. God is the greatest ear for us. If we talk and think and pray, we can find the strength to continue in life. If we believe Jason is in heaven and we can speak with his soul and love the eternal Jason, it makes losing the mortal body a little easier because he is here with us and inside us. Not in a box but within our memory of him. He lives when we catch the muskie. Remember how every summer for several weekends Jason lured muskie at his family's northern cabin. He said once, 'in his second life he would have been a fishing guide.' He fished for browns on slow mornings before sunrise. Many times, he brought his beloved Lani. Their unborn baby. He was teaching the baby how to fish then as Ned swam inside his own waters." A sob broke from Lani. Her sister rocked her and Ned.

"Jason took baby Ned on the banks of Hollows' Creek. It is up to you to take Jason's son into your arms and teach him about his father. Tell him stories. Bring Jason back in memories. And his love, Lani, must have your support as she raises Ned. She needs this community's help. Luckily this is a community where many of you are related to Jason or knew him or his family. We must use our communal strength to raise up his child." The country pastor's dark hair glowed red in the light as she finished.

The people outside heard the organ and knew it was close to over. They could smell the crocks of warming soups and tables full of casseroles, their glass lids glazed with condensation. The Wisconsin funerary potluck: potato leek and cheese curd soup, tuna fish and tater tot, chicken and broccoli, spiced macaroni and cheese casseroles, pulled pork and soft buns. Jars of dill and sweet pickles, dilly beans, pickled eggs, asparagus, cloved beets, and sauerkraut. Pasta salads and Jell-O with glowing fruit and fresh whipped cream. Marshmallows in too many dishes. Then the platters of bars and cookies and pies both seasonal and strange: rhubarb, strawberry, peanut butter, chocolate, coconut, lemon, even a bloody-colored pomegranate, too odd to try. Tables set inside and outside, far from the falling cotton. Esther, her grandmother, Marie and other women setting everything days before, beginning their crocks and mixers as soon as they heard the news.

Before the food came, the burial began out in the pristine cemetery. Clean, modest stones looked over the Clayfields and corn. Jason would rest as the others worked in his surrounding fields. No longer *his* fields. Corn roots were sipping the waters and broad leaves changing sunlit energy to chlorophyll.

The hole had already been dug by a small backhoe, easier in the summer months than a winter death. The people behind the scenes had gone for coffee since no one wants to see the work behind burying a person. Plastic green grass covered the mound, not much brighter than the grass. The backhoe parked behind the small, stone building, which held lawn accoutrements and mowers. Those workers were aware of how death should look despite the technicalities: unnoticeable, easy, and done only in sight of God.

"For," the one gravedigger said at the McDonald's since Marie's on Main had closed for the funeral, "this body is beloved and no one wants to know the crawlies and dirt dump on him." He said this to his young partner just learning the way. The young man seemed as far from death as those tractors in the fields. He was having a chocolate shake, for his metabolism and energy were high. He didn't like the bitter bite of coffee. It was his old uncle with his Styrofoam coffee cup and creamers who looked haggard after his umpteenth cigarette. The kid and uncle knew of Jason and maybe were remotely related since their families had all lived in the Clayfields for generations. They were outside being gravediggers, though they did other excavation work. "Just two men and an excavator," the old uncle had said to his kid nephew.

Back in the churchyard, folks swam down the concrete steps after the coffin. It looked like a boat, the pallbearers its sailors. Lupine and Geirolf helped Etzel down the concrete stairs. A walking procession fifteen feet from the church in a corner beneath a white pine, planted over a hundred years ago when the church was built. It was a good resting space for a man who didn't rest. The hole couldn't be too close to the pine for the roots couldn't be dug through. One could imagine its roots reaching out to the coffin, to Jason. Just as the arms waved upward. The pine crown a perfect foundation for an eagle's nest. It was a good spot to be forever. As these things go, many couldn't see it this way, sobbing out their loss of control, his loss, the tractor's.

"Dust to dust. Ashes to ashes," the pastor spoke. Roses were passed out to all who wished to lay them on Jason's casket, which sat atop the hole on a silver gadget made to lower him down.

The same fellow who nastily mentioned resting, whispered to his buddy in the way back, "You think those things ever fail?"

And his buddy snorted and choked to stop his laughter as he imagined the collective scream at a dropped coffin, the body tipped out. For as we know, life and laughter move on after the dead are wrapped and buried.

Jason's mother, a wide woman, pressed her hand on the coffin's warm side as though it were her son's body she was bringing back and not the sun warming the wood. She laid the rose. Jason's father led her back. The grandmothers, old but of strong, Norwegian stock, sister, uncles, aunts, and cousins laid their blooms where Jason's chest might be hiding.

Then the pastor opened her arms. The white gown hung like wings, and the embroidered purple sash trembled as she said, "Everyone is invited to a great feast in celebration of Jason's life. Just as our souls need sustenance at a time like this so do our bodies. I invite you all to take a plate downstairs and eat from all the glorious dishes our community wrought."

The women found Hiran in the crowd and wet his shoulders with their sobbing. They petted his cheeks, thanked him then moved on to fall on Coach Frank, the last people to see him alive. Emile sought out Lani and hugged her, letting go of their arguments.

The funeral done, everyone could relax their ties, take off their suit jackets and sling them over folding chairs, or slip off heels. It was permission to laugh at the cruder things about Jason—the drunken horse ride back from a bar or the time he skied through the cornfields but fell more than skied. It was permission to live again. Live and nourish and drink up the warm, enduring sun.

EARLY SUMMER

Strawberry Moon

On Love and Horses
Emile and Jed

Sweat tickled the hairs on Emile's neck, near the base of her riding helmet. She ignored it, driving her Appaloosa, Imogene, to attack the large, wooden barrels. The horse nearly skidded as she dove around one and then another barrel. Quick, tight circles and then a gallop back to the finish line. Emile's head low beside Imogene's neck, the reins closed in her hands. A yellow number swatted her back. The movement helped her keep Jason's death at bay. It helped her forget about the phone call she had to make. The apology to Lani and then how to help Lani shoulder such grief.

Emile and her horse both wheezed after their time. The horse championships had gotten harder these last five years. Emile's hips a little more generous. The horse stouter too, less agile. After she caught her breath, she accepted the silver trophy feeling fat beside all the willowy girls. How could she not have noticed herself aging? She'd spent too much of her meagre bartending wages on entering these contests, boarding her horse. She wiped her face on her cinched sleeve. One hand on Imogene's bridle, the other on the medal.

Once by the horse trailer, she unbuckled Imogene's harness. She lifted the saddle and removed the blanket beneath. She filled a netted bag with fresh hay and rehung it from the trailer side for Imogene. While the horse ate, Emile brushed her down. She unlaced the ribbons and plaits from her mane and brushed 'til the horse shone. She unwrapped the slim legs and lifted each hoof, inspecting. She couldn't help it: the tractor accident washed over her.

"Hey," she heard Jed say as his hand skimmed along her spine. Her muscles quivered. She hadn't realized how tight she was, and she quickly wiped her nose.

"Hey back," she said from beneath Imogene. She felt her chest expand with Jed here; he had no idea what it meant to her. Jed didn't move any closer forward to help her. The horse stamped once Emile set the last hoof down. It was the first time he'd come to one of her competitions. She felt this truly was her last.

"You looked great out there," he said his eyes on her tight, dusty jeans and tighter blouse. "You're really good."

"I used to be great. Shoulda seen me when I was eighteen. C'mere," she took his hand. How she loved him even more now after knowing what could be lost. His huge blonde head looked tousled. His face feverish from the spring sun and his eyes brighter because of his burn.

"Here's how you touch a horse," she pulled at his hand, but he barely inched forward. "You're scared shitless of this horse." She stared at him until his face burned redder and his eyes dropped to look at his work boots.

"Shit on a stick, I had no idea," she breathed.

She understood now why he'd never come to her competitions, something that hurt and she'd hid. But this wasn't like her daddy who'd never be caught dead on a "hay burner." And never did before he'd died. Jed was honestly afraid. She felt her heart expand at his fear. It made her love protective.

"Jed, I'm just gonna have you pat her nose. I swear she's a good girl. And her nose is real soft. You wouldn't want to miss it."

He allowed her to move his fingers to the end of Imogene's snout.

"Oh," he said, "you're right. It's like velvet."

He smoothed his fingers down, and said he'd come to show her something. Could she come with him now, he wondered?

She watched his thick fingers sweep across Imogene. She said if he gave her thirty minutes to drop her horse off at her mother's place, he'd have a deal.

Then they were in his truck rushing down a gravel road between farmlands.

"Can you guess where we're headed?" he asked excitedly, gesturing out his open window.

"Nope."

His fingers tapped the steering wheel. Excitement filled the cab. She spun up the radio volume, hoping to break some of his anticipation. She loosened her braids, let her hair float out with the wind. Long frizzy tendrils escaped from her fingers as she combed through the mess. She unsnapped the tight, plaid blouse and slipped it off. She sat in a damp tank, jeans, and dusty cowboy boots. What a hot early spring. She knew farmers had planted corn already. She watched fire numbers blur past the window. Basic farmhouses overlooking patterned hilltops. They were nearing Painted Turtle Lake, above it on the river bluffs. Jed turned onto a gravel drive. A sagging blueberry sign hung from a post behind a fire number.

"It's not blueberry season," she said and jerked up higher in her seat.

"Nope, but I thought you might wanna look over this property with me," he said.

She had never imagined herself as a berry farmer. But the acreage unrolled itself in front of them like a plush, green rug. Immense flower gardens with first perennials poking up: lupines with their little green hands, iris, tulips, daffodils with their bright heads.

They jumped from the truck. They walked around the American foursquare, which could use several buckets of paint. The steps invitingly crooked. Emile glimpsed a barn and walked toward it. Jed trailed her. It appeared sturdy with a solid, new roof. A few sagging lines but nothing structurally wrong.

"I was thinking this could be Imogene's," he said from behind her.

She felt a prick at the corner of her eyes and snorted. Yes, this was perfect. She imagined filling the dark barn with more horses, maybe a chicken roost, egg boxes.

"Come look out back," Jed pulled her to the hillside where hundreds of waist high bushes lined the slope. Glossy leaves were just beginning to show. Little white lantern-like blossoms moved with the breeze. Blueberries.

He led her to another green overlook: the view of Painted Turtle Lake.

"Well," he said low in her ear, his arms wrapping her waist.

"Well, what?" she asked smiling out at the expanse of water fanning out below them. She wondered if he'd get on a knee in front of her. But she told herself not to rush it.

"Should we buy it?" he asked.

In the back of her mind, she knew if they purchased this place they'd be signing on to years of weeding, trimming, picking, and planting. But the thought couldn't stem her excitement about owning land. And really, she'd grown up on a dairy. She knew hard work when she saw it, and it never scared her none. Plus, blueberries weren't cows. She wanted to say to him: see me, Jed, see how I'm with you on this. See how I'll never leave. I'm not her, Jed. But she didn't say a thing. She looked over the bushes just beginning to show lamps that would drop in time, leaving a green nub of fruit.

Forward Ho

Terra and Lupine

"What's this billy goat like?" Lupine asked as she jumped into Terra's pick-up, on their way to check out bucks at a nearby farm. Morning milking done. Animals fed. Full of coffee and cereal and possibilities. Their moods shining with the mid-morning sun.

"Stay on that one," Lupine said as Terra flipped through stations. Then she sang, "I ain't gonna make it to twenty years old."

"What crap lyrics," Terra said checking the side mirror before she passed an enormous tractor with a fertilizer attachment. She waved to the young farmer driving.

"What. Why?" Lupine went back to singing but turned to look at Terra's face while she sang. "The woman has pipes, literally." She turned up the volume.

Terra kept her hands on the wheel though she wanted to flip the song down. She really was getting old, she thought. But the song irked her. Somehow culture had gotten younger as she'd aged. Everyone set on the massive promise of the young.

"Didn't think I was gonna make it to twenty years old," Terra scoffed, "Literally?"

"Okay, she has crazy biceps, triceps and vocal chords. You knew what I meant. Are you laughing at me?"

"No. I'm laughing at that piss poor field."

The field was piss poor and they gazed at the new uneven rows of corn. Planted late with poor germination and wash-out. Without saying anything they both felt for the sorry sap who'd have a bummer of a year.

"Yeah. Anyway, she's this amazing singer before she hits twenty-five. At first listen, I thought this has got to be a man."

"Sure, she's got a great voice, the lyrics bug me. Come on. Twenty-one?"

Twenty years ago for Terra. If she went by what she accomplished at twenty-one…well, there was no need to go into any further memory of her twenty-first year.

"Thing is we'll be listening to some other superstar with pipes in another month," Terra said.

"I suppose, but Billie Holliday is still known."

"Billie Holliday was revolutionary."

"Sure. Darn, now we just talked through her song," Lupine leaned out her window, "Those fields were awful though. Must of planted late."

The pick-up became quiet after Lupine snapped off the stereo. She stuck her arm and hand out against the wind. A great rushing came through as her hand was pushed back by the force of air.

"Didn't see you there," she said, looking at her hand.

"At the funeral?" Terra looked over at her and then back at the road ahead of them, "Yeah, I couldn't seem to make myself go."

"That's what I thought," Lupine said, and they were quiet while the wind sang against Lupine's hand.

At times Terra thought Lupine was hiding some sadness of her own, but Terra couldn't dig into that, not yet at least.

She had too much of her own grief to manage, which felt like her job.

It was good to be on the road with a specific direction. A fine day to pick up an animal. The heat hadn't yet broken into spring, changing plants to summer. Lilacs had dropped, but nights were cool. Terra and Lupine had lifted the large animal crate into the back of the gray goose the previous morning. Using bungee cords and rope, they secured it close to the cab back window. They'd fussed with the cords and added rope which Terra tied into weird knots. She admitted tying things down wasn't her craft. Lupine couldn't help much with the tie down either, and she mentally noted she should study knots. Keep things in place.

They turned down a dandelion-dotted drive. The farm was much larger than Goat's Back Ridge with a couple dozen grazing Jersey cows, golden in the sun. A brick silo, new pole shed, and barn caught their eyes before the farmhouse. A forklift parked in sight. It was the way of Wisconsin dairies. All monies invested in the tools of the trade: buildings, tractors, implements, beasts, and land. The dogs came out to greet them, herding the truck like any critter on the property. No person in sight, though large pens of bottle-fed kids stood up on their fencing for scratches.

"Gert's a real dairy goat operation," Terra said. "I bet she's back here." She motioned Lupine to follow.

They walked past a pile of kittens, another staple on a dairy and back to a handful of animal structures connected to a sturdy fence and even studier gate.

Terra leaned over the gate and called, "Hey Gert, its Terra and Lupine. You back there?"

More than a dozen does rushed the gate like oversized puppies. They responded immediately to the new voices.

"Come on in," a voice trilled from inside one of the structures. "I'm just cleaning out these pens."

Terra unlatched the gate and pushed into the goats. Lupine followed and snapped the gate shut. They walked toward the small barns. A stout, open-faced woman and her eleven-year-old daughter threw down fresh bales of straw inside the first. The air was musty sweet and full of particulate. Mangers held hay for the does and the floor was golden with clean straw.

"We're almost finished here."

They continued spreading out hay then stepped out.

"Hi Terra, Lupine," Gert took their hands, "this is Charlotte."

Gert gave her shirt a shake and finger-combed her short hair. Charlotte was a thick child with strong legs and back. She copied her mother's moves stomping her feet to free the flecks of straw from her pants. One of the does bumped into her side. She scratched between the long ears, talking to the goat.

"Whew, we're covered. It's good to see you, Terra," Gert embraced Terra then inspected her face. "I'm glad you're getting back into the saddle."

"Me too."

She hadn't seen Gert since Simon's funeral. It'd been a rough year, but she felt more like herself most days. It was good to see her old friend. Someone who knew how to work even through difficult times. Gert never spoke more than necessary, but she said enough with her arms.

"Lupine's my 'intern,'"Terra smiled and moved back from Gert, pulling Lupine forward for a handshake. Charlotte scratched another doe listening to the exchange.

"Ahh," Gert's eyes measured Lupine's, "whereabouts you live?"

"We're the next farm East of Terra."

One of the biggest does placed her forelegs on Lupine's chest demanding a chest rub. It made talking difficult. Goat musk permeated Lupine's T-shirt and jean shorts. Her boots were caked with wet manure. The farm never stayed outside, infecting the whole person. She rubbed the speckled chest, loving this kind of immersion.

"My house used to be her grandad's," interjected Terra.

Terra wondered about Etzel's move to the old folks' home outside of town. Lupine used to retell his stories while milking, but she hadn't as much anymore. But then, he was old and sometimes stories do just die out with the person.

"We heard about that tractor accident your way," Gert said, "Bad thing."

They all nodded. Quiet but for the goats against them.

"You know him then?" Gert asked.

"Yeah, Jason helped me out with my fields after Simon."

"Damn shame that," Gert whispered, and they all stood watching the animals and Charlotte. Gert rubbed a speckled-faced doe, "You farm then?" she asked and pushed another doe back to her hooves, away from Lupine's face.

"Yup. We milk about a hundred head."

"Ahh, so you could teach us all," Gert laughed.

Lupine and Terra looked at each other. They both knew she wasn't following Geirolf or Etzel's milking principals. It was at once frightening and rousing.

"Actually, Lupine wants to know more about small farms, goats, and making goat cheeses."

"I see. Well, let's look over the bucks. I got two nice fellas chosen 'cause I know you haven't been following a breeding plan. I'll have to show you mine before you leave."

They left the does after Charlotte showed them her favorites and their biggest producers. Names like Portia, Olivia, Viola, Juliet, Lady Macbeth.

"We're studying Shakespeare," Gert winked.

Then she latched the gate and led them over to another enclosure with barrel-chested males. Most fought for a spot closest to their visitors. Even more ardent than the does. Musk and urine struck nostrils as Lupine's hand stopped mid-scratch.

"Phew."

"Hi stinkers," laughed Charlotte. She rubbed one butterscotch billy. "You should smell them in the fall. They pee on their bellies and beards."

"This one, here," Gert fingered a dark ear, "Is Malvolio. We were thinking he'd do well for you."

"He was born last spring," said Charlotte.

"His mother is Beatrice, a solid milker and his sisters are calm milkers too," said Gert.

A thick-chested Nubian, he fell on their fingers, loving the attention. His forehead curls coarse and free of horns.

"Malvolio can't win ribbons at the fair," Charlotte said, "His ears are on backwards."

Gert demonstrated how the ears should lay by pulling them forward. Then let them flop back into position.

"I used to bottle feed him," said Charlotte as she pulled some of the long grass. All the other bucks butted to get at the fresh greens. Anything over the fence better.

"We'd need another pen."

"And this fine fellow is a Kinder buck," said Gert. She pulled the collar on a stout creamy animal. His legs shorter and thicker than Malvolio, without the Roman nose and pendulous ears of the Nubians.

"This is Valentine," said Charlotte.

Lupine and Terra scratched Valentine, admiring his smaller body. It'd be easier for them to deal with him than two Nubian bucks. Simon had always been in charge of breeding schedules. Terra figured it'd be good to bring in a different breed, change easier to generate when working for herself.

"Why not," Terra said.

"Kinder milk is sweet, creamy. I bet it'd make a great chèvre. Maybe you could try making brie."

"Oh, I love brie," said Charlotte.

"My next cheese could be Queen Charlotte," It was the closest Terra got to ruffling the girl's hair. Somehow Terra knew this child wasn't one to be petted, too used to a working life. Charlotte smiled and changed the contours of her round face. Her cheeks dimpled. Her eyes shone. Maybe Terra was wrong. If she didn't feel tired from so much human interaction after days of so little, she might have asked Charlotte more about Shakespeare. If the character's names had anything to do with the personalities of each goat. Maybe she'd read Shakespeare as a girl, but she couldn't remember.

"So, what do you think about these two guys?" asked Gert. "Are they a pair?"

"Only if you have an extra crate."

"Sure. Charlotte, can you grab one of the dog crates from the garage? I'm going to show these two our milking operation."

"Where do you want me to put it?" Charlotte asked.

"Just throw it next to my truck," said Terra.

"Don't actually throw it, Charlotte," Gert added. Then she whispered to Terra as Charlotte walked to the garage, "She's sometimes too literal with directions. We've become more careful about how we phrase things." Gert motioned them to follow her, back past the does to a small barn. She opened the door and they walked inside a white, concrete interior.

"This is new since I was last here," said Terra admiring the gleam of white paint and new enclosures for each doe's head.

"Ed built it for me with the boys last spring. Look, I can have all my does in a row rather than having only two set up at a time."

"Wow Gert, this is the real deal."

"Yup, just like Ed's Jerseys. Now I'm selling milk commercially. I was just selling to some Amish fellows. Now I have a tank back here in the milk room."

They walked away from the head clasps into a small white-washed room with stainless sinks and large metal container.

"You're not milking by hand anymore?"

"Nope. I only miss it a little."

Terra patted the big drum, "So how much milk can you keep in here?"

"About 500 pounds. They pick up every two days."

"Imagine the cheese we could make, Terra."

"We haven't even bred our does yet," replied Terra.

"No, but we will this month." Lupine said admiring the charts on the wall. The clean organized milk room, a scale model of her father's dairy.

Terra smiled and said, "Impressive, Gert. You can't still be working in town then."

"Nope. Ed and I had that big talk last year, and we came to a decision. I could be a full-time goat dairy. We both felt we could get a loan from the bank to back it, which we did. But Ed's still working for the fire department and the county highway road service. He loves it too much to quit. Me though, I couldn't stand working as a personal banker anymore, getting gussied up every morning after milking at four-thirty."

"It's good to be able to do what you want," said Lupine.

Charlotte trotted up, "Crate's by your truck."

"Thanks, Charlotte," said Terra.

"Hey Charlotte, you want to walk them through the cow milking parlor?"

"Sure."

They walked out of the barn and across a swath of green to the red pole shed. One half of it enclosed for the milking parlor and another half open air where several fawn-colored Jerseys lay on shavings in divided stalls. They were beneath the roof instead of grazing outside with the others. They had the choice to pasture or hunker down, the gate open for the cows to come and go. Silage remains on the concrete floor in front of the metal dividers.

Charlotte pointed out the step-up parlor, speaking with authority about how they'd constructed it. She had Terra lift one of the milking vacuum pumps hung beside an industrial sink. Each weighed about five pounds, and they all agreed how they preferred the dainty does and their smaller equipment.

"They're making milk," said Charlotte as they walked by the chewing Jerseys. She grabbed an industrial broom and swept away their breakfasts. Moments of idleness rare for a farming family. Silage, hay, and manure sweetened the air.

Gert asked Terra her feed ratios while opening an enormous square bale to show the green of alfalfa. Then it was time for Charlotte and Gert to clean water troughs.

Terra and Lupine separated the two bucks from their crew, which was like stemming the flow of the Mississippi. All bucks pushed against the fence. They crated them separately and secured the ties and bungees to the truck. Charlotte threw in a stack of alfalfa and timothy and mixed grains to adapt the buck's rumens to Terra's flock and feeding regimen.

The truck bumped back along country roads with two new genetic codes in tow. Visions of fattened does, fattened udders, and full milk pails danced in Terra's mind.

The Question of a Grandchild

Meg and Paul

Meg thought Helen was pregnant. Some sixth sense, she said after coming home wiped after singing all day.

"It's Evan's," she said. "I know it is and I want her to come back."

He knew it was Evan's too but felt some sort of ugliness soar up his throat and said, "It's somebody's that's all we know. And we won't know even if she's doing the telling."

"Well, Emile's doing all the telling all over the Clayfields. LaVonne told me Vern's heard it at the Junction Bar and now everyone's talking about Evan being a father."

"LaVonne don't know when to shut it," he slammed the cupboard door harder than he intended.

"LaVonne's a loudmouth but she's also a good woman," Meg pinched her mouth together in the that way she'd been doing more and more often.

It made her look old and prudish, he thought. He knew he was being unfair. It was he who was to blame for the girl leaving. For Emile taking her away from them. And he felt sick that he'd pushed out his own grandchild. He saw in his mind the bulge of Helen's belly as he'd worked at her belt along the trout stream. He should have known. Evan should have known.

"Do you think I should call Evan?" She broke into Paul's thoughts and the bag that sat beside her chair spilled out folders and sheet music as she leapt up. She acted as though Helen's pregnancy was his fault. That Evan leaving had been his idea. He never felt so guilty.

"Where did you say she went, Paul? Please." She grabbed his arm, insisting that he tell her.

"Emile's going to introduce her to Terra. She's probably gonna work for Terra," he said.

"Oh, thank goodness," she said, covering her mouth with her hand and laughing.

Her joy surprising.

"We're going to be grandparents, Paul," she said and hugged him close to her.

SUMMER

Hay Moon

Skirting Wool

Terra with Lupine

Terra plucked seeds and hay from wool at one long chicken wire frame which balanced between two sawhorses. Lupine worked at another. They'd sheared Terra's two sheep earlier, a struggle because the last person to shear had been Simon. He'd sheared quickly on his own. He'd easily flipped the Icelandic sheep on their backs, working the claw-like shears through their fleece like butter. He talked about his time in Iceland shearing, the unspoken wife there like mercury lodged in the sweet fat of large salmon: a slow poisoning.

Terra imagined the pretty girls and wife with Simon. She imagined them huddled over simmering stew in that tiny Icelandic cabin. The musky warmth of mutton. Or they were in front of a rock fireplace in a cottage in the mountains. Everyone in red and blue ornamental costumes because she couldn't exactly picture Iceland. Because she didn't really know where they'd lived and couldn't ask. It wasn't fair, she knew, to take his memory in sour bites. It is a part of his life she can never enter. He'd wanted sheep, and Terra had balked as much because he and his former family had them together in Iceland for that year. But she truly didn't want to work with such elusive animals.

Goats weren't easier but they were more like dogs. Terra enjoyed their personalities, how they'd lean into your hip for a scratch and stick their noses into your pockets, feel your coat or gloves or fingers with their lips. Sheep were sheep. And yet here she was working the wool with Lupine, Lanolin softening her parched hands. It'd been over a year since she'd worked with wool. She realized she missed it.

Between the other two sawhorses, Lupine pulled sticks and grain free. Terra showed her what parts of the fleece to discard. They'd hacked some of the long wool as they sheared. Hunks littered their feet as they threw out the shorter pieces. Wool from the sheep's legs and butts lay on the ground too. Lupine and Terra were able to set up their wool cleaning on the brick patio just outside Terra's door. No sign of rain for days. Some years Terra needed to set up inside their old pole shed, which was more like an oversized garage. She hated working inside. She moved back to her straw-colored fleece and methodically picked plants and sticks, handling a whole year's worth of seasons. She missed this. She missed him.

Simon's daughters were grown when they'd met Terra. Had no interest in her. Made her feel like a kept woman. Younger. She always felt to be competing with them for him. She shouldn't have. Simon was their father. Simon was her partner. Was this her doing, the girls', or Simon's, she wondered? What did it matter. Simon was dead. She was as good as dead to her stepdaughters.

She glanced at Lupine. The ball cap shaded her face. Her slim nose, high bones, and wide eyes shaded. Faceless. It gave Terra a jolt. She put the image out of her head. Terra'd had premonitions before. Nightmares whenever Simon rode the tractor or used the wood splitter. Images of him like faceless Lupine. He wasn't flattened by his tractor tires or hacked by the splitter. Then she had these about flights and long drives too, calling her brother in weird terror in a different time zone. And what good did the worry do. If one worried enough and about enough, there would be a day the worries would be founded. She now wondered if it were just seeing people's eventual end, which would happen for everyone.

After a year, Simon's face had smudged a bit in her memory. Parts of him were so engrained: his hands, freckled to the point of tan. His voice. His strange laugh. She could still hear him. But the eyes, the nose, the lips. They wouldn't fit together like his face in her mind. His face was now just out of reach. There. But not there. Pictures didn't give her the total sum. They were flattened arrangements of his face. Like his face as a young man holding two red-headed daughters. It is a different man. It is a different happy. She feels guilty having the picture of a father and his two children taken by the mother, the wife, she guesses. It is a different kind of happy than the happy she holds from their life together. She is not so much jealous or even angered by the girls' relationship with their father. She really has no right to it. Their aloofness even at the celebration of Simon's life held here at Goat's Back Ridge hurt, though.

His daughters are full, like Simon was, full of songs, stories. They gathered people because of their volume. They don't talk with Terra. They don't like her. Have they made a pact against her? She wondered. How could she have known Simon and his wife were only separated, taking a break. How was she to know?

At twenty-five, she was dragged to see a speaker at a MOSES convention. Farming had just been a fling in her mind as had ceramics. When was the last time she'd pulled a pot? There he was like a lumberjack. Twenty years older. His ex, as he'd called her, didn't want to farm anymore. She was a graphic artist who worked on computers all day and commuted to the city. Terra would never commute, never work in a cube, never on computers, she'd said. Their affair began by the bonfire with three too many PBR's.

Terra decided she was a farmer that weekend because of that man. And now here she was on the land he'd bought before her, cleaning wool as he'd wanted. Her wants and his had entwined. It became hard to know her mind.

Lupine, for all her largeness, worked quietly, absorbed in her thoughts. Terra silently thanked her. Lupine was eager to know about cheese, about wool, though she didn't need to fill space with unnecessary talk. Terra would teach her how to spin. Lupine would show her how to cable knit.

Gravel crackled. Terra and Lupine lifted their heads to watch a rusted, white pick-up park. Emile opened her door. Another woman opened the passenger side.

"Hey," yelled Emile.

"Hey," Terra and Lupine yelled back.

"This is Helen, who I was telling you about at the Junction."

Helen hauled a large pack from the bed of the truck.

"This is Terra and Lupine."

"Hey, I go by Hel." The woman strode to Terra and reached out a tattooed arm.

Helen's frame was swathed in a man's large, worn shirt. The T-shirt hung everywhere but around her middle where Terra's eyes hooked and could not be freed. What in the hell had she organized at the bar? She ran through their conversation. She'd acted interested. Now here was the meddlesome Emile with a locked and stocked situation.

Lupine smiled wide, flipping off her hat to wipe her forehead like an old-time farmer. She came into focus again for Terra. Larger even than she was before.

"So Hel, when are you due?"

Summer Events Page

Esther and Katie

At the River Valley Daze, June Bug Days, and UFO Daze they found fried cheese curds, fried and powdered elephant ears, and fried anything stuck on a stick.

"Just like any county fair, anywhere in the Midwest."

"Yes, but fried food makes it Midwest," Esther said as she licked powdered sugar from her fingertips, oil between her fingers. She liked knowing what an elephant ear was before ingesting. The familiarity made it a tasty friend. Well, not exactly a friend, she amended.

And Katie had replied, "That's exactly the problem with you people. These are supposed to be weekend celebrations of a town and yet everyone is trying to make it perfectly the same as the next town over because it had been sooo fun, which makes every event worthless, safe, and no fun."

Which made Esther think *that's what you think* but she said, "But that's the Midwest."

Esther was really wondering what she was seeing in this girl. She'd gone weird, one time even ranting about Days versus Daze. At least with Daze, you knew what the town council had planned: street dancing and beer tents.

"Did you know of the top fifty drunkest cities, Wisconsin has three in the top ten?" Katie said.

This wasn't surprising to Esther. In fact, she'd heard it was five and didn't know why it was important to say. She liked quite a few of her relatives better after they'd knocked back a half dozen beers. She liked how their lines fuzzed at the edges—disappeared into the framework of a deck chair or the rolling corn behind them. And then the laughter came to them. What was wrong with a little laughter? A little unbuttoning of the personality?

"But see these beer tents could be stocked with local brews, and you could have the brew masters run a class or something. Or give a talk."

"Yeah right," Esther said.

Like Uncle Barry would choose a beer talk over a beer in hand. Katie was too much with her flowered thrift store skirt and T-shirt cut into a tank. It was really starting to get on Esther's nerves that boys came up to Katie to ask her to the mainstage or some puny, kid-ride while Esther nibbled on elephant ears, chili dogs, fried bananas and took notes about differences. Of course, Katie said no. But it was the point: Katie had the possibility for fun while Esther was getting fat.

After another cheese curd basket, she had to admit the lack of home baked pies and cakes made her glum. She hankered for real food. She'd thought she could enter a contest or two. Bolster her confidence as a baker. But there were no bake offs—just eating contests of cheese curds. Men and boys stuffing face with nothing of real substance. She felt empty. Maybe Katie was right. It wasn't a huge change Esther had in mind simply a nip and tuck like her pie crusts. Midwesterners might accept small modifications.

After a weekend off tiny town events, they recruited at the Creamery, stepping beyond the window and dividing wall whenever they recognized a customer. Katie had typed up fliers she wanted Esther to hand out. Esther enjoyed chatting. Hearing about graduated grandkids, cows, crops, the weather before enlisting them in the bake-off. Esther's grandma and Hiran's grandma would judge the baking competition (Katie's idea). Between those two grandmothers were twenty kids and an unfathomable amount of grandkids, great-grandkids, cousins, sisters, and brothers in the area. "Half the town," joked Katie. And Esther knew she was close. It was a good move to involve the old women. Half their publicity work done.

Katie was good at getting the high school girls enlisted, and Esther knew how to work the oldies. Katie had a clipboard list of email and phone contacts which spanned an entire front and back page.

"Even if they don't want to enter the contest," she said, "they can help in some way."

"What way," Esther asked feeling at once excited and dull-witted at how this could work.

The Visit

Meg and Terra

Terra was in the gardens pulling massive weeds. She'd been kicking herself for leaving the gardens fallow the fall before. Nettles, burdock, and others had gone to seed and now she was breaking her back for it. A car climbed her drive. She pushed the hair from her eyes. Yes, it was still moving toward the house. Her throat felt squeezed; every time a strange car visited, she saw trouble on the horizon. The car parked. She saw a trim woman walk toward the house, a plate in her hands. Maybe it was one of the neighbors bringing more bars, or casseroles. It'd been a while since the last dish. Terra stood and the woman shaded her eyes. Saw the movement and saw Terra in the garden. The woman changed direction and came at her. Terra saw it was the tidy music teacher, Meg.

"Hello, Meg," she said and opened the garden gate. Dusted dirt from her hands and knees. Tried unsuccessfully to straighten her hair.

"Hi, Terra. I brought you some lemon bars," Meg said and then, "Oh, you look like you could use a little extra fat on you. How are you doing, my dear?"

"Okay, better than last summer, I think," Terra motioned to the gardens, "I'm out trying to make something of this mess."

Meg grabbed one of Terra's hands, "I heard you might have a helper."

"Helen? Yup, she's been good to have about. Lupine too."

"Ah yes," said Meg as she pushed the plate of bars toward Terra. "This is for everyone," she paused. "Would you tell Helen I said hello?"

Meg said it in such a way it made Terra look closer. Meg might have been crying if she wasn't looking at her straight. There was something desperate in her tone.

"We miss her. I miss her, I mean," Meg said.

"I think she's just inside," Terra moved toward the house with the lemon bars in hand.

"Oh, don't bother her. Really, I just wanted to make sure she's well. That the baby's well."

"Really, Meg, I'm sure it's no bother," Terra said but Meg was walking backward toward her car, waving.

When Terra brought the lemon bars inside, Helen was in the kitchen pouring out glasses of sun tea.

"These are for you, I think," Terra said sliding the lemon bars across the counter to Helen.

"Huh, who'd bring me lemon bars," then she stopped pouring and set the glass pitcher down. "Did Meg come here?"

Terra nodded, "Yeah and she wanted to be sure you were okay. The baby too."

Helen seemed to be glaring at her then she picked up her tea and walked briskly outside, away from Terra.

Seeing Chickpea

Terra with Helen and Lupine

The baby was out there between them, or at least the idea of the baby. It thrust out its mother's abdomen. Brain, eyelids, fingernails forming. They didn't talk about it. The belly was the first thing Terra saw when Helen walked into a room, her man's shirt not wide or long enough to hide it. Her world will explode, thought Terra.

"Morning," said Terra already milking the first doe. She'd gotten into a new habit of waking earlier and earlier each morning. Needing time alone before the other two helped with the chores and cheese making. For the most part, though, Helen kept busy on the farm or kept to the spare room in Terra's house. Doing what, Terra didn't know. She didn't peg Helen a reader. She was an orderly person. And she cooked. More than Terra had managed since Simon's death.

"Yup," said Helen as she opened the door into the milk shed after five.

"You know," Terra began, her upper half hidden by the doe, "You may want to prepare for your baby." Terra had been thinking this since Helen pulled out her duffle bag. She'd had this conversation with Helen in her head for over a month now. It came out rougher than Terra intended.

Helen stopped washing her hands, her back to the stanchions, "I never asked you for money."

Terra could tell without seeing, Helen had frozen. No good. Terra didn't want her to go. She craved to hold that baby. It was an ache nearly similar to the ache she felt for Simon.

"That's not what I'm saying."

The door swung in again. A rush of morning air brightened the room. The doe lifted her head, inquisitive as a cat. Hair standing up at first to the loud interruption. Hay hung from her lip. Leave it to a goat to lift the spirits.

Lupine blared, "You wouldn't believe the fish I hooked yesterday," she spread her hands to gauge its length, "like a human baby."

"Funny you should say that," said Terra trying to lighten her comment.

Over to the sink strode Lupine. She shoved her hands under the faucet where Helen stood. It wouldn't surprise Terra if Lupine stroked Helen's big belly. She'd never do that. Helen wasn't a person one stroked. She concentrated on the even stream of milk. The warm teats of the doe between her fingers.

"Quiet today. How's Chickpea?"

"I'm leaving at the end of this week."

"Come on," said Terra. She stopped milking, placed her ear against the doe's full rumen. A low rumble from the goats' insides.

"Why?" asked Lupine.

"No reason," she dried her hands on a towel. "I think it's time to find my own apartment," Helen's voice sounded cold.

"Hel," said Terra. She stood and moved from behind the goat. She stood in front of Helen, wanting to grab her arms.

Shake her. "All I was asking was about the baby. It's obvious you're having a baby. If you're staying with me, you need to start thinking about where the baby will sleep. What it's gonna wear. How you'll transport it from place to place. You have absolutely nothing for it yet. It's like you're deluding yourself that you're not pregnant."

"That's my business," snapped Helen and pulled the T-shirt down over her protruding abdomen. The does were watching the three women from their stanchions. Hair on end again, their eyes wide.

"Yes, it is. If you're living with me, it becomes my business."

"She's right, you know," said Lupine softly. "You need to prepare for a baby."

Helen pushed her way to the door. Terra blocked the door with her body so Helen couldn't leave. In her mind, she thought Helen was pretending the baby wasn't there.

"Let me out," she said and pulled at the handle.

"No," said Terra.

She moved between Terra and Helen and grabbed Helen's shoulders. Everyone in the small milking room knew Helen had nowhere else to go. It seemed like a stage production. They were all acting out this scene before the climax.

"Maybe I don't even want it."

"You do," said Lupine, "I can tell."

Lupine brushed a lock of hair from Helen's face. Helen swatted at her hand.

"We can help," said Terra, "if you let us."

Baking with Gram

Esther

Katie wouldn't let Esther enter the contest with her grandmother judging. "Too much at stake." But she never said Esther couldn't sell. Esther was in her gram's fifties, sea-foam green kitchen cutting fresh butter into flour and crushed almonds for blueberry tartlets. Sour cream, cream cheese, and hand-picked blueberries chilled on Gram's stuffed second refrigerator. A third beer fridge sat empty in the garage which used to house Gramp's homemade swill.

Gram's policy was to always serve a full course dinner every noon for any of her stray children, grandchildren, or spare change relations. And she never forgot dessert.

"Dosey doats and little lambs eat ivy," Gram sang.

It was just all the lullabies and biblical verses Esther had to wade through to get to recipes and critical advice.

"I stack the bowl with butter and flour inside another packed with ice to keep butter icy cold. Ceramic is nice; metal better," Gram sang in the same tune as the weird, goat song.

Two jersey cows in the barn were milked by some relation, and Esther's cousin Emile churned butter and ice cream. Gram's hands had swelled and twisted over her years, so the offspring gave her their hands. She didn't use measuring cups or spoons, favoring her eyeball and broken hands or the small scale tucked inside the new-fangled, red microwave. The device some ill-fated dream by a daughter.

It hurt Esther's heart to know her mother's rose-inlayed measuring cups were deemed unnecessary. She loved how they nested together on the shelf in her mother's kitchen. How her mother passed on her baking along with her tools: the Cuisinart, Kitchen Aid, blender, 'thunder wand.' She had so many tools Esther and her sisters bought her. Recently they'd pooled their collective wages for William and Sonoma. It was Esther's kitchen dream. She snapped pictures of pumpkin orange mixers, coffee makers, bowls, and spatulas for her Facebook page. Her kitchen-dream selfies. Gram would have pooh-poohed color schemes, "Nothing to do with a crisp crust." Esther had begun to think she might not want a farm kitchen. A country husband. Kids. Maybe she'd leave. Maybe she'd bake in a city somewhere beyond her farm, her cousins' farms, even Gram's land. A terrifying thought.

She concentrated on baking. What most excited Esther about her tartlets was the sugar and egg white glaze she brushed on each blueberry. They looked more like themselves—ceramic forms of blueberries. Kinda like how her selfies were a prettier, glossier version of herself. Tomorrow she'd help Emile mix a salted caramel ice cream for pies. She knew she'd have to convince her cousin on the flavor before she worked on the town's palate. In her way, she felt bigger than Katie because she was changing more than an event. She was changing the communal tongue and that was like the bread. The wine. She remembered when Gram told her own story of bringing in her homemade Limpa rye for her Lutheran congregation. Now that was another kind of small town, small church ordeal. As Esther's dad told the joke, "How many Lutherans to change a lightbulb?" he'd pause and then add, "You can't change that lightbulb! My grandpa bought it."

LATE SUMMER

Grain Moon

Pizza Party

Emile and Jed

They'd entered in on the team boondoggle with the mortgage on the hundred-year-old farmhouse and acreage. They worked the flower beds, started a vegetable garden. Jed's heirloom tomatoes already bearing fruit. They'd had snow peas, radishes, lettuces, and spinach. Imogene was settled in the barn.

Emile felt they'd grown together, outsized the apartment where they used to rent. Still, she imagined she needed to test him. They'd been preparing for blueberry season for two months, and he hadn't asked her to marry him. Look at what could happen she wanted to say, just look at Lani and poor, dead Jason. She planned to push Jed a smidge: gather people together and show Jed what he might be missing. Be her best self that had first drawn Jed to her after his wife left him.

When she'd first met Jed, he'd been stationed at the bar drinking every night after work until she finally got him to smile. She, Pauly, old Etzel, and Jed swapping stories, or maybe it was more Etzel's songs she remembered. Until one night it was Emile and Jed.

Time for a summer shindig, said Emile. A pizza party where couples brought their toppings while Emile and Jed provided crusts and sauce. She thought it was the perfect way to further cement their togetherness: a dinner party with summer drinks and summer vegetables.

"You've never baked bread," Jed said when Emile explained her vision two days before the party.

"Crust isn't bread," she said removing flour, yeast, and brown sugar from grocery sacks.

"Damn near close. Okay. You've never made pizza crust either."

"Good time to try," she said and set out a big bowl on the counter, a spoon, and began flipping through pizza crust pins on her smartphone.

"You always drink too much with your high school friends." He turned off the stove burner she'd left on with a full kettle of cored and peeled tomatoes. "You burned the bottom," he said.

"Phooey," she said and pulled out measuring cups, spoons, salt. "I'll take care of it. Don't be such a stick." She'd been thinking about Lani. How she needed to get out of her house and away from her baby for one night. She'd set her up with someone fun, Emile thought

"The first tomatoes are the sweetest, you know. I wanted to eat them with fresh mozz and garden basil." He stomped outside to check any damage to his tomato plants from her picking.

It was funny to Emile how frothed men got over their gardens like rearing a flipping kid. She didn't have that kind of patience. She dumped tomatoes into a fresh pan, scoured the blackened bottom in the sink. She would have a damn fine sauce Friday no matter what. She wanted Jed to remember that first time at the bar when they realized there was something other than beer that brought them together. She called her cousin Esther for advice on making a mean crust. This was going to be the best pizza party ever.

That Friday, four large crusts waited on the dining room table for guests to "decorate." She'd begun mixing margaritas, Long Islands, and Piña Coladas that afternoon to taste test after one couple texted that something had come up and another was on their way to the hospital to deliver their first child.

"Didn't even know she was pregnant," she sputtered as she handed Jed another Long Island, which he set on the counter to sweat and melt. She was oblivious to his mood. She'd forgotten how his ex would be delivering soon. "Oh well," she said, as she threw ice in the blender, "more drinks for us." She spun it.

This way too she could spend more time on Lani. Maybe she'd offer to babysit and get her out again. The oven had been preheating to 450° for over an hour. The kitchen was stifling. She wobbled over to Jed and lifted her glass. She saw herself testing him, making sure he knew who she was. She was not his ex-wife. Emile felt she was being her worst self, uncontrolled and drunker than she'd ever been with Jed and other people. She couldn't stop herself from drinking more, pushing him further. She needed him to show her that he loved her more than that other woman. That he would love Emile always.

"To tomatoes, blueberries, and horses and all things non-knocked up gals can do," she winked.

They clinked glasses and had a cold, wet kiss.

Lani and Keith arrived an hour late. To teetotalers they were obviously mid-argument. Canadian bacon, pineapple, black olives, Titus sardines in plastic baggies. Emile nearly lost her drinking belly, but persevered through loading the oven.

"You'll have to take the leftovers to your parents. Share the wealth," she yelled.

Jed's pizza with red peppers, olives, and sausage, she carried out to the grill. She'd researched this, she told Jed. It'd be like a wood oven, "Open flame shit," she'd said over her shoulder and almost tripped over a crack in their walk.

"Mind if I take over this one?" he said, and she could hear his frustration with her drunkenness. But she couldn't stop herself.

Proudly she refused to freak-out, allowing that perhaps she'd had one stiff drink too many. Needing to catch the others up, she headed back to her mixing station. Liquor bottles littered the kitchen counter. She ran a clean rag through simple syrup and ice chunks before beginning a drink for Keith. Lani in the upstairs bathroom throughout the mixing.

"You think she fell in?" she asked him.

"Hell if I know," he sipped at his muddy drink. "Strange taste."

"Maybe it needs some lime," she reached for his glass.

"You know I might just go with a beer," he said and sat the drink on the counter.

"Sure. Jed filled the fridge. Think I'll take this up to Lani." She squeezed a little lime, a little lemon, stirred it with a long spoon before ticking the side several times, leaving a puddle.

"Good. She needs it," he said as he opened the beer.

Emile was too focused on not spilling Lani's drink on her way upstairs to react. Using her toes, she rapped at the door. A sob spilled out. She pushed inside. Lani sat fully clothed on the toilet seat.

"Man," Emile said frozen in the doorway. She'd always got the heebies from tears.

"I can't do this," cried Lani.

"Oh man," Emile set the drink beside her friend. "Take a sip. It'll cool ya down."

"He's not Jason," Lani sobbed harder.

"Hey, that's okay. Let's you and me have fun. Eat pizza. Ya know, get smashed."

Lani cried, "You're already smashed."

Not exactly, thought Emile. All the same, she felt her hot cheeks and throat with her fingers. Sheesh, she was sozzled, and she'd promised Jed she wouldn't be. Well goodnight, she was already bombed. She didn't need old Jed telling her that. She lifted the drink straw, offering Lani the drink. Lani blew her nose and gulped like the drink could take her away.

When she finally came up, Emile hugged her and said, "It'll be okay. It won't be the same, but it will be okay."

"Thanks, but I don't agree," Lani studied her eyes in the mirror. Then looked at Emile's image watching her face in the mirror. She steadied herself then turned to Emile and said, "That was out of your character."

Emile shrugged, "Maybe it's Jed." She looked away from Lani and drew up her blonde hair into a tight roll at the back of her neck, cinched it with a band. The back of her neck damp from the heat.

"I don't think Jason was ever going to marry me anyway. I mean I loved, love him, but man that really sucked not ever getting married. And him gone half the time." Emile looked at her friend again and nodded, Lani grabbed her wrist, needing to say more, "It was the damn farming. I think."

"Maybe," Emile said feeling tired and a tad sober.

Lani turned on the faucet. She ran water over her forefinger, rubbed under her eyes. "I'll never get over him," she said to herself in the mirror. "But at least I have Neddy."

Emile nodded, her lips pinched. Maybe this wasn't the best idea.

"Emile," Jed shouted from downstairs, "Lani. Pizzas."

"Oh man," Emile swatted her forehead, "the pizzas."

"Go ahead," said Lani, needing another minute.

Emile showed her where she kept her make-up and placed the drink in Lani's hand. Lani grimaced but guzzled and grimaced again. Emile squeezed her arm. Lani grabbed her into a hug, equaling the small arm squeeze to an invitation.

The grilled pizza turned out climactic, so Emile said after every bite.

"You guys really got to try this," she said mouth full. "Should I put another on?"

They ate more since nothing would shut a drunken Emile. She yammered about a bolstered income through her own stallion breeding company. Jed mentioned that this company didn't exist yet.

He sipped his beer slowly and asked, "Where'd you keep a stallion?"

"In the barn of course. Need a few new stalls and a new pasture plan."

He lingered on a bite of pizza and knew this meant more work for him. Emile would start out with the post-hole digger, make it halfway round before something else took her fancy. It both bridled him and made him laugh. Her spirit was bigger than the property.

Keith smiled at Lani. Every drink had them imagining they could make a go at this evening together, Jason fuzzy in their heads as they jointly tried to forget him for the night.

Emile said she'd sell stallion services and semen, making all the money back from his hay and then some. She even had billboard lingo in the works although in the morning those slogans would meander and confuse her. Now she was drunk on possibilities. The whole table buzzed with it. They sweated and ate and drank with open windows. The fans blew across their damp skin.

Emile mixed more drinks, while the three finished their pizza. Then she was onto slicing peppers, pears, goat cheese for another pizza. She opened a jar of Jed's pickles. He came up from behind and wrapped one arm around her waist while his other covered her hand and the ugly knife.

"Guess I made a pretty mess of those," she said.

"Think you're too tanked for cutting." He seemed more father than lover.

"Pooh, I've been stone drunk slicing lemons at the bar."

"I'm sure you have, but let's not have an amputated finger this evening."

Jed persuaded her to put down the knife and half-cut vegetables. Uneven chunks of peppers stuffed into baggies broke his heart. He liked orderly cuts, nothing wasted. Emile liked excess. She pulled out two pails of ice cream as Jed swiped the sticky sludge off the counters. In the other room, Lani turned up the Big Pink and pranced around the living room. Keith gazed at her hips and bum as he sucked down another, his chair turned to her. Their relationship aligned for joint enjoyment.

"Blueberry sundaes," shouted Emile as she carried two cups out to the table and returned to the kitchen for two more. Jed swallowed. All the work of picking for a party of young drunks. He quickly returned the ice cream to freezer and dutifully brought out spoons. The main focus for five minutes: spoons, ice cream, and mouths.

Soon after, Lani and Keith rode off into the long-extinguished sunset on a borrowed four-wheeler, avoiding roads and cops. Riding with them: ticks, burdock, and crawlies. That wouldn't be noted 'till midday tomorrow. Even then it couldn't be in the forefront of their brains for headaches banged foremost. *Lani's grief put off for the night*, Emile thought.

As soon as they were out, Emile stationed herself next to the blender. Basil and pickle butts in her hands.

"My spin-off on a bloody," she slurred, sloshing tomato sauce where Jed just cleaned. He was at the sink washing dishes, but he lifted the vodka bottle from her hands before any poured. He slid it onto a high shelf where Emile couldn't grab without a chair.

"You're done drinking."

Which Emile promptly agreed to, vomiting drinks, pizza, and sundae into their kitchen sink, thinking she'd ruined everything with Jed and poor Lani too. Her ideas always bigger and better than reality.

Bake-Off

Esther and Katie

They hung streamers from their canvas tent's awning and sweltered. Niagara Falls surged between Esther's boobs. Esther thought the streamers were unnecessary. They wilted in the humidity. It was her blueberry tartlets that worried her. The crusts would become soggy with filling. The cream cheese melted in the heat, making a bluish pond.

"Seriously, Esther, this thing has to call in the people."

"The food should. Not the deco," replied Esther.

Esther swiped sweaty bangs to the side and blew upward to her forehead. Good luck with getting people to come. All she wanted was a spring-fed swimming hole and a popsicle. Freakin' 95 degrees and a little hot air wouldn't cool them down for anything.

"The dairy barn at our shoulders is more problem than streamers. We better hope the wind shifts," said Esther. The smell of fresh manure and wet cows hung around their tent as they decorated and sweated. Kids scrubbed their cows within sight of their tent. You could see the flecks of manure spraying off their coats. At least the washing should be done by this afternoon.

"Can't set anything up right without a fuss," Katie said. Esther felt her complaints honest-to-goodness problems. Who wants to eat pies or tartlets with a cow-crap breeze?

"Hold onto this string of lights, would ya?" Katie dangled them from the ladder where she teetered. Esther found the electrical plug and ta-da. Lights for the afternoon. She was beginning to sour on this whole thing. Wouldn't it be the end all to have Katie topple and break a foot? *Where were Katie's boyfriends when she needed them?* thought Esther.

"I think what we really need," Esther said, reaching for the strand, "are some industrial fans and ice water." She struggled to hold the lights up to Katie who had dropped them again on the summer-green grass. The ground was the only thing appetizing about this space. The tent scrunched between Jehovah's Witnesses handing out New Testaments and American Family Insurance handing out policies. Maybe the two should combine for a whole new approach, she thought crabbily.

"Hey."

Esther turned toward the young male voice. She wished she were just a water droplet in the air. Or nothing. Or hot air so she could force out a bead of sweat from his face or neck or . . .

"Hey back," said Katie from high above, not at all smelted by Hiran's greeting. Esther felt her sweaty face redden more and wished she'd applied a second coat of mascara and deodorant as both slipped off her damp skin.

"Grandma thought you might need muscle setting up your tent," said Hiran, who didn't melt in the heat. He had on sturdy shorts, a tight-ish sports-themed shirt, and running shoes. Lots of satiny skin exposed, but without any pomp. Esther might just swoon if she wasn't mid setup.

"Looks like you got things under control, though," he said watching them work for a moment.

"Actually," Esther sputtered, "could you find some industrial fans and a big water cooler?"

"Try Paul first. Or Sue at the library booth might have an extra water cooler, or try Marie's."

"Sure, sure. What time you gals starting this?"

"Three hours."

"Seems doable. Better jet then."

"Thank you," Esther felt her cheeks ignite and then the fire break over her chest.

After he left, Katie clucked at her. *As if Hiran wasn't her crush too*, Esther thought and stuck her tongue out at Katie, who stuck hers back. They finished the wimpy streamers and unnecessary lights. Then they struggled with long folding tables and chairs. Esther had to snitch cardboard boxes from the recycling to insert under some of the table legs that kept sinking into the ground.

Hiran lugged two fans over only twenty minutes later. He plugged them into the full surge strip.

"One to blow the manure smell outta here," he said as he flicked on the first, "and one to cool it down," he said, situating the second. Then he was off to find water. Katie instructed Esther to blow up balloons. All Esther wanted was to share good food.

"Wow, this isn't just a food tent," Hiran said driving up a gator with water in back, "It's an extravaganza."

"Try a circus horse," Esther said under her breath.

Katie smiled and taped another balloon.

"Where do want this?" he said motioning to the cooler.

"Right on the back table," Katie said.

He moved fluidly with the heavy cooler. Esther rushed in to help, her strong arms as capable as any boy's. Her pulse ticked a little faster each time he appeared. She sucked in her belly and pushed out her breasts which she imagined her best feature. At least that's what her mother seemed to think when she tried to get Esther to wear sports bras that mashed them flat. Her mother was of a puritanical mindset. She wanted her daughter to hide those fleshly sins.

He didn't forget the cups and pulled them from the front seat after setting up the water. They arranged them prettily on a doily. Hung up a final sign.

"Kay. Break a leg. See ya then."

"Thank you so much, Hiran," Esther said, trying to look him in the eyes without flinching in the sun. Hiran drove off in the gator with a back wave, heading to some other part of the fairgrounds. Music from a polka band could already be heard revving up inside the gazebo. At the grandstand, something rougher, maybe metal. Esther wondered where Hiran would hang. Katie broke in, shushing her. Esther grunted back.

"Let's see," Katie checked her schedule, "baked goods should arrive in 45."

"Well, then I'm off to shower," said Esther mentally flipping through her sundresses.

"You gonna wear a dress?" asked Katie as she scrutinized Esther.

"Maybe."

"Good I think we should wear these aprons too," Katie pulled out two atrocities from her backpack.

"Oh man."

"Seriously, I think they'll be cute on."

"I don't want to put on a stitch more than I hafta."

"C'mon. Or I'll make us wear these bad boys," Katie pulled two brilliant canvas shapes from her bag that sprung open into huge hats. Katie pulled the teal-and-hibiscus print down on her head. She couldn't stop laughing as Katie tied on her apron and flounced around the tables. Esther remembered why she liked her.

After an icy shower, Esther's skin prickled. She misted, rubbed, and dusted her skin 'til her mom came by to tell her, "Sometimes too much was too much." She sponged off some perfume before checking her trays of tartlets splayed across the downstairs fridge.

"Don't worry Esti, Dad will bring them right at 1:45."

"Will he keep them covered?"

"Sweet Potato, you left written instructions on them…"

"But Dad is…Dad."

"It'll be fine," her mother smoothed Esther's damp chignon. "Let's blow this pop stand."

Back at the fairgrounds, Esther noticed Katie hadn't changed. Must not have left. It was a good thing since old and young ladies were carrying in pies. Esther dutifully slipped on her apron and joined Katie in accepting and labeling contestant's pies. Katie used post-its to cover each name so the judges weren't biased. Esther wished she'd thought of it, realizing again theirs was a good partnership.

The tent became a bustle of bakers, so she didn't see her father set down the tartlets until Katie asked for a price. When Esther paused, Katie pulled out a Sharpie and recipe card.

"OK. Fair price 3.50," and scrawled the numbers across the card.

She then wrote Esther Baumgarten in calligraphy. People were buying and commenting on her tartlets, so she hardly had time to prepare for Hiran.

When he came up to Esther, her hands were full of coins and pastries. Too full to feel empty as she should. Hiran and the lanky homeschooled girl, both with half-eaten tartlets (Esther's tartlets). They sandwiched her. Those two easy-as-pie beautiful people at each of her country-sized hips had her gutted.

"This is fabulous," said the girl, her mouth full of crushed blueberries.

Did no one chew with their mouth closed, Esther wondered. At least Esther had the good sense to shut her lips. She wanted to hate the girl for being skinny and pretty and with Hiran. But then the girl was glow-y and devouring her tartlet and chummy.

"Don't tell my grandma, but you're a better baker," he whispered in Esther's ear, breaking her ear drum along with her heart, no doubt. Then louder he said, "Hey, you know Lupine, right?" the blueberry-stained tongue licking his glazed upper lip.

Lupine looked at Esther's full hands. Esther looked at the tartlet and smeared blueberry. Lupine smiled.

It just didn't seem right that on Esther's best moment should emerge her worst. She smelled her own perfumed body. She saw her loud dressy dress stretched over her hips. The girl, Lupine, wore cutoffs, tank, and braids. Simple.

"Really," the girl declared, "I don't think I've tasted anything this good."

Esther plastered on a smile, sucked in her belly and said, "Thanks." Then she picked up another tartlet with crisp pastry paper and without tears said, "That'll be 3.50."

Katie squeezed her damp hand into Esther's shoulder, "You're baking bigger things than boyfriends."

The Bear

Lupine with Hiran and Etzel

The assisted care center followed lines of some waterway, though there was no stream. A Frank Lloyd Wright mash-up named Whispering Pines or Laughing Pines or some sop-name dedicated to the trees or farmland that had been paved over. These elder hostels, as Lupine liked to think of them, were always on some thoroughfare. The developers guessing their old guests heard waves instead of traffic. Right off the highway in the Hollows was different than near the Twin Cities though, which gave Lupine some comfort. Packed between two working farms, the care center was rural enough.

A storm had toppled several aging spruce on fences, which an Angus herd took as an opportunity. Police, volunteer firemen, and the farmers had to herd them off Highway 12 one morning. Those kinds of stories always got Etzel, so Lupine searched for them in the police blotter. Like the momma bear whose head was caught in a bird feeder. Her cubs watched from a tree as people greased her neck, then rigged up ropes to pull her free. Off she ran stinking of French Fries. Or the woman who called 911 to report a badger blocking her car and her way inside home.

Etzel's stories were drying up somewhere in the pathway between his mind and his mouth. Lupine had to fill in her own narratives. When she brought Hiran to Etzel's room, she guessed there'd be little dialogue. Little of him left.

The blanket was pulled tight beneath the starched pillow. His trout and deer mounts on the wall. Light shining through his colored glass bottles that she'd packed in newsprint. The revolving beer sign shut off. It gave her as much a jolt to see the clean, empty space without her grandfather as it did when she'd begun moving him into this place. His hold on the world shrinking. He'd come to this country with nothing, built a dairy, signed it over, and now was stepping back to nothing.

"Should we check the dining room?" asked Hiran.

"Yeah, he must be on his third cup. Should be ready to sing for ya," she drew a smile on her face. Tried to make the best of this place.

They walked down the hall to an open, dining area. Old Etzel was surrounded by bent, white-haired women. Their mugs in front of them, coffee pots center. The nubile staff, mainly women, mainly Latina, clattering dishes close by, aware of the giggling white hairs.

"Good day for Etzel." A woman in a printed smock and slacks moved in between Hiran and Lupine as they looked inside the dining area.

"Yeah, I hate to break them up," she said. "This is Hiran, Mary."

They shook hands, but had nothing to say. They watched Etzel with the women instead.

Animated as Etzel was telling long ones, Lupine could see the structure of his face as a young man. His skin glowed in his excitement and didn't hang.

"Today must be a lucid day," she said. Mary nodded and squeezed Lupine's arm. Mary was a good sort. She was careful with old Etzel, and laughed at his stories

"And here I'd been practicing my German," said Hiran. Lupine hated to interrupt, but she didn't know how long he'd have his mind today. She strode over to her grandfather and hugged his flannel back.

"Lou Lou, skip to my Lou," Etzel sang as she squeezed. "This is the most magical lass in the county," he smacked a wet kiss on her forehead. Lupine let him as Hiran stood back.

"Come let me have a look at you," said one old woman.

Another fingered Lupine's braid and said, "Oh I remember when my Gwen's hair was this long. She hated me to brush it, had to run around the house after her. But then she loved braids."

"Oh yes," said another, "used to make those French braid crowns. Oh my, and stick dandelions inside. Look at Dahlia, here. She always has such a pretty black braid," the old woman patted the young hand of a woman pouring more coffee.

"Now, who is your young man?" asked a woman in a blue sweater. Her hands fluttering like they'd like to take off and land on Hiran's shoulders. Pull him in, her fingers said.

Etzel eyed Hiran for the first time and said, "Young blood to take my hens away."

"Introduce your cute boyfriend, dear," said the blue sweater.

Hiran flushed, "I'm a friend of Lupine's," he turned to Etzel, held out his hand, "I'm Hiran Biswa, sir."

"Ahh," said Etzel, "Hiran, good name young sir of the round table." He took Hiran's brown hand in his crooked one and shook. Then all the women had to inspect, comment, and touch Hiran. A consuming of youth. Lupine knew her grandfather didn't want to lose his light, so she and Hiran wedged in chairs.

Etzel boomed, "Nobody can make fried eggs and bacon like my Lou, sorry Liza."

Liza looked like she ran more marathons than cooked. She replied, "Don't make me jealous, Etzel. And here I thought I was your sweetheart."

"You were yesterday. Keep being sweet to me, and we'll see about tomorrow."

Etzel watched everyone arrange themselves into a new order around the table, and then as if they'd all come for him began a story Lupine hadn't heard.

"When I was twenty, not too long after leaving Oldendorf I met a bear hunter. At that time the wild animals were wild here. Bears and wolves were SUVs then. The woods, I guess bigger and trees too. Strong, I had a young back then," he straightened and looked at Hiran for a clear case.

"It was a time when I could catch a big fish out of a little stream."

Lupine watched him disappear inside his story and the rest of them disappeared from his view, the assisted care center, the nursing staff and ladies. She could see she was gone too.

It was fall of 1948, two hours north of Eau Claire beside the cold stream. Etzel was sicker than a dying bear from last night's booze at an old roadhouse.

Randy directed the hunters to their spots after showing Etzel the claw marks on trees, "Big fella been coming through. Keep your eyes open, Kraut." Etzel looked up to where the grooves ran through the old cedar bark. If he weren't so woozy, he'd have run his thumb over the wide-spread trails, and imagined the paws. He'd always liked the tracking part of hunting or fishing. Looking for the creatures that left traces of their life. But this was different than deer hunting, the scoured trees purposeful not furtive. The animal big, powerful, bright. His brain felt like it was in the middle of a c-clamp. Someone kept screwing it and screwing it tighter.

"'Bout eight feet, I'd say," said Randy.

They split off in different directions. As he crouched under balsam fir branches, Etzel worried he might shoot one of them instead of a bear. One-eyed Louie might shoot him. He hid and wondered if this was an elaborate game to kill the Deutschman. They could leave his body in these woods. No one would care except his mother in Oldendorf. She wouldn't know. Maybe the old, Norske lady he worked for would send out a notice when he didn't return to milk her cows. Most folks would just pretend to respond. The bears ripping him apart as he rotted. The people kept hidden. So did the bears.

About an hour in, he was asleep. He kept at least two of Randy's instructions: quiet and downwind. The dainty lady bear tip toed below, snuffed where must have been bait earlier and waltzed out. He woke and adjusted the binoculars just as she scratched a tree on her way out. He wouldn't shoot such a small sow. Not worth the work of skinning. No shots followed her as she walked through the other's range. The others must have felt the same. Let her make more if she wasn't already pregnant.

Etzel dozed again, dreamt of his life back in Germany before the war. He wrote a letter in his head to his little brother, an apology for stranding him. When he escaped, he knew they might not see one another again. It was something he swallowed. Now he felt the guilt.

He startled awake. A big son-of-a-gun. Without thought, he lifted his rifle. The ole beast of a black bear shone brown in the sun—looked half-grizzly. He shot without squaring up—missed. Bear ran quicker than grease. Another shot. Another miss. He mumbled, "Scheisse." Not shocked by his aim, but the fact he shot at a bear bigger than any man. Brain and fingers trembled. Lucky he didn't maim the huge creature. It took several breaths for the world to settle and Etzel within it.

Crack. A shot fired from Louie. Etzel was sure of it since the bear loped in Louie's direction. A bellow like a man's voice, but lower and massive enough to loose the tree under his hands. Quiet except for cracking brush. Another gunshot then a scream. It took Etzel a moment to realize it was human, not the bear. Randy. He was sure. The next in line. He wouldn't let his mind slide back to Germany, his mother and brother who he'd left to another bear.

He followed the shrieks, cracked branches of pine and maple. Snagged fur, puddled blood. Rifle in front. He'd shot moving targets before. He could do it. He could, he muttered, though his muscles shouted no, stop here, hide. Screwy Louie nowhere near his post.

Etzel tracked the tufts, the dark pools, fresh scat. Then an opening in the woods. A meadow. He froze on the periphery.

Before him: the bear reared up like a man. Back muscles bulged beneath fur. Paw size larger than a man's head. He realized a man was behind the bear, hardly visible. Fighting it off with a knife. Etzel wanted to shoot, but he couldn't find an angle. He remembered to look for the vital organs. Aim for the middle of the chest. Hit the lungs, heart, or kidney. Randy's head was too close to the furred body. Randy had said don't track an injured bear unless it's mortally injured. Nothing more dangerous than an injured bear. Louie must have miscalculated his shot.

Bear and man danced. They grunted and howled at one another with a slow-time one-step, two-step. A blow from a knife. A blow from a paw. A roar. Nothing but the two. Louie, finally beside Etzel, took aim. No one spoke. Etzel wondered why he and Louie weren't fighting with their knives, honed blades. But it was self-preservation. Etzel aimed. Again, he couldn't find a spot. He scoped and breathed as shallow as possible, but the gun moved on each exhale.

Deb blew in, a red scream of force and love. Bowie blade in paw. A bear of a woman. What a woman. She stabbed between the bear's ribs, pulled free as it reared away. She leapt from the great paws, which fumbled as they flung out toward her. She stabbed again and again. Randy thrust from the other side. The bear howled. Perhaps it was Randy, Etzel unsure anymore. Deb in the mix with her blowing red hair. Prancing back and back with the knife. The bear stumbling now. Then a blast and crack, more metal inside the furred body.

"I think I got 'im," Louie said.

"God," Etzel said.

"I hope I got 'im," Louie said as the bear fell. Randy fell back, and Deb fell to her knees beside him.

"Lucky you didn't take off her head," Etzel said.

"I know," Louie said. Then he vomited and spat. Wiped his mouth.

"Must be a god," Louie said. But Etzel wasn't so sure there was a god. Randy was red as Deb's hair. Her hands were covered in bear blood. Louie strode over to the downed bear and shot and shot and shot again. The hide a mess. Blasts reverberated in his brain.

When Etzel realized he was telling this story to his granddaughter and a whole table of folk, he couldn't remember if Randy survived. He couldn't remember if he left after Louie's rounds. Couldn't remember the Berserker Deb wrapping Randy in her hair or was it her shirt. Ill is what he remembered. Hate is what he remembered. He couldn't remember the extent of Randy's wounds though he could still see the gaping, clawed flesh. The woman deftly hiding them.

"Never did hunt bear again," he said, "too much like hunting man." Etzel sagged into his chair. Lupine poured him water and looked into his faded eyes. The old women and caretakers clamored for him to finish the story, "Does the bear man die?" "How did they get Randy out?" "What about the bear?" one of the younger women asked.

"I don't remember," he mumbled.

"You don't remember if the bear man survives?"

"Hiran," Lupine urgently whispered, "let's get him back to his room." Hiran leapt up from his chair to help her. Lupine's face was pinched, only aware of her grandfather. The ring of younger women found walkers for their patients. An aide asked Etzel if he'd like a wheelchair. His eyes closed.

"Yes."

Lupine's heart thumped her ribs. Using Etzel's belt the aide lifted him from the dining chair to wheelchair as Lupine held it steady. His face shifted back into crevices and hollows. Lupine pushed him back to his room. The aide and Hiran followed. She didn't need their help. Didn't want it. It was her grandfather. All of his stories and the people inside them dying or dead.

Lupine unlaced his boots and pulled them off as fast as she could. They lifted him into bed. One leg and then the other. Lupine pulled up the crisp sheet and the bright wool blankets. She turned to Hiran and motioned for them to leave the room. The aide closed the door softly behind them.

"I wish you could have talked with him," Lupine said leaning her back against the cold, hallway wall. The abstract flowers on the carpeting hurt her eyes. She closed them.

"I did."

"No, I mean a real conversation."

"Maybe another day."

"Maybe," though she thought, this may be his last lucid day.

The Hollows Library

Sue, Meg, and Terra

Terra splashed through the small parking lot to the library, her hands blocking the rain. The library was a brick building snug on a hill.

The library, the bar, the church: the only communal spaces where pure conversations and group movement took place. Unless one counted the fair. The librarians knew the literate underbelly of a farm town. Sometimes shocked at what public figures read. Or did not read.

Meg exited an aisle of books, her arms full. When she saw Terra swiping strands of wet hair from her forehead, Meg's throat flushed. She beamed at Terra, but pulled the books to her chest, hiding the covers.

"Hey Terra, looks like the storm came through after all."

Terra slipped a hand down her graying braid. "Started right when I parked the truck. Good for the crops, though. Been a dry summer."

"Yup, been hearing that from Paul," said Meg and adjusted her books again.

"He still farming, then?"

"Well, he was going to do some CSA with Helen, but I think that's on the back burner now," Meg paused, "I want him to slow down. He'll be sixty-six this year."

"Young man around here." Terra and Meg laughed which eased the awkwardness.

"How is Helen then?"

"Good. Tired though."

"Has she been seeing anyone in the area?

"No. no," Terra busied herself with her hair again.

"Where do you think she'll deliver?" Meg asked. In her excitement to hear more about Helen and the baby, Meg set the books down on the front counter behind which the library director, Sue, stood. Terra's eyes glided over a title, *Birthing From Within*.

"Are you and Paul expecting a grandchild?" Sue scanned each birthing book while Meg and Terra watched. Sue's teal and copper scarves trailed down her arms echoing the cascading rain down the front windows.

Sue continued while Terra and Meg's faces reddened, "You know I had a terrific midwife in the area with Tev."

"I'm not sure about a homebirth. I mean it'd be my home," Terra stuttered. Meg watched her. Without looking up from her computer where she was typing in a search for more birthing books, Sue continued, "Yeah, your tub. Sure, I understand. My mother-in-law is a doctor. You should have heard our discussions, well, debates. We have fundamental differences. It's funny, though, she was at the birth because she couldn't stop herself."

Sue stopped, realizing it had been Terra talking and not Meg. She looked between the two women. Of course, she remembered the rumors about Evan. About the girl trailing Paul around town until she wasn't. And now she was at Terra's place.

"Well, for what it's worth," she scribbled a name on a post-it note and set it on the counter, "this was my midwife, and she was wonderful."

Terra picked up the note and read, "Meredith, is she close?"

"Yeah," she pushed her glasses up her thin nose, "and I have some more titles if you'd like, Terra." Sue grabbed a plastic bag to wrap Meg's books inside, "You need a bag, Meg? Looks like a watershed out there."

"Actually," Meg said, "I'm going to give these to you," she turned to Terra, "Do you think Helen would read these?"

"Honestly, I don't know, but I can bring them to her.'

"Do you think we, Paul and I, I mean. Could Paul and I help in some way? I feel bad about how everything has gone." Meg's face seemed to plead with Terra. Sue went back to her computer trying not to eavesdrop on the conversation.

Terra studied the books, "I'll try to convince Helen. Thanks for the books, Meg."

Meg's face dropped. Then she righted herself and said, "Hope to be seeing you around, Terra. I'm glad you're back out and about." Meg was out the front door before the other women could say goodbye.

"Well, do you want to look at some of these other books," Sue breathed out from behind the desk toward the stacks. It was the place she felt most calm. Titles and authors surrounding her watery form. She pulled out several vivid spines. Her glasses slipped down her nose as she looked over them first to make certain they were the ones she intended to pass on to Terra. And Terra followed her; she stewed about Meg and Paul and Helen.

"I loved reading this one," she handed a book to Terra who flipped through it.

"You may also want to think about buying this great daily journal. Gosh," Sue put her hand to her mouth, shocked she couldn't remember the title. She paused waiting for it to come. "Hmm. Anyway, it goes through all the incremental, daily developments. And it has information about childbirth from different cultures, quotes. And space for your own comments. You know weights, feelings…"

"Um. Not sure," Terra turned pages in a wide, paperbound book.

"Here's another good one about nutrition. It includes some recipes. And it breaks down protein consumption for vegetarians, too."

"Sure. sure," Terra seemed to understand the portion size and protein better than emotional, abstract commandments. She nodded and flipped, nodded and flipped. They carried the stack back to the desk, and Sue scanned each volume. She wrapped them up with the other books.

"Are you coming to the Artists' Corner next Thursday? We'd love to have you speak about your work in ceramics." Sue was a recovering artist.

"It's been years since I've thrown. I guess the last hand-built piece was last year. Simon's urn," Terra turned as if she would leave but Sue's hand was too quick. She pulled Terra's and squeezed. The scarves fell over their wrists: water echoing water. Drowning. Pulling back. It was nearly closing time. The library was empty but for the other librarian shelving books in the back. Lights flickered from an electrical surge. A long holding on without words.

"I'm feeling better these days," Terra said. "It helps to have Helen and Lupine on."

Sue nodded. She sucked in her lips and seemed more solid. More earth.

"Helen is having the baby. And it's. It's. It's something to plan and think about."

"Yes," Sue squeezed.

"Thank you," Terra said. They held for a second longer.

"Well, I should get out so you can close before another person comes in looking for some obscure movie," she laughed. When Terra turned and walked out, Sue wiped behind her thick frames. She wanted desperately to get home to her husband and son.

College Visit

Hiran with Lupine

Hiran visited the small Wisconsin school to appease his grandma. Twenty minutes away. A school known for education and agriculture. It wasn't a place for pre-med and certainly no place for him in a town of bars and raw drinking. Puke on the sidewalks. At least that's what he knew from high school guys, which admittedly in the Hollows were only outwardly interested in one-hands-worth of activities.

Lupine took the walking tour with him since she was a future farmer. Hiran's mother was against a local school. She had high hopes for Berkeley or Harvard. *A stretch*, he thought. His father wanted Hiran to visit University of Iowa because he'd heard good things from their physician, "Good medical school and in the Midwest, too."

Really, Hiran knew it was a little silly to tour a school only twenty minutes north of your door. He guessed it irked his parents. Even a good kid wants to get in a little irking when everyone is telling him what to do. Plus, Lupine was excited. He liked Lupine's excitement.

"I was looking into Iowa State, too," Lupine said. "But I don't know if I can leave this state."

"Why, you got a restraining order?"

Lupine burst out laughing, which stopped the torrent from the tour guide. Potential students and their parents frowned. She didn't notice. She laughed more. Then she drove up the bill of her baseball cap. Lupine patted Hiran's arm; her face looked like the sun. Her emotion still surprised him. His comment wasn't so funny. He liked the response, though. He wasn't getting anything from this tour other than face time with Lupine.

"Are you getting a GED, or how does your homeschool thing work?"

"Yup. I'll take similar tests, and I'm taking the ACT and SAT next spring. I mean there are state standards. I just skip the silly steps. Work at my own pace. It's not for everyone. I think I'm a pretty motivated person. Sometimes I think school is overrated. I mean, I think I could feasibly run a small dairy now," she regarded him with serious eyes. Her eyes appeared older than most of his classmates. Still, he wasn't completely convinced, though she'd spent her whole life in the milk parlor. He looked away, toward a brick clock tower, the surrounding flower gardens and the kid on a gator watering them. Some people might care for a response. Lupine didn't seem bothered. She didn't care about his belief. She believed. The guide glared at them again.

"We should shut it," Hiran said and elbowed her to look at their plump guide, Bailey.

"We'll look on our own now, Bailey. Thanks so much," Lupine said, and the followers seemed pleased to have her leave. She adjusted her hat again, rubbing the sweat and grime into her forehead. Damp curls sprung out over her ears, braid swinging behind.

"I guess it doesn't matter if I listened. I'm not going here."

"Let's grab a lemonade and walk by the Ahnapee," Lupine said, and strode toward the angular, fieldstone building blocking them from the river. It looked more like a ski lodge.

"It's strange that there's all this green construction," Lupine said as she opened the heavy double door. "It seems counterintuitive. Any new construction by a waterway is gonna be destructive, right? And yet they have all these green signs." Like most college student centers, the entry had about twenty feet of headroom. Huge unused space above them just to entice parents into buying in on their kids' craniums. Like all that air allowed each student to grow when all Hiran saw was an expensive emptiness.

"Yeah, I have a funny one: Leonardo DiCaprio builds a completely green, exclusive hotel on some island for only the wealthiest to spa and he's given some kind of eco medal." They walked past the long information desk with a studying student and a convenience store to a coffee shop.

"Yup. Our world is weird. But then anything humans do will screw the environment."

One guy stood at the counter ordering. Hiran stood behind him. Lupine's shoulder hit his shoulder. He watched her profile. "Guess I shouldn't cure age," he said.

"We live. We let live."

He didn't know exactly what she meant but left it. He ordered two lemonades and paid. They quietly sipped and walked out of the student center toward the path between prairie grasses. Shade from swamp oaks cooled the river bridge. They leaned over the railing, looking into the moving water. Sandy bottom with small rock outcroppings. Clear. A small tributary to a larger stream that people kayaked and canoed to the St. Croix and then to the Mississippi. All these waterways leading south, coursing into one another until they met the Delta.

"I heard you can catch big browns here," he said.

"Nah. I think a lot of city folk fish this. I know an unnamable creek to try and Hollow Creek is better too. The DNR rehabilitated it a few years ago—lot of big holes with structure. I can take you to a few spots if you want," she looked at him.

"Do you fly fish?" he asked. She leaned further over the worn railing, her long fingers waving at the water like she wanted to slip inside.

"Nope, too complex. I use the simple stuff like worms. We can look for night crawlers this week. It's supposed to rain."

"You *do* want to live here," he said.

"Yup," she propped herself up. Looked at him. Sipped.

"I don't," his face froze as he watched oak limbs sway in a good breeze. Trees moved millions of miles in their lifetime and no one even noticed.

"Why?"

"I can't. I just can't. I can't farm after this year," his voice cracked and he was afraid he might just break right there on the bridge beside her while drinking a stupid lemonade. He pushed himself off the railing, began walking. She stood on the bridge watching him stride away. He felt he should turn back to her.

"People die," she said louder.

"I know that," he snapped and kept going.

"You will watch people die as a physician," she said louder still.

He stopped, "I've thought of that. I'm thinking lab technician,"

"Oh. But that's removed. You don't seem like a person who's removed. I think you're a person who wants to do."

She didn't understand him at all, he thought. She had not a clue into his personality. How he'd have backed away from

Jason that day. Maybe still would have today. He shivered, though it was warm. He was cowardly. He needed to get outta this place. He began walking again.

"Hey," she shouted. "Why don't you stay?"

"I can't," he yelled back and started running. He wasn't sure if she meant stay on the bridge or in the surrounding Clayfields. He couldn't stay either place. The drink sloshed as he ran, so he set it along the path thinking he'd take the loop and come back. It was his car they'd taken; he'd have to come back for her eventually. She was looking over the bridge at the cold water below. He ran faster. *He couldn't stay*, he thought again. If he stayed, he'd ask her to marry him. Not that they'd even kissed. But he knew. He knew. He was just eighteen. He couldn't do this now. She was sixteen and wanted to farm. Jesus, he needed to find himself. It couldn't be here. He'd never even considered dating girls. His mother had driven into his head to leave. And his father to become a doctor. He could not stay. If he stayed, he'd always wonder if he'd made a mistake. But what if he left? He ran faster and faster, ignoring the straight, red pines along the river. Passing the stone partition and student gardens. His muscles singing like strings on a violin. Lungs and blood chanting faster, faster. Go go go.

He needed anonymity. He wanted a school where no one knew his grandma made prize pies. No one would comment on his father's weekly editorial letter. He wouldn't be a star football player. He wouldn't have been "the kid who tried to save Jason." As if Jason could have been saved. Jason's mom, sisters, and girlfriend wouldn't have wrapped him into their sobbing circle. They wouldn't have garbled, "Thank you thank you thank you" while pressing his back, his hands, his cheeks so it felt they were marking him, one of the last people to see their Jason alive.

"Thank God," his mother bawled, "Jason died in the arms of people he knew." It was enough to burn him like their words were flames and he the burning building his soul had to escape.

He sprinted, curving back among the sumac even though he wanted to follow the path right out of town. Past the horses on the gravel path. He ran back to Lupine because he owed her a ride back and an explanation. She was the type who'd find something to occupy her while she waited and not even mind, which made Hiran feel guilty. He ran back to her because he had to talk with someone even if he would eventually leave. He picked up speed as he saw her. She was curved over the bridge with a weed in her hand, strumming the water. Humming. He spun her. He kissed her hard. *Almost too hard*, he thought. He couldn't stop himself.

"I can't stay," he blustered, clear out of breath and heart thumping.

"I know," she said and kissed him back.

EARLY FALL

Corn Moon

The Midwife

Terra with Helen and Lupine

Labor watch. Terra's alarm rang at one and then again at 4:30. She slid out of bed and pulled on some crusty jeans. Stumbling downstairs, she heard Helen's feet hit the floor inside her room. A prick of unease had her holding the railing. She'd been leaving holistic pregnancy and birthing books at Helen's door when she was too pissed to talk. The books made a vibrant building outside Helen's bedroom door. She passed it on her way to the kitchen. It looked like Terra would have to birth this baby. And she couldn't even mention Meg or Paul without Helen shutting down. She just couldn't understand why Helen wouldn't want more help. Everyone already knew it was Evan's kid Helen carried. Why pretend? Her throat constricted whenever she had these thoughts. Just this afternoon they'd had another argument.

"You've delivered goats. You'll help if I get stuck or the baby gets stuck," Helen said while they milked does at their separate stanchions. Lupine was out feeding and watering the other animals.

"I don't know about that. I assist goats. Most times they don't even need me." If Terra ducked her head, she could see beneath the doe over to Helen's stool, the expanding belly sitting on her thighs.

"Yeah, like I probably won't."

"Probably not, but the hospital is twenty minutes from here. I'd rather not risk it, and I'd rather not be responsible for two lives." It had felt like she'd wound a damn long scarf around her neck that stupid one she'd knit early on for Simon. She and Simon laughed at how many times it could be wrapped. Like that constricted. Only now it felt like she'd bound it tighter and tighter so she couldn't breathe. This wasn't good.

Terra cracked the back door slowly and stepped into her boots. She was on her way to check on Inga whose soft ligaments and dropped belly indicated babies were on the way. Helen slammed the door. At the butt-crack of dawn, she was not the person Terra wanted following her to the barn.

Inga was a tall speckled Nubian on her first kid. Simon bought her as an early birthday present last April. They'd been on labor alert since last week with a handful of does ready. Terra told Helen there wasn't any need for both of them to be up. But Helen wanted to be present at every birth. For her own education or for the good of the goats Terra wasn't sure.

The sky bloomed; if Terra looked up, she'd notice the pink, orange, and purple. She didn't. She opened the barn door and stepped inside the dusky warmth.

Inga struggled and huffed on the straw. Terra had seen enough labors to know Inga was in trouble and had been for some time. She pressed her heaving sides and guessed the kid was turned or tangled. Helen knelt beside Inga while Terra ran back to the house to fill two buckets with warm water. When she returned, Helen was stroking Inga's nose. Terra took betadine and obstetrical lubricant from the supply box on the wall. She added the correct amount of antiseptic to each. First, she washed Inga's back end with one bucket then smeared the obstetrical lubricant around her sealed vulva. She attended to her own hands and arms while Helen observed.

"What're you going to do?"

"We'll see."

Inga stretched out straining and moaning. Terra noted that her vulva wasn't opening even as the doe pushed. But the cervix was complete. She probed. Her fingers like eyes tried to locate the pointed front hooves and the narrow snout. All she could feel was the little tail. Breech. She sweated as she worked, careful not to tear the thin uterus. Still watching, Helen moved to Inga's face and stroked her nose. Goats nudged one another in the other pens. Helen whispered and rubbed the one wonky ear. The sky changed from red to pink to blue.

"Red sky at dawn, sailors be warned," said Helen. Terra kept silent. Robins and grosbeaks sounded out their territories, ready for a day of foraging.

"Hey," Lupine's voice was unusually low, "I figured there were problems."

"Yup, it's Inga."

Lupine walked slowly up to the doe, massaging her flanks.

"Hmm. Inga, you got a topsy-turvy baby don't you. Poor girl," murmured Lupine.

"Kid's breech and stuck good." said Terra.

"Can I take a try?" Lupine asked as she washed her hands and slipped on gloves. She nodded to Helen.

"Have at her," Terra said stripping off her own gloves, rubbing her strained hands.

"Could I have you two help me stand her? I think it may help to change her position."

"Sure," Helen and Terra said in unison and moved together to help lift the doe to standing. They gently muscled her up, sweating with the effort.

"Hey honey. Hey love. Poor Inga girl." Terra smoothed the long neck. She trusted Lupine. Trusted she'd grown into a careful, competent midwife by observing her father and his hired men do this very thing with much larger, more expensive beings.

Terra stroked Inga as she steadied her, "Lupine's going to help you get your baby out."

"Alright, I have a hold here," Lupine groaned like she was in mid-labor with the doe.

"Let's flip you round and get those hooves up here. Good girl. Good. Okay I found one. Here's another," she continued her low monologue to Inga as she worked the baby's hooves out without hurting the doe. Terra knew they weren't in the clear yet. With the bag of waters broken and their hands inside the doe, there was risk of infection. She'd have to give her vaccinations. Maybe she could have Lupine help.

"Inga girl, now it's time to push," Lupine said louder and she guided the two black points from the doe.

"Come on honey," Terra joined in until finally the exhausted doe pushed. Her breath ragged, she pushed a large kid free. Lupine caught the slick kid and lay it on the straw. Inga turned, nickering at it and cleaned its sodden hair. It bawled, and breathed.

"Yes," they said.

Inga's sides began heaving in contractions again.

"I kinda thought I felt two," said Lupine.

Terra and Helen rubbed the first with a towel and lifted it to standing.

"Here she comes," said Lupine. Two more hooves emerged. Another great heave. The second kid plopped into Lupine's hands. Again, Inga turned and nosed her second baby, licked the quiet nose and mouth.

"Not breathing," said Helen.

"Got it," said Terra first suctioning the mucus from the nose and mouth with a syringe. Still silent. She grasped the kid's hind legs and swung it round like a weird amusement ride. The others stood with the doe and her first baby. They stared. The small, swinging kid squalled. Terra slowed. She set her on the straw beside Inga's teats.

"Scared it outta death," said Lupine.

"I've done it before with lambs but never with goats. I'm not exactly sure how it works, but it's a picture I'd never forget," breathed Terra.

"Me either," said Helen, "But you're not doing that to my kid."

"What does that mean?" Terra turned to her, leaving both babies beside their weary mother.

"Maybe it forces air into the lungs," said Lupine as she fetched clean water, fresh hay, and removed the bloodied straw. Unaware of what was going on between Helen and Terra.

"You win. I'll see the midwife."

Terra bit her cheek to keep back a smile. She checked the doelings to see they were nursing.

"Hmmm," she said.

Later, Terra slid Helen the number and name of the recommended midwife she'd gotten from Sue. Helen flipped the yellow note with her nail as if more information were on the back that she'd missed. Flick. Flick. Back and forth with the note and Terra knew she was some kind of stormed.

Lupine perched on a kitchen stool, "Good choice then Hel. 'Spose you'll have Meg come too then."

"Oh? I don't think I need advice from a 16-year-old virgin."

Lupine ignored the knock, "Don't call it advice then. Call it thoughts."

"Okay, thoughts from a 16-year-old virgin."

Lupine lifted her spine, her long neck.

"Helen, you're being too hard on her," Terra cut in.

"Hard? Shit, I'll tell you what's hard," Helen stopped talking. "Never mind," she closed her eyes and sat for a long time. No one spoke as they focused on their cold drinks, but Terra kept one eye on Helen as her face altered in color. Lips and eyes tightened. Helen reared up, tipped her chair and bolted for the stairs, "Oh go lay your own egg," she shouted as she slammed her bedroom door.

"Let her alone," Terra said as Lupine flew off her stool.

"Nope," said Lupine, "she needs us" and she dashed upstairs.

Returning the Office

Gin and Lupine

Lupine crawled under Gin's bed among the dust bunnies and dark. The lace bed cover--a veil between her and the rest of the old house. The wood floor cool on her belly. She shoved the boxes of papers and books toward Gin who helped pull them out into the middle of the sun-filled floor. They carried them downstairs and into Gin's old office. Yellow pillows sat on the bed to make it into a sofa. The pillows looked like fat yellow cats. The desk and shelves were crowded by papers again. Nothing was Etzel's.

The two walked back upstairs and hauled down two more loads. Lupine followed her mother's narrow hips. Gin had not visited the assisted care center. Lupine set a box on the sofa bed.

"Gin?" she turned to look at her mother who was riffling through papers.

"Hmmm?"

"Mom?"

Gin turned halfway toward her daughter, her eyes downcast.

"Why haven't you visited Grandpa?"

"You've visited," Gin looked at Lupine.

"I'm asking why you haven't."

"Some things are hard to explain, Lupine." Her fingers went back to a box.

"Mom," Lupine kept her tone even, "But, he's dying."

"I'm aware of what he's doing," Gin said as if he were dying to spite her.

"Why?"

She turned to Lupine, "Because he made my mother leave is why. She never came back is why."

"She left," said Lupine, "She did it."

Her mother brushed by her as she tried to leave the room, but Lupine grabbed her wrist, pulling back. Gin shook her arm, "You'll never understand what it's like to lose your mother. I've always been here."

"You're wrong," said Lupine. "You've never been here."

Gin smacked her, "How dare you talk that way to your mother."

"How dare you not visit your dad." With the absurdity of it, Lupine laughed. This was the stuff of bad movies. It was ridiculous. It was funny.

"Stop it. Stop it. It's not funny," Gin laughed.

"I don't want to laugh," Lupine snorted.

She jacked a pillow at Gin's head. Gin struck Lupine in the face with another pillow.

By the end of it, boxes toppled, crushed paper littered the room. They sat on the floor among crumpled bills and breeding charts.

"C'mon, I'll fix you tea," said Gin holding her hand out to Lupine.

Across the table, cups between them, Lupine drank tea and thought about throwing tea. Not that she wanted to burn her mother, just hurt her a little. Push where Etzel hadn't.

"I'll go," Gin said.

"What?"

"I'll go," she said again.

"Really?"

"I said it didn't I?"

"Okay," Lupine stood.

"Not now. Tomorrow. We'll do this my way, not yours."

So now Lupine had the night to ruminate. She sat back down and thumbed the tea bag label.

"I used to be like you,' Gin said.

Lupine thought, *I don't believe you know me*, but said, "Really?"

"I wanted to see the world."

She thought there was no reason to set Gin straight. It might be more interesting to hear her out. She'd never known her mother to explain her past.

"It got me into trouble after my senior year."

"Was that Henrick?" Lupine asked assuming 'trouble' was a reference to her oldest brother.

"No," her mother sniffed, "I guess there's no need for me to continue with that part of my story, though it did set me back and Etzel didn't tend to things that well."

Lupine sat down and waved her hand. She didn't want to hear about her grandpa. She picked at the wood laminate where it was coming lose along the edge of the table.

"I shouldn't try to ruin your thoughts of him especially when he's too old to defend himself. If you're unlucky enough to get old, the least people can do is forgive you for it." Gin's understanding confused Lupine. It wasn't like her mother. She looked at the beer steins above the cupboards with tiny scenes of villages and bucolic pastures. Little heads with little hats peeked out of windows at her. She wondered if they'd been Etzel's.

"Hell, Lupine. You want to know what really happened? Etzel gave me her address after I was pregnant. He had her goddamn address. Only when I was pregnant did he give it to me. Said I needed advice from my mother. What about all those years when I needed her." Gin was crying now. Lupine's eyes were on her mother's, the streams on either cheek. She didn't bother to swipe at them just let the tears run over her jaw, down her neck and wet her T-shirt.

"I walked up to her pretty little house and rang her bell."

"What happened?"

"I said, 'remember me? You named me after your favorite drink.' She was so happy she invited me in and gave me chocolate chip cookies and a glass of milk. She said she loved me and missed me and asked if would I stay."

"Why didn't you stay?"

Her mother's face was red from her crying. She wiped her nose on her wrist.

"Because I never went. None of that happened. I just drove by her house and looked in the windows for a weekend. Watched the damn house like a stalker and never saw her. Never went back."

Lupine watched her mother cover her face and wanted to embrace her but knew it couldn't be done. She slid her hand across the table. Fingers inviting her mother, waiting for her mother to look out from behind her palms.

The next day Gin changed her mind about visiting Etzel. It wasn't until the weekend Lupine could convince Gin to go. Finally, Gin stepped out the door dressed for a visit. Lupine wished she had an aunt or Gin's friends to explain her mother, round the edges. Old stories of laughter and trouble would help her slide inside this woman's head.

Gin opened the passenger door, "Let's pick up some cheese on our way out."

"It'll go soft in the truck."

"We won't be gone long," she looked at Lupine, "Anyway, Etzel could use some good cheese in that place." Lupine tightened her grip, but drove to the Creamery. She waited in the truck while Gin bought up curds and aged cheeses. She wondered if it was Gin's purpose to keep her hanging. The asphalt parking lot had her sweating. She rolled down the windows and propped a bare foot outside. A man twice her age with a dusty little mustache followed the ankle. Country music swelled from his old truck. Lupine watched him and wondered if he was waiting on his wife. Gin plopped in beside her before the man finally turned away.

Gin read all the cheese labels aloud to Lupine as she drove them to the assisted living. She read the towns from the labels and the awards. It was the most she'd spoken to Lupine all day. They pressed the little bell to enter and wrote their names in the ledger on the front desk. They passed wheelchairs and walkers parked beside the dining area. Once they reached the hall most every door looked like every other door but for the plastic adornments. A nurse stopped them as Lupine lifted her fist to knock.

"He had a hard night and was still sleeping when I last checked. Give him a half hour, and I'll be back to wake him for you." She turned and hurried down the long hall.

It made Lupine uncomfortable to have a stranger know more about her grandfather as though she and Gin were intruders. She felt she had to prove her love to this new nurse, though she never had to prove it to Etzel.

Gin and Lupine slumped outside Etzel's door in plush-looking furniture, which felt more like folding chairs. They passed hunks of cheese from the brown paper bag without conversation.

Finally, the nurse returned and went in to rouse Etzel. They sat longer.

Then she poked her soft, pink face out, "Come on in. He'd love to have your help shaving."

Etzel wasn't singing when Gin and Lupine entered. Already the bed was neat, the room musty, in need of an opened window. Lupine would have lifted the shades and opened windows if the nurse weren't so solidly in charge. Etzel was parked in a wheelchair and pointing at Gin's brown bag.

"Got some good stuff," Gin said, "aged cheddar, curds, baby Swiss, and smoked gouda."

He waved Gin to him, and the nurse pushed Lupine out the door.

"Let's have some coffee in the dining room," the nurse whispered into Lupine's ear.

"I don't drink coffee."

"Tea then."

Lupine wasn't used to commandments, but she let herself be convinced that the father and daughter needed to be alone. She worried Gin might become angry or impatient. That she wouldn't hold Etzel's skin tight while shaving and cut into his cheek. Maybe he'd be speaking German today or not speak at all.

Lupine and the nurse sat with a cup each at a round table with pressed, fabric napkins.

"I know you don't want to hear this, but he needs time alone with his daughter."

Lupine sipped and nodded.

"I could tell he wanted to see her alone."

"Hmm?" she wondered how the nurse thought she could tell.

"Listen. He's been talking about her. All the night nurses know he's been asking for his daughter."

Lupine slugged down more tea, choking and sputtering until the nurse whacked her back. Her throat was raw and scalded like she'd barely escaped a fire.

"I know you know he doesn't have long. But Gin strikes me as someone who doesn't realize."

"More like she doesn't care," Lupine struggled out.

"Nah," she rubbed her stomach, which Lupine suddenly realized was a baby and not fat, "I've seen people who don't care. She looks to me like someone scared to care." She paused, "Whew, gotta tell you feels good to sit down and get off those varicose veins."

Finally, the nurse let her walk back down the hall to Etzel's door. Vibrant barn pictures hung on the walls, and she wondered how many still stood. Had any barns been knocked over for this building? She rapped three times before the door opened.

Etzel, small and remote in his chair, waved her away as Gin said, "We just need more time."

Blueberries

Jed with Helen, Hiran, Lupine, and Terra

A Ford Ranger drove up just as Jed had finished counting the pint boxes inside the clapboard shed. He'd order more this afternoon. Emile was fussing with her new stallion. He didn't like entering the barn anymore with that one inside. His idea of buying one milk cow shot down immediately even when he'd said he'd milk. So, he wasn't a farmer, he'd been told again. He still knew how to work.

As he set out a shovel and work gloves, two women walked up. One in late pregnancy. He thought about asking if he could touch the hard protrusion. But he watched her and knew better. The other woman was older with an open face.

"Morning," they both said.

"Good morning to you too. You pick blueberries here before?" He thought the one seemed local judging from the cut of her jeans and beat-up sneakers. And then there was the truck—rusted and sprayed with a film of dust.

"A long while back when I first moved to the area," she trailed off and the pregnant woman cut in.

"Never been."

"You from the area?" he looked straight at the older of the two women.

"I am, she's . . ."

"I am now."

A brief look passed between them.

"Where about's you live?"

"Up north from the river, closer to the Hollows."

"We're on Goat's Back Ridge Farm in the Clayfields area," the pregnant woman said.

"Oh yeah, Emile's talked about you. I'm Jed."

They smiled and nodded but didn't say they'd heard of him.

"I'm Terra," she shook his chapped hands, "Tell Emile I say hi."

"She was around here working with her new stallion. Not sure if she was going riding."

"Helen," her long fingers strong around his.

"This is Chickpea" said Terra pressing Helen's belly as if it were her own.

He looked at the hand spanning Helen's belly and then caught Helen's eye. He pulled the bill of his cap lower, pretending to shade himself from the morning sun. Helen chuckled.

"I've tried your cheeses," he said changing subjects, "I think the little co-op in Green Falls carries it. You do nice work."

"Thanks. What have you tried," asked Terra.

"Montenebro. Ever pair it with the blues? Pretty nice flavor I gotta say."

"That's the plan," Helen lifted her bucket in a ready sign.

"Well hey, Emile and I just bought the place, but I'd say it's been run as a blueberry orchard for going on 'bout twenty years. Trying to run it in a similar vein." He removed his cap, pushed back his shaggy hair from his forehead, and replaced it.

"Have a look around while you pick. Think of it as your place while you're here." He paused then said, "Well, I see you have your bucket. Follow me over to this stretch."

The blueberries grew on a downward slope. Summer-darkened grass was clipped close around the bushes and mowed right up to cliff's edge. He'd cleared much of the sumac, grapevine, and buck thorn the old owners had neglected. They were too old for the back breaking work of an orchard. The relentlessness of invasive plants and weeds.

This morning it was crisp. Fall in the air. The Mississippi below was dark where it opened into a lakebed. He wished again Emile worked with him instead of with the horses or bar. She'd been right that they couldn't both cut back from their day jobs. It'd been enough of a risk for him to become an independent plumber. But then he'd decided to do everything differently this time around with Emile.

He watched the women turn from the view and look toward the blueberry bushes, their glossy leaves and gray-blue berries.

"These first three rows are Liberty and larger, easier to pick. We have Patriot here, nice firm berry. And Tophat. These are like the wild ones up north, compact, small, packed with flavor. You work to pick these little guys from the lowbush. If you want these, it might be a job for Terra. If you're interested in currants, they're closer to the house. Tart taste, perfect for jams and chutneys. Might be another good one for your cheeses," he said.

"We recently put in some fall raspberries, which you can taste, but we aren't selling this season. Just holler when you're finished."

"Should be another couple of folks coming to join us," Terra mentioned.

"Good to know. I'll just be working on the hill by the perennial gardens," he climbed the hill back to his tools, leaving the women to pick and taste the fruits.

Early for a Saturday. Seven. Emile complained about his sign, so early. But he liked knocking off some afternoons for a swim. Sometimes Emile picked before gunning it to the bar. Those were the days he liked.

Early hours cut out the city riff raff. He didn't think they needed any new business. He'd started selling to a handful of places. The previous owners had enough praised views of the lake and limestone faces in all the local brochures.

He watched a second pair drive up in a battered Neon. It surprised him to see the two teens. The girl was open about morning milking: goats for her and then thumbing at the boy, "cows."

"Her dad's. Cows, I mean. The cows I milk," the boy countered. Jed immediately pegged him as the pharmacist's kid. He couldn't remember the boy's mother's name, a fixture in town. Too bad Emile wasn't beside him saying who belonged to who.

"Is your grandma LaVonne?"

Hiran pulled back his hat and grinned, "Wow, she sure is. I'm surprised you pulled that out."

Jed shook Hiran's hand, "Lucky guess. Figured your daddy was the pharmacist and just guessed he married one of LaVonne's kids. Didn't she have something like thirteen of 'em? Shoot we're probably related. If not me than Emile, my fiancé is."

Hiran chuckled, "I'm Hiran, and I'm impressed."

"Well, don't go asking me your daddy's name." Jed turned to Lupine, "And you gotta be an Olsen?" recognizing some of her features.

"Yup. Geirolf's my dad."

"Oh okay, I went to school with your older brother."

"Yah. Henrick or Anders?" she studied him, looking for his bloodlines.

"Henrick. He was one mean quarterback."

"Huh," she said looking out toward the blueberries. "Just looking for our friends."

Jed pointed out their floppy hats down the hill. A radio sang predatory bird calls.

"We're planning blueberry tarts," she said. When Hiran twisted his mouth, she elbowed him.

"C'mon, man. Terra wants to make them for Hel," she looked at him. "She's craving blueberries." They all looked toward the hats to glimpse a belly like a red balloon stuck between the bushes. Its own red heart.

"Blueberries are easier to pick than ground berries when you're that pregnant," Jed said like he knew and surprised himself by feeling some sort of longing. Emile in the blueberries' full belly, a small girl tugging at her pail. He'd have to remember to tell Emile. That'd get a good laugh.

Hiran and Lupine came prepared with ice cream pails too. After a quick weather exchange with him, they ran downhill, or the girl ran to meet the two. Hiran's hesitancy made Jed will the kid to run, catch up with her. He should ask Emile; he knew he had to take that chance.

It wasn't that he felt he'd missed chances just that he'd seen thirty full summers, and they counted. He admired the consistency of his fruit. Sure, there were good and bad years, but the fruit always came. The old apple trees on the property still wore fat apples.

Jed went back to digging briars and stinging nettles. The nettle's seed heads hung in fat crumbly bracelets, hard to kill without reseeding. He'd missed this section in the spring and now he'd have more digging next spring.

He wanted to start over after his first marriage. He wanted real country. He meant living off the land like Emile's daddy. He couldn't tell her how badly he'd wanted that baby he'd seen pushing out his ex-wife's abdomen. Emile couldn't understand that it wasn't his ex-wife he wanted it was the life that she'd promised him. See that baby was supposed to be his; that life was supposed to be his. He'd realized in the store that it wasn't the life his ex-wife had been rejecting, it was him. Jed had fallen short in some way, and sometimes he couldn't help replaying where he'd gone wrong.

The foursome, Jed could see far below, were quick pickers. Not the talkers who came as much for the views as for the blues. He knew before he set the shovel down, he would ask if they would come back. Ask if they might just bring that newborn baby. What could it hurt to try?

Hearing Chickpea
Terra with Helen and Lupine

The three of them rode to the midwife's house. A long gravel road south of town.

"No dairies, I guess," said Lupine

"Nope, must be one of the rare unpaved roads in Wisconsin."

Helen just held her belly against the bumps, her other arm steadying her body on the open window.

"Won't be using this truck much longer," Lupine said, eyeing Helen.

"No, guess not" said Terra, slowing to check a fire number. She edged the truck forward, "I've been meaning to ask how your grandpa's doing these days."

Lupine let out a sigh before she answered like testing the air first, "Oh, he's hanging on, though we had a scare a few days back."

Terra stopped the truck between fire numbers and looked at Lupine, but she wouldn't go on. Mature branches bridged the road. Shadows fluttered with the breeze. Finally, Terra said, "Give him a hug from me, will you?"

Lupine nodded but said nothing else. The truck crawled up to another entry into the woods.

"W6748. Looks like this is it," Terra checked the note in her hand. Mosaic ornaments littered either side of the drive. Ceramic, wood-fired creatures hung from trees. Wind chimes sounded the moving air.

"Looks like you found a damned artist," Helen bit out. Terra and Lupine glanced at each other. Lupine placed a hand on Helen's arm. Terra parked close to a maintained bungalow. Cats and dogs wove around them as they jumped from the cab. A tidy lady wove down red steps.

"Ignore them. Scoot gals," she spoke firmly. The animals backed off.

"At least she can train animals," Helen whispered to Terra. Terra ignored Helen's comments, not even bothering to roll her eyes.

The little woman was older than Terra expected. Her khaki pants pressed, lawn-colored shirt buttoned to her throat, black and gray hair twisted into a silver barrette. No hugs, which Terra knew Helen had feared. The brazen familiarity with a pregnant woman. People rubbed her belly for their fertility or good luck. Terra thought *it was just the draw of new life, which was okay wasn't it?*

After introductions and handshakes, Meredith, the midwife, asked them in for tea and fresh yogurt. She wanted family medical history, but she knew how to make a person frightened of medicine comfortable.

Helen settled between Terra and Lupine. The creamy, fruit-topped yogurt halfway eaten. The home was spare. After the mess of clay works played upon the drive, Terra thought the display would creep indoors.

"Are you the artist?" Lupine asked.

"No. My partner was a potter, but she works in glass these days."

"Does she have a glass studio here?" Terra asked.

"Yes, we just had one built last fall. Alex is going to teach classes this winter, maybe even rent out space to other glass artists in the area. Glass blowing is a bit expensive, you see. You can peek into her studio after we visit my office. Alex is teaching at the U today."

She turned to Helen, "Are you ready to move to my exam room?"

Helen stiffened.

"Your friends are welcome too. We won't do anything you don't expect or want." They followed Meredith through the kitchen and a sunlit living room to a back hallway and door. Except for the wood-fired pots and soft chairs, the room was similar to any physician's office. A wood desk overtook one corner. Most of the room centered on the white exam table. A bookshelf with disorganized books stated that books were read not displayed. A cupboard above a small sink. The only window looked to a large vegetable garden. Beyond it, sugar maples.

"You can sit wherever you like," Meredith turned to Helen, "I'd like to feel your baby now if you're comfortable with me. Then we can move on from there."

"So, you'd like me up here is what you're saying?" Helen said stepping toward the big table.

"Yes, and I'll explain everything I'm doing."

Terra helped Helen up.

"And if you could just unbutton your pants. I'll have you lay back. I'm just going to lift your shirt up over your belly here so we can determine this little one's position. And I'm going to touch your belly here. My fingers aren't too cold. Still warm out there." She pressed and molded the small figure inside. "Okay, head is already down, though you still have some time yet. Baby may change positions on us."

Meredith manipulated Helen's lower abdomen, her hands tracing the fetus.

Helen lay the back of her head on her arms. She looked up to the ceiling, at the poster image of a woman seeing her newborn for the first time. The woman's face was worn but her teeth shone.

Meredith massaged and continued "Here's baby's spine, good. Here's baby's bottom. Here. Bring your hand over if you'd like to feel."

Terra and Lupine leaned out of their seats. The mound compelled them like the sun.

"Helen, I'd like to listen to your baby's heartbeat. I could use the Fetoscope or a Doppler fetal monitor." Meredith took both out of a cupboard above the sink. She held them in her hands so Helen could inspect them. The Fetoscope looked similar to a stethoscope while the Doppler was a boxy device with a tiny screen, curling wires and what looked to be a small microphone.

"I'm not Amish. Go ahead. Use the electric thing."

This surprised Terra considering Helen's take on everything else. As she'd aged, Terra found more and more the little surprises in behavior refreshing. No one could be boxed and labeled.

"Alright."

"Do you have Amish patients?" Lupine asked.

"Some. Not many." Meredith removed a bottle from the counter. "Helen, I'm going to squirt some warm gel on your belly. Let's find your baby." A dull thudding filled the room. "That's Mom's heartbeat."

Terra and Lupine leaned in closer. A higher, faster thrumbing sang next to Helen's heartbeat.

"There it is. About 150. A strong, solid beat."

And Helen smiled.

Chickpea

Helen, Terra, and Lupine

Extreme pressure in her hips and low back began that morning as Helen tried to catch some shut eye. Sleep had become impossible. Always too hot and only comfortable in one spot for minutes. Her bladder felt squeezed. She fumbled out of bed. The quilt and wool blankets caught around her legs. She didn't bother changing into clothes and struggled inside a huge sweater. Then she hobbled to the milk shed, forcing her feet into a normal gait.

Terra noticed as Helen tried to slip inside, "Go back to bed," Terra said as she pushed a full pail of milk inside the refrigerator. She shut the door and washed her hands.

"I can't freaking sleep," Helen moaned as she stood in the middle of the concrete milking shed.

"Well, sit down at least. You look like you're in pain."

Helen lowered herself on a milk stool and nearly missed, "Sitting's about as awful as sleeping."

"Lupine, you finish milking today, I'm taking Helen inside," Terra said to Lupine who was methodically milking a large cinnamon-colored doe.

Lupine nodded and directed a steady stream of milk into the pail. Helen stood back up in her oversized cable knit sweater and sobbed, "I'm a mess."

"Oh honey, let's get you some tea. Come on inside the house," Terra grabbed her arm.

She led Helen slowly back into the warm living room where she'd started a fire this morning. The wood floors were chilled at five when she first woke up.

"I'm miserable," cried Helen.

Terra helped her into a soft, worn armchair and smoothed her swollen fingers. She pulled up a foot rest, switched on the classical station.

Back in the kitchen she filled a tea kettle. She could hear Helen groan, "I'm never gonna have this baby. It's too enormous."

Terra wiped down the counters as she waited for the water. She grabbed a handful of almonds from a glass jar and crunched on them. She dug in the cupboards for some essential oils, keeping busy. After the whistle sounded boiling, Terra walked back to her with tea and lavender oil dabbed onto a warm washcloth.

"Can I rub the back of your neck?"

Helen sniffed.

"It's lavender," Terra coaxed, "I think you'll like it."

Helen shut her eyes, "Okay."

"Were you able to sleep last night?"

Helen's eyelids were bruised and swollen. Terra rubbed the cloth behind her neck. Helen barely responded, but the lines on her forehead and between her eyes faded.

"No, but I feel like I could sleep now."

"Good. I'll let you be. I'm going back to the milk shed. I'll check on you in about an hour."

Helen had only energy enough to nod. Terra left the steaming tea on the side table and the cloth in a bowl.

Outside, the grass still wore white from the first frost of the season. It crunched beneath Terra's feet. The sky was brilliant without a cloud to mar the morning. Migrating birds arrowed overhead.

"A good day for a baby," Terra whispered before entering the milk shed where Lupine was working. Two does were secured in their stanchions. Lupine sat beside one. Terra came up behind Lupine and took up her braid, let it slip through her fingers.

"You want to talk about your grandpa, honey?"

"There's not much to say. He's not doing well. Good to be here, though."

"I'm glad you're here." Terra squeezed her shoulder then readied for milking. She couldn't force Lupine. She had to let her talk on her own, "Who's next?"

"Suni and Totie haven't been milked yet."

"I'll grab them," Terra motioned to one of the does, "Is Nexus done?"

"I'm just finishing Zion, here, and then you can let her out. Still need to milk Nexus."

"Great, I'll wait for you then," Terra rubbed both of the does' ears and noses as they ate the hay in front of them.

"How's Hel?" asked Lupine her voice muffled by the doe's side.

"She's feeling pretty low. I think she may be sleeping now, though."

"Good. Do you think you should call the midwife?"

"I'm wondering. I kinda think things have shifted. I didn't want to disturb her, but I have this feeling the baby dropped. It would make sense with her hip and back pressure."

"I bet you're right," Lupine said. "Well, let me finish this girl off."

She dipped Zion's teats in a cleaning solution. Terra opened the head latch and let Zion sneak a mouthful of hay before she jumped down. Terra led her out into the yard as Lupine moved on to clean Nexus's teats and udder. Suni and Toti danced nearby already aware they were next. Terra exchanged Nexus with Toti and Suni before working alongside Lupine through four more rotations of does. The work was slower without Helen. Quiet but for the milk and chewing beasts. This afternoon would be devoted to cheesemaking unless Helen progressed.

They began the cleaning process after all animals were fed and watered. Terra fidgeted, dropping a bucket of grain.

"Go on in and check on her," said Lupine, "I don't mind finishing up in here."

Once again, Terra was reminded how adult this child was with her perceptions at times when they were most needed. In social situations, Lupine embarrassed others with her honest replies or questions. But she read the emotional landscape like she read animals.

As she was becoming more used to doing, Terra said, "Thank you for being here."

"I want to be here," Lupine simply said back at sweeping. She'd sanitize the pails and cups next, then the sinks. Terra was relieved to hurry away without a glance back.

The day was warming. Most of the tomato plants black from the night's frost. An end to another growing season. They had sauced all the heirloom tomatoes Simon had once loved. Terra felt an ache that couldn't be fixed, but it wasn't as close to the surface. Simon was gone. He'd never again save seeds, plant peat pots in late February. The fragrance a musky wet during the scentless white winter. Terra would have to save and plant for him. She had help and she would live. She would enjoy his tomatoes without him. It was the nature of this life.

Back inside the fire had gone out. The large cabled sweater lay over Helen's thighs. Her legs stirred against it. Terra closed the chimney flux and took a hot shower. When she came back, Helen was awake.

"I think it's coming," she said.

"Okay. Can you explain what you're feeling, so I can call Meredith?" Terra kneeled beside Helen and placed her hand on her protruding belly.

"It's a tightening and cramping every so often."

"Have you begun timing them?"

"No."

"Do you want me to?"

"Not really. Not yet. But I would like Meredith to come."

"Alright, I can do that."

"Could you get me a glass of water too?"

"Sure," Terra filled a glass from the kitchen sink for the reclining figure.

She was reminded of Degas, the hidden window he'd peek through to watch poor women bathe inside his rooms while he secretly sketched them. But this was where she belonged. She would help Helen and the baby for as long as they needed. If she were open, she'd say she never wanted Helen to leave. She loved the warmth of two people in the house. The dinners Helen prepared. Helen was a natural cook like Simon, experimenting with garden vegetables. Terra missed the mutton kebabs Simon used to prepare a little less with Helen.

"Here you go," Terra said and set the glass beside her.

"I think I'm going to shut my eyes for a while again," Helen said her lids already closed, "I'm just so tired."

"Sure sure. I'll call Meredith from the kitchen."

Already in the rock-bottom sleep of motherhood, Helen didn't answer. The stolen hour of sleep between labor pains and nursing.

Terra started her coffee and called. Meredith said she was on her way. Lupine blew inside. Terra put a finger in front of her lips. The waiting began as Helen and Chickpea worked together for their new, independent bodies.

It was quiet in the kitchen, but there was electricity in the air. Terra focused on filling the teapot. She placed teaspoons on the counter and then a butter knife like she meant to use them. Then she nestled them back inside the drawer. She slid a chair over to a hard-to-reach shelf and took down a thrown teapot to steep the tea. She rinsed out the dust and poured it full of hot water and tea leaves. She opened the towel drawer and then closed it. Finally, she sat beside Lupine at the counter.

Perched on stools sipping coffee and tea, Terra and Lupine peered out the side door. Steps sounded on the deck. They both cornered Meredith at the door. Her hair was twisted up in a clip, her white shirt buttoned to her throat and covered by a down vest. In contrast, Lupine and Terra's hair had flyaways. Their jeans and flannels marked by milk and dirt. Meredith gave them a pert hello, but hurried to the source. She strode into the living room to check Helen's vitals. Lupine and Terra drank more tea and coffee, waiting to hear their roles. Low tones from Meredith's questions and Helen's lower replies carried in from the living room. They tried to stay out of the midwife's way.

Meredith dabbed scraps of material with a brown glass vial. A mild lavender mixture wafted behind her as she moved room to room, tucking the scraps on bookcases and shelves between large ceramic pitchers and bowls. Back in the kitchen, she asked for clean towels, and if the bathtub was clean. Meredith was in and out, carrying back a birthing ball, stool, another bag.

Set to work, Terra was in the bathroom washing the tub again even though it had recently been cleaned.

Lupine collected clean towels and carried them into the living room. Then she scrubbed the kitchen sink. It felt good to work at something while Helen labored in the other room.

Soon Helen was up and moaning. Quickly they were all beside her, forming a cocoon of strength.

"Would you like me to check your cervix?" Meredith asked.

"Sure."

"Do you mind if the others are here?"

"I don't care," Helen's breath hitched.

The women stopped talking, offered their hands to squeeze. Helen blew through her lips. Her body loosened.

"Some call these rushes. Some call them contractions. What would you like me to call them?"

"I think we talked about this before," Helen grunted, "Call them whatever. It's the uterus contracting to push the baby out. Call it that."

`"Okay. Have you been aware of your contractions for a while? Have you been timing."

"They began this morning; I haven't really been keeping track, but they're coming more frequently, maybe every five minutes."

"Can we help you move to the couch, so you can lay back while I check your cervix?"

"Okay."

"Lupine," Meredith directed, "Would you please spread out a towel?"

"Sure."

"Helen?" Meredith asked.

"Yeah?"

"Do you have a comfortable dress or skirt you'd like to have on during your labor?"

Helen surprised them by saying she had a dress picked out on her dresser and would Terra please get it and her mother's necklace?

The room was neat except for the twisted sheets. Helen's few shirts and jeans were hung in the open closet. A single pair of sneakers lay on the closet floor. There was very little to show that this room now belonged to Helen. All the pictures of Terra and Simon's families. There was Simon as a child on his mother's lap. Another framed oval of Terra's great-grandmother, the one who died in Panama as a missionary. On top of the old bureau, a folded soft purple material with a necklace draped on top.

Once Terra returned, they helped Helen pull off her worn stretch pants, her underwear that crept beneath the drum of belly, her man's tee, and expansive bra. It made Helen feel like a great ship breaking on rocks.

None of them were mothers, but they knew what the becoming mother needed. They slipped the purple material over her head. It billowed out over her girth. Gold brocade at her neck. The soft cinch beneath her breasts. Terra clipped the freshwater pearl necklace around Helen's throat. She held it in her fingers, warming the pink and gray seed pearls.

"You look beautiful," said Terra.

"Like a queen," said Lupine, "Can I braid your hair?"

"How about I check first," said Meredith, "and get a hard part over."

Helen sucked in her cheeks, and set her back teeth. Then she loosened her jaw and blew. Quietly the women let her work as the midwife whispered, "Lovely, relaxed breath."

They let her finish. Her shoulders slumped; they put out their arms for support as she walked over to the couch. With help she lay back. Meredith washed her hands in the bathroom sink and slid on gloves.

"Now this may cause another contraction. I know you're very sensitive right now. You'll feel my touch and some pressure."

"Alright, I'm ready," Helen whispered.

"Here's my touch. Now pressure.'

Helen grunted and writhed as the midwife found her cervix with two gloved fingers.

"I would say about five centimeters. Totally effaced, soft and supple cervix," she took her hand away and stripped off the glove. "You've been doing some good work, my dear."

Helen groaned, chin to chest.

The morning swept into afternoon as Helen labored. Terra baked a chocolate cake, the dark warm smells mingled with clean lavender. Creeping left and right, Helen slumped on the birthing ball with her head and arms resting on the fainting couch. Lupine wiped her exposed neck with oils. Meredith pressed her fists into Helen's back hip sockets whenever prompted. Quiet moans. The ball crept on the wood floor. Helen became sick and the midwife held out a bowl. Lupine held her hair. Terra returned to the living room to see if her help was needed.

"Good you're transitioning. Picture this as all necessary work before you hold your baby," Meredith said.

"Good work. Good. Good," Lupine and Terra murmured.

Mumbling, Helen said she wanted to try getting into the bath.

Water splashed inside the claw tub as Lupine filled it with warm water. Terra and Meredith gave Helen their shoulders and arms, so she could shuffle to the bathroom. Helen stopped to hold a desk and then a bookshelf. Minutes of walking down the hall to the bathroom as Helen paused for contractions.

They lifted the soft purple dress exposing the large breasts sleeping on the taut belly. Pink thumb-sized nipples surrounded by moons. Body ready for baby, ready before the brain.

Time became irrelevant as Helen tensed and relaxed, rode the contractions and opened herself for her baby. Terra poured warm water over her stomach whenever Helen's eyebrows cinched together. Meredith took over while Terra and Lupine milked in the evening.

The day suddenly disappeared into dusk. Terra whipped frosting and warmed a mutton borscht and carrot soup for dinner. Lupine called from the bathroom, and Terra came with a cup of ice chips. Helen began to push. Her face flushed. All muscles engaged to push out the small figure. She was no longer riding but steering, sliding the baby through the birth canal.

With a growl, she felt the burn of head as Chickpea crowned. Out slid the head, then the shoulders like a fish into the tub between her thighs. She pushed again and the entire form came free. She and Meredith pulled him up and out so he could shriek out his hello to the world.

MID FALL

Blood Moon

The Third Day

Terra, Helen, and Chickpea

Terra woke early, believing she'd heard the baby, Chickpea again. Chickpea's second night surprising them as he realized his hunger and loss of that perfect space of his mother's womb. The midwife had warned them about this, suggesting they call her with any concerns.

"It is never too early or too late to call," Meredith said first to Helen and then with a hand on Terra's arm.

Helen's door was slightly ajar. Terra put her eye to the opening. *She'd take the baby if Helen needed sleep*, she thought.

Helen's body spooned the little body—her hair wild on the pillow, mouth open. Beneath her eyes the color was smudged purple. Chickpea nestled by Helen's half-exposed breast. Terra felt she should snatch up the baby, so Helen wouldn't smother him. Helen looked like death. She talked herself out of such an invasion: goat kids, lambs, and chicks slept with their mothers. Unless a mother were drinking, she couldn't see why they couldn't sleep with their newborns. She shut the door and crept down the hall. She'd take the grinder and coffee out to the milkhouse.

After chores, Terra opened the kitchen door and was met with the whistling teapot. She shut off the burner and walked into the living room. Helen sat in a chair humming while Chickpea nursed. Her top was open—her head leaned back, eyes closed.

"Did you want tea or coffee," Terra asked her.

"I wanted coffee, but I couldn't find the grinder."

"Oh, I have it. I just didn't want to wake you," Terra said. She noticed tears sliding down Helen's cheeks.

"I was going to turn off the kettle, but he won't stop nursing, and I can't remember the words to any lullabies."

"Oh, honey," Terra rushed over and stroked her hair, "Meredith said it'd be like this for a little while. Chickpea's so new right now."

Helen sobbed, "My foster mom sang me such beautiful songs when I was sad. I can't remember a single one."

"That's okay. We can sing new ones," said Terra looking at the tiny head smooshed against Helen's breast. She wondered how the baby could breathe like that.

"I've been so afraid to be a mother," said Helen, "my mother was horrible, and I know I'm like her."

"No, you're not, Helen. You're going to be a great mom just look at you nursing this guy now. And I'll help you, I promise. Now how about I take Chickpea for a bit while you take a bath."

The baby looked asleep, Helen's nipple sliding out of his mouth.

"Yes, that would be good," whispered Helen as Terra slipped her hands beneath him. He was warm and slightly sweaty where his cheek had pressed against Helen's bare skin. Terra slid down into the chair that Helen had been using. She leaned over and smelled the downy head. He smelled sweet and musky where he must have burrowed beside Helen's underarm. Though he was wrapped like a sausage, Terra knew his limbs were long and lean, not like the plump babies she'd seen before. Really, he wasn't cute at all: his nose smashed and slightly coned head from his long entry into the world. Terra thought he was astounding. She bent to him again, sniffing the sweet, sourness of milk beneath his chin where it had collected.

She didn't want to wake him or she'd touch his lashless lids and brow. He let out a sigh. He stirred. She hummed. A tight, small fist mashed up to his cheek then his mouth, completely out of his control. Eyes opened, dark blue which bled into the whites. They were wobbly and unfocused. Terra was stabbed with an urge to protect him.

Bakery by Bike
Esther

Esther huffed, her toes pumped the pedals against the steep incline. Once at the top, she stopped with the bike between her thighs. She looked behind her, and caught her breath. Katie wasn't far back, but that didn't stop Esther from ringing the new silver bell she'd just installed. She moved to the bulb of her horn and honked for good measure.

"Shut up, dude," Katie heaved out as she parked beside Esther.

They looked out over all the new duplexes in the subdivision just north of town. It was just nine a.m. Their front and rear bike baskets brimmed with saran-wrapped baked goods to sell.

Against Gram's wishes, Esther was saving up to buy the pumpkin orange Kitchen Aide which she felt necessary for a proper pound cake. There was no way she'd mix all that butter by hand. Sorry Gram.

Esther began "The Bike Bakery" through Katie's resolve. Esther had to admit it was a good plan. She and Katie were just 16 and without cars. They pedaled through the streets and cul-de-sacs Sundays before and after church. Petite pound cakes, muffins, fruit breads, anything hardy enough for a bouncing bike. Esther stayed away from exotic goods like scones, croissants, or biscotti.

Now she could hardly keep up with all the ingredients, baking, and biking. She was close to purchasing the Kitchen Aide. She could imagine the silver etching rimming the warm pumpkin. The silver bowl gleaming back at her as the whir of the mixer beat egg whites into a stiff, white mass.

"Beat ya there," Katie yelled as she pushed off down-hill.

Esther sat back down on her seat and thrashed after. She'd noticed an accentuation in her calves and thighs. How her waist bands slipped from her slimming hips. She was happy at this surprise.

Katie rang her bell as she sped ahead. Esther managed to plow after and honk her horn. Several houses knew their route. People stepped out onto their porches in anticipation of fresh baked goods.

Thursday after school, Esther biked to the Ronnigan household. Before she had time to knock on the door, the twins had swung it open, nearly braining her. Their mother smiling behind them as if to say to Esther, "aren't they something else?" Esther thought, *aren't they just*, as she entered the house avoiding the flailing limbs. They were explaining something big about their day. She couldn't understand either one as their voices rose and overlapped.

"Maybe you want to try the library music today," said Mrs. Ronnigan.

The two jumped up and down at the thought, their story changing subject, voices louder. Esther looked around the living room with its couch pillow fort and sleeping bags and children's books.

"Well, I better run," said Mrs. Ronnigan and slipped her bag over her shoulder before kissing the bouncing, blonde heads.

To hasten her purchase of the Kitchen Aide, Esther started watching the Ronnigan twins. Babysitting once a week gave her a handful of cash that she used to buy ingredients on Fridays. Then she'd bake petite pound cakes Friday night and fruit breads, wheat breads, and muffins Saturday morning, leaving the packaging up to Katie Saturday afternoons.

With the little people, Esther forever looked for some two-bit entertainment. Hard to find in a small, farm town. She checked the time and began looking for shoes. Helmets and backpacks were more important items to them. They ran around the room with their helmets. She loped after with shoes, begging them to stop so she could wrangle them on.

"We can't go if you don't have shoes," she said sternly, "I thought you wanted to hear the music and dance."

"Yes, yes," they chanted but then were jumping on the sofa.

Easy pickings, Esther thought, and grabbed one little boy, sat him on her lap and pulled on his sneakers. She blew hair out of her face, scooped up the other Ronnigan and slipped on his sneakers. Then she wiped sweat from her brow. They had helmets, jackets, and backpacks with emblazoned names on the back. Perfect for yelling out the appropriate name as they biked down to the Lutheran church where the larger library events were held.

"Okay peoples, I think we're ready to move out. Should I invite Katie to come with us?"

"Yes, yes."

The boys approved another playmate. Esther texted her. Then it wasn't nearly like babysitting. It wasn't like Katie was making much headway on her letters to the editor or bullet-point manifesto to the cheese festival committee.

Katie texted back "sure." Esther's cell rang. It was Katie.

"You'd think we'd have some kind of in, working at the Creamery," Katie groaned over the phone.

"That's not how it works here. You need gravestones," replied Esther.

Katie had been working on Esther to join the cheese festival committee.

"Listen," said Esther. "We need to get out the door if we're gonna make the music. Can we talk there?"

"Fine," Katie sighed and hung up.

Esther pushed the boys out the door. They ran around the house while she pushed their bikes out of the garage.

"Boys," she yelled, "Boys, come here now!"

She hugged one to her and dragged him over to the blue bike.

"That's not mine," he said.

"Fine," she huffed, "Get on the red one will ya."

When the other boy saw his brother on his bike, he came running. At last, they were on their way. Esther chose to run alongside them rather than bike herself; she couldn't trust they'd listen.

Katie already leaned beside the church entry. Esther and the twins blew in beside her, and Katie straightened. She helped park bikes beside a whole rack and grabbed one of the small hands. They were late. Already a handful of children were running around the large room. Parents sat in metal folding chairs ready to stem any blood. A taped-out stage had guitars and drums. *It was only so long before a big header*, Esther thought. But they let go of the twins' hands. The twins zoomed off.

A man dressed in a huge chicken costume walked into the room, which stopped the screaming as the kids eyed the strange adult. Katie and Esther sat down, far back from the stage.

"Only in the Hollows," whispered Katie.

"What, a chicken costume?"

"No, a public library, church combo."

Esther hissed back, "Where else would you hold it?"

"The library," Katie hissed back.

"It's not big enough for a man-sized chicken," said Esther. Katie rolled her eyes.

"Although this is unexpected," said Katie "maybe he'll pass out drumsticks. You did make me miss dinner for this."

Granted Esther had texted Katie that this musician played banjo, fiddle, guitar, and mandolin. Esther guessed this pointed out culture, and she knew Katie was a sucker for culture. But then here was the fuzzy, man-sized cluck with orange, rubber feet.

The twins jumped and squealed, as did five other kids. They hopped within wings' reach of all those instruments. At least the twins weren't head butting.

"Not a bad showing," said Esther.

Katie rolled her eyes, so Esther swore to ignore her during the performance.

"Can you watch the kids a sec? I gotta use the bathroom."

On her way to the bathroom, Esther spotted a tall, skinny teen lift a boy to drink from the bubbler. The boy had been at it a while; his front was dripping wet. She slipped into the women's noting the teen's unfamiliarity. On her exit, he still fought the little guy. He turned to her.

"You'd think he'd wet himself with the gallon he's drunk."

"Sure does."

Esther had never seen puffier lips on a boy before. Like all his body fat sat there in his mouth. His high cheekbones pointed into that same mouth. Esther knew she had to feed this guy, needed to connect with him somehow. The little boy was still going at the bubbler. She supposed it might be the teen's brother. She'd help them both: she grabbed the boy's hand as she described the large, singing chicken in the other room. She had an extra red helmet the twins could share, she cajoled. The little boy and his brother (as she soon found out) followed her back inside. Esther was only a smidge worried about beautiful Katie until the teen said, "Hey, don't you bake all that awesome pound cake every Sunday?"

Esther knew he'd be hooked.

LATE FALL

Hunter's Moon

The Wedding

Emile and Jed

The horses were perhaps a bad idea, she thought. They quivered side-by-side under the erected canopy. The pastor stood in front of them at her lectern, young enough and inspired enough to agree to Emile and Jed's jamboree. The wind lifted the most carefully coiled, tresses. But the bolt of blue sky and horse trails behind the pastor looked like a strong sign. The tulle whipping from the canopy raised an opposing view.

Emile shifted on the stallion. Jed sat stiffly atop the mare. When she'd first insisted that she sit on her stallion, he called it pure Emile boondoggle. Why, he asked, pay hundreds for a white dress if you're riding a horse? She'd never get the horse-sweat out, but she loved the idea of the wedding itself leaving marks on them. It wouldn't be a wedding if she didn't get a little dirty. That was her point. The point of it all. She wanted everyone to remember this day.

She reined in the stallion, pulling his head from Jed's mare.

Jed had already been through this act before. That old saw. He'd wanted something intimate, something small. Family only. He wasn't exactly a horseman either, which is why Emile sat on the stallion in the first place. Plus, her new stallion "bought" the dress. The first successful stallion in her burgeoning business plan. She wanted him featured.

It was a day when she actually missed her father. Not that it'd ever happen, but she coulda tried to force that dairy man on a horse. He coulda cantered up the aisle. Instead, she'd convinced her mother to ride with her on the mare. The ride made Esther and her mother cry. She deposited her mother to tulle-covered chair. Her mother was one of a few who sat on chairs. As it was Emile had convinced many of her bridesmaids on horses, the groomsmen on mules and burros. Family members sat on or behind a variety of four-legged beasts. Most people had ridden over by horse or parked off-site.It was just animals and people in front of the listing trails. The stream behind held two sorry fishermen battling the wind with their fly rods and fluorescent lines.

God, she loved wearing cowboy boots, Emile thought. The prospect of the trail ride in her mind: She and Jed on their own path together. It was a lovely hollow with rocks and clay closer to the river. Woods and a neighboring farm field lay uphill. On weekends, fishermen from the city filled the gravel lot. Only a handful of locals casting in this stretch. The horse trails free. Emile used to ride beneath the branches when she was fourteen.

The horses pranced before the pastor who refused to preach on a horse. Like Jed, the pastor said she preferred her own two feet. When Emile found this a breaking point, Jed found it perfect. They needed one solid and fixed point out there. And it was his church. His preacher. So, all was well. One for. One against.

It had the makings for a beautiful marriage. She couldn't decide what Jed quote she'd toast to first. Maybe all of them. She'd hold a bottle of champagne between them. Drink and toast and drink. But then there was the stirring stallion again.

Jed looked at her horse who kept nosing and disturbing his. This was perhaps not what Emile had anticipated. Jed's face didn't appear loving. It wasn't the look of someone entering into a new life. He seemed freaked. It struck her as funny. Jed was a large man.

Here they were before the pastor, and the horses were acting up. They whinnied and shook their heads like the marriage was an impossibility. Emile clung hard to the stallion and spoke in a low commanding voice. Finally, the stallion calmed. Jed's face warmed again as his horse settled.

After their vows, Emile's mother forced her to remove her veil and train. Then up the rocky trail Jed's and Emile's horses climbed. The wind picked up again around the awnings and the crowd. Between the trees on the rocky trails, Emile and Jed were sheltered from the wind.

Etzel's Last Hunt

Etzel and Lupine

He'd been asleep most days Lupine came in to see him. Sleep healed only to a certain point. Then it became the alternative. She wondered what he dreamed about. Was she there or was it his previous life in Oldendorf? Was his brother there? His mother? Up until this year she hadn't heard of them. He'd never spoken about his brother's love of radio music and how the program changed. No more France. No more England. No more America. The world become infinitely smaller to German families for a time. His mother used to grill potato pancakes on Sundays with applesauce and sour cream. It was only one small part of his life now that the years were laid out. Was that where Etzel was today—his German farm—far from this collection of last stake folk and their absent families?

When Lupine arrived, old ladies pinched her cheeks with their wrinkled fingers. She walked into Etzel's room expecting him to be asleep. He was up singing "Louie Louie" as soon as she opened the door. Standing-dressed, shaved. He grabbed his Carhartt coat from the tiny closet.

"Grandpa!"

His change was a shock. He was slow, but he was moving. He hadn't been this lucid for weeks. He hadn't even been out of bed. He looked thinner, but he looked more like himself. The grandpa she knew.

"We need to grab my Remington from Ginny."

"She won't give you a gun, Grandpa."

"Got a itch to hunt, ma dear," he opened the cheap door out into the hallway. Old barn photographs lined the gray-blue walls, an oncoming storm.

"Step up Lou, I'm needin' you."

For a moment, she felt a jolt of happiness as if he had recovered from old age. There was that niggling trouble with reality. This was no good. She ran to catch up with him.

"Grandpa, we don't have hunting licenses."

"Never stopped me before," he paused to look at an old stone barn.

"Hell, this one always bothered me." He ripped it from the nail, slid it inside his coat.

"Grandpa!"

"New England barn. See Lou, they feed you all kind of shit when you get old. Like I wouldn't know."

He slipped out two sets of doors where visitors buzzed in. Lupine hurriedly signed him out at the visitor's desk. *What a lock-down*, she thought.

Outside, Etzel was dissembling the plastic frame by the trash cans.

"Paper," he roared as he ripped and broke it. Everything made to look nice, cheap in the end.

They drove to the farm. He said again he needed the old rifle and his pistol.

"I don't know where the keys are kept," she insisted, even though she did.

Guns were a bad idea, but he kept on about how he'd like to shoot cans with her, maybe squirrels, rabbits. No deer.

He swore, no deer. He couldn't even remember the last time he'd shot a deer. Corn-fed venison sure was good in stew, he mused. She had to agree, though she'd never shot a deer herself. Her brothers always let her tag along. Until they didn't come home anymore.

Etzel worked his angle about a last hunt. Everything taken from him. After all, the guns were his. Eventually she saw it his way. He was old, but he wasn't dead. They were his. The guns couldn't be at the care center, that's why Gin had them locked in her office.

Lupine ran inside her house while Etzel sat in the car listening to oldies. She was lucky: no Gin. She dug for the keys inside a dish above the fridge and snuck into the office. She clicked open the old glass cabinets. The Remington oiled and glowing. Like a living thing. She slid it and the pistol inside a cloth bag. Next, she unlocked the desk drawer with boxed bullets. She put the key back above the fridge, grabbed a hunk of cheddar and several landjägers. She shoved it all inside her coat pockets and ran back out to the truck.

Etzel unzipped the bag and petted the guns before she could stow them behind the seats. She was nervous Geirolf or Gin might see them. How would she explain this virile grandpa? What of the gun cabinet she'd unlocked without permission? The guns?

"Hello friends," he said to the guns in a strained voice, and she wondered if she'd done something wrong.

They drove north. He wanted to hunt on Geirolf's land. Forest land which had been for a cabin that never was built. Hunting land. It was an overcast day with a fine mist. Wipers clicked back and forth. Etzel fell asleep. The cab warm as a nest. She drove and drove.

When she pulled into the gravel drive, she didn't want to get out. Etzel still slept after she turned the ignition off. Perhaps they'd just sit here and turn around. She watched him sleep like at the home. Chalky cheeks. She put her hand in front of his nose to make sure he breathed.

"We're here."

He snorted, shifted, sat up. He gazed through the windows, "Missed these woods."

The trees she'd planted as a little girl rose up beside a crippled wire fence and pitted drive. Twenty-foot cedars, skirted by deer. They'd planted Fraser fir, white pine, and Norway—soft needles. Etzel made fun of their tree choices at first as deer feed. They'd fenced them in for the first five years. Time tracked on. Now they were solid trunks.

Etzel and Lupine zipped up their coats. Even though it was early fall, the wet was bone-cold. The forest floor still soft and damp. Only some of the leaves had dropped. Etzel removed his guns, cradled them while Lupine grabbed unopened cans of beans. She didn't notice the pistol slip into his pocket. They crouched under the first tree limbs. Once they reached growth, they walked easily beneath the pines. A solid stump was enough chair for Etzel, and he sat.

"You want any cheese?"

"What you got, Lou?'

"Six-year cheddar and landjäger."

"Sure do."

She used her jackknife to carve the cheese and dried meat. They ate silently. She felt tired, sure that he was exhausted.

After he stood, she set up the cans. He talked through loading his old Remington then aimed. She let him explain even though she already knew. He lowered the rifle without firing and nestled it in her arms. Stepping back, she aimed, shot and missed.

"Even your stance."

She widened her feet, aimed, shot, and missed. With the third shot, beans blew out the back. Etzel laughed as he took the gun and shot the next two. Pop. pop. No problem. His eyesight still good enough.

Back at the truck, she found full cans of PBR her brother had hidden. Etzel only let her blast one. He cracked two others, handing her one as he gulped and swiped his upper lip. She took sips, the needles outlined more clearly for her.

"You know what my favorite tree is?" he asked without waiting for her response.

"Northern White Cedar. Reminds me of primordial times. Man, that smell. Nothin' better."

He walked over to a cedar that was near one hundred. He set down his beer and rubbed the flat leaves between his fingers, lifted them to his nose. The green fading into a golden green.

"Scatter me here," he said finishing one beer, snapping open another. His false teeth poked out his lips, "Keep these beauties on your shelf to remember me."

Laughter didn't come easily, but she pushed it out for him. Into his pocket went the crushed can as he guzzled the second. She worried the beers would alter his ability to walk the uneven ground. This had been a bad choice. She pulled out the last of the cheddar and lined several crackers for him. He crushed the second can in his hands as if to say he was still strong. Farm hands.

"True little Lou, but let's first take a look see at these deer trails."

There weren't any defined trails. The forest maintained by the big conifers shut everything else out. She followed him just the same. The rifle unloaded and in her hand. They walked until Etzel sat huffing on another stump.

"My dear Lou," he began and then coughed a bit.

"Grandpa, I think we should get back to the truck."

"Let an old man sit in the woods a while."

She sat down against the trunk of a white pine. She with the Remington draped across her lap. He with his elbows on his thighs. Head down. It was an unusual position for him.

Her fingers were numb so she tried again, "Best we get back."

He lifted his head. His glasses slipped down his long nose. He looked at her and then said, "Just gotta take a whiz quick, Lou. Help me up would ya."

It took them a moment to right his body. He shuffled off. He was long out of her sight. She sat back down among brown needles and stroked the wood stock of the rifle. *Pretty gun*, she thought.

A single shot rang out. Loud with a slight reverberation among the trees.

WINTER

Long Nights Moon

Dinner and a Movie

Esther and Katie

Inside Katie's bedroom, Esther feigned irritation but she wanted Katie's support. She was the only completely honest friend. Katie, Esther, and Guy would be driving one town over, and Esther enjoyed the rare attention of both people.

"You gotta make sure he's legit," Katie said from her bed, laying on her belly.

"I'm pretty sure we're in the twenty-first century," Esther said to the full-length mirror version of Katie as she yanked on the fifth, tight Black Keys T-shirt. She smoothed her uni-boob, another try-fail in the bra department.

"This sports bra isn't going to work either, dude."

"No," Katie laughed then covered her mouth. "I don't mean to. I mean I'd love to have tits like yours."

Esther lifted the boob roll high so the curve burst through the scooped neckline.

"You shouldn't borrow my clothes."

"So, I noticed," Esther flopped onto the bed, Katie's skinny jeans making it hard to bend her knees.

Katie scooted next to her, "You just gotta make sure this Guy isn't a Republican," (they'd gone back and forth making fun of a guy actually named Guy.)

Esther turned awkwardly toward Katie thinking *where does she come up with this crap?* and said, "Most of my family is Republican. Most of our town, our county is Republican."

"I know, but I couldn't take it if you were dating one."

"I'm sixteen. I don't even know what I know."

They were facing one another. Watchful faces on level. Body to body. Katie's long feet and longer legs hung off the mattress while Esther's just met the edge. Katie thumbed Esther's hair back from her eye. A stomach growl broke between them and neither knew whose body belonged to whom. Abruptly, they both sat up.

When Esther changed back into her own shirt, she turned from Katie. She admired her own red, tight jeans and cool high tops. She liked her curves. She sat between Katie's legs while Katie braided Esther's hair. Methodically, Katie brushed Esther's hair and scalp. This was no mother. No abrupt pulls. No rush. Just languid fingerings of hair and nerves. Fresh jeans and lavender lotion.

The doorbell startled them. Katie's dad shouted upstairs to them and went back to his den. They tromped downstairs, down the hall to the tall, skinny boy.

"Wow," he smiled, "you look great."

He stood flat-footed on the woven rug looking at Esther. She felt her neck prickle, felt her friend's stare.

He opened it up to both girls, "You both look great. A guy's never been luckier."

"Not if we're bitches," Katie said as she unhooked jean jackets from the coat rack and pushed one at Esther.

His smile slipped and Esther felt injured for him.

"She's just joking."

When he turned to open the door for them, Esther pinched Katie's bony side and hissed, "Be nice." Katie yelled. When he looked back, she explained she'd just hit her elbow.

"Hate it when that happens," Guy said.

The girls laughed. Esther knew it would be a difficult night.

At the next town over, Guy urged them to sit together across from him at the greasier of two pizza places. Salads with more than chopped iceberg and mealy tomatoes for Katie. Thin crusts and sweet marinara for Esther. Something for everyone, he'd said and looked directly into Esther's eyes.

He tried luring them into a conversation about their Bakery by Bike, "Would they be skiing with their bakery packs?"

"Absolutely, skis," said Katie.

"Absolutely not skis," said Esther.

Guy laughed.

"Hey," Esther insisted, "Do I look like a person who exercises?"

"It did take a lot of cajoling to get her on that ten speed," Katie conceded.

"Well, it'll take a lot more to get me on skis."

The waitress set the pizza on a tiered rack. Katie made a big deal out of dabbing little orange ponds of grease from her piece. Esther had to pinched her again. Guy shook red pepper flakes on his slices and encouraged the Scandinavians to leg up their taste buds. The little plastic jar getting more dance than ever on both girls' plates by an overeager Katie. By the end of the meal, their noses were running. They finished their third pitcher of pop.

At the single screen movie theatre across the street, they threw three whole dollars apiece at tickets. Then they spent one dollar each on popcorn, dots, and junior mints. Esther suggested Guy squeeze between them. He held the popcorn in his lap while Kate and Esther's hands dove inside. They licked butter from their fingers and passed the cardboard boxes of candy back and forth.

By this seating arrangement, Esther wanted to rub something she couldn't quite wrap her thoughts or heart around just yet.

Grandmother

Lupine

When she began looking for her grandmother's information, she sorted Etzel's things into piles of items to be tossed, kept, or sold. Nothing to be sold. She kept his fishing poles, tackle, gun, and fillet knife.

As Lupine lifted the books off his shelf, pictures fluttered out. On the floor were pictures of a woman sitting on the hood of an old Ford. Lupine knelt and picked up the photos of her grandmother. The woman on the Ford must be her grandmother, Bernadette, around Lupine's age—legs crossed, dark lips and glaring teeth. Another one showed a baby in front of the old farmhouse: the woman's hand holding hair out of her eyes. One arm on Gin, Lupine guessed. No smile. Three snipped out newspaper articles also included photos of this woman. Lupine's grandmother lived in southern Wisconsin. She ran a bar.

As Lupine fingered the brittle papers, she realized the articles were after her grandmother left Etzel and Gin. Etzel had watched for her in newspapers. He knew where she lived and never contacted her.

Her grandmother couldn't have known about Lupine. Couldn't know about Etzel's death. It hurt her. Their suffering hurt. She dug into Etzel's books and papers with purpose. Nothing. No address book. No letters. She briefly wondered about Etzel's long-lost brother and mother, but there was nothing of them either. All these broken connections. All she had was a city and a bar from twenty years back. Slight chance. She needed more.

Midnight that night, a time when most dairy folk are in full REM, she snuck into Gin's office. She quietly pulled out drawers and flipped through the papers. Folders of receipts. Accounting books. Her mother rigid in the written form, only the breeding schedule on the hard drive. Not one personal item. No pictures. No notes. No address book of friends. Lupine shut drawers and closed the heavy roll top. Everything was in its space.

It felt treacherous to rifle through her parents' room but necessary. While her parents were occupied with farm work, Lupine went through her mother's dresser drawers.

The carved wooden pulls opened easily to the clean scent of lavender. They weren't a family who held or folded one another's underwear. She roved through the dark socks first. She dove her fingers into her mother's simple beige and white bras. It surprised her to find silky black with lace overlay and pink and purple brassieres. She pictured the cups around her mother's own small breasts, and she shut the drawer quickly. No notes or pictures or cash in among the panties, of which a handful again seemed bolder, sexier than the woman inside them.

She dug through drawers in the side table and looked under the bed. Nothing. She opened her mother's closet, the foreign life she'd never led and moved through tweed slacks, pencil skirts. She'd never seen her mother wear these clothes. She'd never known her mother had these things. It felt like worming inside her mother's brain. Brilliant heels, heeled boots alongside sneakers. She told herself she was looking for her grandmother's address, but truthfully, she was labeling Gin's things just as she had with Etzel. She noticed on the shelf above her head two shoe boxes. She rose on her toes to tip one into her hand. Envelopes and papers flew everywhere.

Quickly she shoved envelopes back inside after looking at the addresses. Her grandmother. Her grandmother had written Gin hundreds of fat envelopes. None were opened. The loose papers all had a different version of Gin's scrawled handwriting. They burned Lupine's fingers. She couldn't allow her eyes to read them. Too much. Too intimate. She could not understand. She took one envelope and stuck it down the back of her jeans, but couldn't make herself leave the room. She crawled beneath the bed, wanting to watch this mother. She fell asleep after waiting an hour.

She woke when Geirolf came in wet from his shower. It was late. She must have slept for several hours. Instantly she wished she hadn't hidden under their bed. His white toes and furred legs stood by her face. For a moment she was afraid he'd spotted her. The bed creaked with his weight above her. Hardly ever this close to her father, she listened to his breathing. He opened a newspaper. Gin came in next.

"Did you see Lupine today?"

"Nope," he said and a page turned. She felt warmer, like a bonfire burned beneath the bed with her, the smoke engulfing her heart.

"Wasn't in the milking parlor today."

"Huh," Gin said. "Must be with those women."

Terra and Helen, she guessed that's who her mother meant.

"Ja," he laughed at them, their inexperience.

"Takes all kinds."

"Ja, I'll say," another page turned.

Gin pulled down her jeans and stripped off her socks. Lupine watched the slim feet and ankles as they shimmied into pajama pants. The lamp clicked on and the overhead light snapped off. Her mother's weight sunk into the bed. The space seemed tighter since her parents laid down. She wished she hadn't hidden here. How would she spend the entire night under their bed? How would she sneak out? She heard her father rub her mother's body. She could barely stand the picture.

"I'm reading," Gin said. The newspaper crinkled again.

"Gold is up," he said.

"Hmm," Gin answered.

"Ever thought about antiques?" he asked.

"Hmm?"

"I don't want to hear about Etzel," Gin said.

"You want to sell them?"

"I don't care what you do."

Gin snapped off the lamp, and Lupine waited, her heart thumping her ribs. She waited for her parents' breath to even, so she could escape.

She woke to movement above. The first thought was she'd been buried. She choked down her scream when she realized she was beneath her parents' bed. Perhaps it was worse than being buried. Her father stood up from the bed—there was a groan from the bed frame. This is perfect, she thought. The door would already be ajar. She could crawl out and down the hall to her own room.

She scuttled out from beneath the bed then out the door into the dark hallway. A blunt heavy object slammed into her side, crushing her. Geirolf. He howled as he smacked the floor and Gin screeched in response. The light flicked on in the bedroom. Gin plowed through the door.

"What the hell," Gin yelled.

Lupine and Geirolf lay stunned on the floor.

"Girl, what da devil?" he roared.

It took Lupine a moment to note her legs, arms, wrists, and back were fine. She wasn't as sure about her father.

"Ack," he sputtered again.

Gin helped him up from Lupine. He stood in his white underpants, which glowed along with his chest and legs. Lupine couldn't look at him even in the dim light.

"Did you just get in?" he asked confusedly. She knew he'd been to her bedroom to check for her.

"Yes, sir," she said still on the floor.

"Go to bed," Gin said.

"We'll talk about this in the morning," he said too quietly.

Geirolf shook her from a dream the next morning, his face smeared with sleep. The morning verdict: She wasn't allowed off their land after getting in so late. She couldn't milk the goats. This all would make it worse with her plan. After the evidence that her grandmother wanted to contact Gin, she had to try to find her grandmother. What if Gin refused any such connection?

Lupine would feed calves and finish any other odd jobs today. She pulled on yesterday's jeans and checked the pocket. The letter she'd grabbed had a postage stamp from two years ago. She couldn't believe her luck. It was likely her grandmother was still alive, still in the small town with her bar.

LATE WINTER

Hunger Moon

Finding Her Way Back Home

Lupine

On the road to the Driftless area, Lupine sat shotgun in Manny's pick-up. They listened to his music and didn't talk much. She didn't feel like talking. He understood.

He'd have to leave her somewhere and head back in order to be back for morning milking. They pulled into a McDonald's near eleven. Already they were tired. Lupine hadn't been sleeping well, and they were both used to an early schedule. Two Cokes and hamburgers sat on the plastic table in front of them.

"Will you walk to her house tonight?"

"Nah, thought I'd read a book and eat fries."

"Promise me you'll stay inside tonight."

She was sorry she talked him into this. He'd gotten up early and his eyes were red-rimmed from driving. She worried about deer and ice. She realized she didn't even know his status. Was he working on a green card? She'd been careless about his safety. She relied on her father's honesty and hoped Manny wouldn't be pulled over.

"You got some more tunes to keep you awake," she asked.

"Yup, yup. Got some great ones from Hiran."

"But you didn't tell him where you were going?"

"Oh no, no one. This our secret," he pointed to his chest, then hers.

She smiled as she sucked her Coke, "You have your cell?" He nodded.

"You'll call me if anything happens?" He pressed his chest again.

"You better run so it doesn't get too late. Lots of deer out there."

"Yup, I know. You're sure you'll get a ride back from her?"

"She's my grandmother. She won't let me hitchhike."

She figured she could always take a bus back if she were wrong about the address or about her grandmother. She wasn't sure. This she couldn't divulge to Manny. He didn't press her about it unlike Terra, Helen, or Hiran would have in this situation. She couldn't ask them.

She touched the envelope in her pocket and sipped another Coke. She tried to read. Caffeine made her jittery. The pages trembled as she held them. She skipped along over paragraphs and looked at her phone. It'd only been an hour since Manny left. She didn't know how she'd get through the entire night. She used the bathroom for the third time, certain the cashiers watched her along her path back and forth. She focused on the coffee and apple pie she'd just ordered. The continued purchases and small talk hopefully earned her time.

She'd almost rather find her way in the cold. She opened up her pack and patted the small wool throw. Maybe she could just find a bench outside to sleep on. She was so tired. She glanced at the cashier. At the empty tables.

A police officer pushed through the doors. She looked down. He ordered. She sighed. But then he loped toward her, the tray in front of him like an offering. He sat beside her at the little plastic table and swivel chair. She gulped her coffee, burning her tongue.

"Not from around here, huh?" he asked as he unwrapped the yellow paper from his burger.

"No."

He chewed for a while, "Where you headed?"

"Here," she said.

"Here?" he raised an eyebrow and took another bite.

"Well, not McDonald's, but this town."

"What for?"

She sipped more coffee, "To meet my grandma."

He stuffed the last two bites in his mouth and chewed. He balled up the first wrapper and unwrapped another burger, "Isn't it a little late to meet up with a grandma?"

"Well, I'm not meeting with her until tomorrow morning."

He took another bite and chewed for a long while.

"What's your grandma's name?"

She flipped the plastic tab on her coffee back and forth with her nail. He swigged pop and finished his second burger, began working on his fries.

"Want some?"

"Nah, I just finished some pie."

"She's Bernadette Müller."

"Huh."

She took a fry and munched it. Then took three more.

"Didn't know Bernie was a grandma."

She didn't say she doubted Bernie knew she was a grandma.

"How old did you say you were?"

He took the paper balls and aimed at the garbage can a little way behind her. Hitting both in. She didn't realize on duty cops did that sort of thing.

"Seventeen," she said fudging a little, "But I didn't say."

"Didn't say what?"

"How old I was before."

He smiled, "I guess you're right," and went back to chewing fries. Ten deflated ketchups littered his tray.

"How about I drive you over?"

She studied her book. The same paragraph she'd been reading the last two hours.

"Oh, it's kinda late," she said.

Giving up with the book, she fiddled with her fingers.

He watched her. "I've known Bernie for quite a while," he stared at her. "Grandmas forgive a few late hours."

She hoped he was right. "Okay."

She just felt she should get on with it. She couldn't sit eating at McDonald's all night. Now that she said they could go, it seemed to take him an eternity to finish his fries. She ate a handful more. Then opened and closed her pack.

"Well, I 'spose," he picked up his tray and tossed the trash before walking over to the counter to thank the staff. The manager seemed relieved to see Lupine follow him outside to the squad car. She zipped her fleece up to her chin, glad that she wouldn't have to sleep on a park bench.

Up front in the squad car, she thought of all the questions she wanted but couldn't ask about her grandmother. Instead, she looked out the window at the piles of snow. A handful of teens loped between the buttery lamplight. The town was still. Bakery, banks, dress shops dark. Even the bars with their neon, Budweiser signs seemed sleepy.

He wound through a neighborhood and parked in front of a lit German framework house. Orderly yard, blue spruce out front. Nothing seemed to state a runaway mother and wife lived here.

"I'll walk you up."

Realizing she'd been staring for several minutes, she dragged herself out. Before she could sling on her pack, he took it for her, which felt invasive. She trailed him. Did Bernie still tend bar? she wondered? She noted several beer cans stacked neatly in a pail on the porch and a turtle shaped ashtray full of stubs.

He knocked. A woman with red hair knotted behind her neck like a walnut answered. Her hair too brassy for her age. The long, lacquered nails flashed under porch lights.

"Hiya Bernie. Just found your granddaughter lurking around McDonald's scarfing down apple pie and my fries."

Bernie coughed. Like a snake before a meal, her eyes focused on the pack then moved to Lupine.

"Come in," she rasped, opening the door wider.

Grateful that she could follow the officer, Lupine slipped off her boots. The cop already sat on the couch.

"Coffee?" Bernie asked.

"Sure," he said.

"You?" she asked Lupine.

"I'm fine," she said realizing Bernie wasn't the type to rat her out. Not knowing of Lupine's existence cast her badly.

The couch was normal grandmother fare with its floral pattern. But the black and white photos above it were close-up shots of flowers. It was hard to decipher the parts, stamens like genitalia. This couldn't be Gin's mother. The blown glass lamps and curios were not usual Midwestern kitsch. Lupine followed the lines on Bernie's face to locate Gin's eyes, nose, or chin. Bernie turned to the cop, the lamps backlit her profile. Lupine saw the thunderhead from years before.

"How's the bar biz been?" he asked.

Bernie shot back, "How's the cop biz?"

He laughed at her, "We don't need to get into the ugliness of it. Business is always good."

"I'm sure you can't. You're no big city cop."

"Nope, and your customers are keeping me busy."

"Two fer one," Bernie smiled a bit and Lupine liked her.

Lupine looked across to the dining room. Vines climbed haphazardly across the wall. It was difficult to determine what types of plants. Leaves and tendrils stretched everywhere.

"Have you had supper?" she asked him but looked at both.

"Golden arches is my ticket to middle-aged heart attacks."

Bernie rolled her eyes, "Want something baked from real ingredients?"

At least they had one thing in common, Lupine thought.

"I'm full of fried goodness," he shook his nonexistent belly.

"Well," he stood. "I best be going. Not the time for visits, though they help me get through the night."

Lupine worried over what she'd say to Bernie once he left. She'd never been good at small talk, and it wouldn't be easy to explain herself without it.

He winked at Lupine, "Be good."

Bernie walked him to the door. Lupine stood up from the couch. She inspected photographs for a signature and reminded her fingers not to touch. She felt this all was part of her. She repeated in her head, This is my grandmother. This woman is my mother's mother. The rounded entries and small leaded-glass windows gave the room an appearance of being a cave. In the dining room white-petaled domes opened their coiled tongues in the dark.

Bernie came back to the living room with a beer and ginger ale.

"Do you smoke?" she asked as she handed her the pop.

"No."

"Well, I do, so let's sit out on the stoop. You can tell me again who you are cause I think I missed a few things the last go-round."

The little concrete porch was cold and Lupine's drink made her colder, but she refused to interrupt Bernie as she puffed smoke through her nostrils.

"I'm Lupine," said Lupine and put out her hand. Bernie kept watching. Lupine put her hand back in her lap.

"I believe I'm your granddaughter."

Silence and the smoke were hauled in and out.

"My mother is Virginia, Gin."

Bernie blinked and kept smoking.

"My grandpa was Etzel."

"Was?"

"He died about a month ago."

"Huh, always thought I'd die first," Bernie waved her hand around with the glowing cigarette. "The smoking, you know."

Lupine nodded, "I was there," she said. "We were," she began and cried, "close, you know."

"No, I don't. Sorry but I don't. Huh, always thought he'd be in this world while I was."

Lupine wiped her nose on her sleeve and poured the rest of the pop into the bushes.

"Now don't do that. Don't fall apart just cause you're sad," said Bernie

"People are allowed to fall apart."

Bernie squashed the first cigarette and lit another. She inhaled and exhaled slowly. Lupine crushed her can. The porch was solid and clean. Windy this evening, perhaps more snow by the weekend. Lupine never felt so unmoored. She'd never been this far from the farm or without her grandpa. She wondered where Manny was on the long trip back, maybe Tomah. She wondered if her dad was looking for her tonight like the night she'd hidden beneath the bed. Maybe Gin too. She didn't like to worry them, hadn't been accustomed to it. There was a good feeling too.

"Time for after dinner drinks."

Lupine frowned.

"That was just my beer supper," Bernie said, "How about I make you a Shirley Temple. I make one curly Shirley," she said with false cheer.

"Mind if I use your bathroom?"

"You can use the upstairs one and put your pack away in the yellow room," she stubbed out her second cigarette and walked Lupine back inside and showed her the stairway upstairs. Then she went back to the kitchen to mix drinks. Lupine felt very tired.

Upstairs in the yellow bedroom, the pictures were of dead daisies. The seeds emerged like loose teeth. It made Lupine clench her jaw. She sat on the bed looking at them. Something cold about the flowers. They didn't give you anything but looks. Carrots, potatoes, and garlic were the plants she loved. The surprise of troweling away the dirt to find the roots of things. She took out her grandmother's letter. She opened and read.

Not the person to connect Bernie and Gin, she folded the paper back inside and wrote a note. The letter lay on the single bed. Funny how the heaviest things don't leave any impression on objects.

She shouldn't have come, she realized now. She was too tired to explain Gin to Bernie. It wasn't her place. She'd let things go. The world was made of so many tangibles and yet most people lived inside their heads, she thought.

She hiked up the window feeling the rush of fresh air. She stuck one foot out. The pack dropped. She bowed under the sash. This was not like escaping her window at home. No tree in sight. But the exposed framework seemed sturdy enough. She clawed to stay on for a handful of seconds before slamming down into the bushes.

Laying face-up to the moon, she assessed her body. Guessing Bernie heard the crash, she lay still longer allowing her fingers to freeze. No Bernie. Her ankle throbbed. She crouched and then stood. Something was wrong with her ankle. She hobbled before realizing she couldn't go far. She was on the sidewalk now between street lamps when she saw headlights.

It was the young cop. He rolled down the window.

"Well, if it isn't the granddaughter."

"Hush your mouth. It's Lupine," she hissed.

The dark interior made it hard to see him as he leaned out to talk with her.

"You don't look so good," he said, "Go back on in with Bernie. She's gruff but she means well."

Lupine stood still. Finally, he opened the door for her to duck inside.

"What happened to you? Did Bernie push you out of a tree?" his laughter waned once he looked at her face.

She kept silent. They drove for several blocks. All the street lamps made wide arcs on the pavement. She was thinking about Bernie mixing the Shirley. Carrying it upstairs to an empty room. Finding the envelope. Lupine had always wondered how it was her mother couldn't forgive Etzel or write back to her estranged mother. She felt she could understand now. It was too difficult to change.

"So, where you headed?"

"Bus stop, please."

And then the Hollows by morning. She stretched the injured leg. A stab in her ankle had her gritting teeth.

"Do you want to talk?" he asked.

She shook her head. He turned up the radio, and they listened. She rested her head on the window with eyes closed. The glass fogged with every breath. Numerous lights brightened the bus station. He parked and turned on the overhead light. Radios, gun, and cage behind her illuminated.

"Bus doesn't come for a bit," he said. "We have time to chat."

To stop him, she leaned over for a kiss. She pictured it as evening things. The skinny man, boy with a baton and guns. Pimples scattered below his high cheekbones. Maybe twenty-five years, she thought. He put a palm in front of her face.

"What are you doing?" he asked.

She sat back and switched off the light. They sat in the dark until their eyes became accustomed to the dark. Black hair cropped close. She realized she didn't really know anything. They sat in silence waiting for the bus to pick her up.

Boneyard

Lupine and Hiran

Hiran and Lupine limped through the crusted snow of the graveyard. She was down to one crutch. They started in the back with the oldest headstones, names worn to smooth ridges. Lupine rubbed her thumb over one white stone with the smudged word: Mother.

"As if she'd been nothing else," Lupine said.

"Huh," he said from another stone.

"It's like she's defined only by what she made. Mother and nothing else."

"Or defined by nothing at all," he said motioning toward the large dark obelisk, surrounded by small white marks on the earth. "My great, great aunts and uncles."

"Babies?" she walked over to look at the unnamed, small markers.

"I think it was tuberculosis," he said. "Only my great, great grandpa survived to adulthood." He walked around his family plot to find the stone. All his mother's dead relatives here underfoot, while his father's dead were across the world. Maybe his father thought these were his dead too, now. He'd probably be comforted by the cornfields stretching out beyond, the white steeple of the modest church.

When he found the gray marble, he ran his hands across the smooth front, the grooves of two names, Albert and Kirsten.

"Always thought it was strange to buy a headstone for two," he said "like the other is always waiting here for you to join them. What happens if one dies twenty years ahead of another like Jason. I'm guessing Lani will remarry."

"I don't think they ever married," she said "Dunno that the two person headstones ever bothered me. Guess I thought it was just a symbol."

They looked at the simple church built nearly two hundred years back. Old for the Midwest. It was his mother's church that her family attended since their arrival to Wisconsin. The fat cottonwoods slated for cutting. The county road to be widened. The cottonwoods most probably rotted at their cores, what with their dropped limbs. It still stirred them to think about cut trees after the permanence in their lives.

They looked out to the edge of the cemetery where the shorn cornfields met with the tall spruce. Gaps in the line of old trees showed where there used to be others. Spruce didn't do well with all the clay; they preferred sandier soils and warmer winters. In the basement of the church hung old pictures of congregations, of the property. There used to be a pretty line of trim, black spruce.

They walked past gravestones with plastic flowers and emptied planters, recognizing family names around town. Hiran found Jason's black headrest, the fresh gray etched name and date of birth, death. The dash between—all his life. A full can of Miller and a cuff of old snow. Wind chimes were hung beside.

Hiran ran his fingers over the chimes. They clattered together like teeth. He placed both hands on the stone, imagining the body beneath him. His chin to chest. She stood back giving him time and herself too since she wanted to visit Etzel here.

Hiran took out a rolled note from his jean pocket. He kneeled and dug away at the snow and frozen dirt with his fingers. Dirt pushed underneath his nails, cold. Not too deep. Just enough space for his rolled paper. He pushed it down inside the hole, covered it. Then he stood and looked down at the cold black marble where his legs shone back at him.

"You ready to see him?" he asked her.

"I guess as ready as I'll ever be."

She had thought about bringing cheese for his grave but knew immediately it'd only bring the coons to him. She had nothing to offer and felt sad for it.

As they made their way between stones Hiran said, "Hey, isn't that Terra's Simon?"

He pointed to a modest white marker that read: My love, my friend, my Simon.

"Wasn't he cremated?" she asked.

"I thought so, but maybe his urn is buried here. Some people do that."

"I guess she's staying then," Lupine said.

She figured Terra couldn't leave if she'd placed Simon here. There was no other reason she thought to keep him in the Clayfields unless Terra planned to stay.

"I guess," he said.

"I mean I always thought she would leave. She has no family here. Does he? It would make sense if she left, but now, with him here," Lupine gestured to the marker, "it changes things."

"I suppose," he said.

They both looked at Simon's stone and had a better feeling about it than Jason's, which only felt wrong and unfinished.

"You ready to see him?" he asked again.

"I guess," she said though she wondered. She wished she'd written a note. Hiran wrote a note for someone he couldn't really know. She only came with her hands. Jason's stone seemed full and even Simon had two ceramic mugs. Etzel's grave would be empty. She knew it, though she'd not even seen the grave on the day of his funeral.

Coming here had been her idea—getting Hiran to face Jason. Maybe he'd apologized to Jason in his letter. She didn't know but she knew he needed to see Jason's gravestone, just as much as she needed to confront her grandfather. Have him apologize to her, she didn't know.

"Okay," she said, "Let's find it."

It wasn't as if she couldn't guess where he lay. It was a small boneyard with only three fresh graves. But it felt right to search for it like his address to a new home. This dead little town unmoved for over a hundred years.

And there he was, Etzel Ulbricht. No inscription. She should have insisted, but then she was too angry with him to give him anything more of herself. Grandpa Etzel beneath this slab of marble. No parents. No brother. No wife. Just Etzel. Behind him all the Lutefisk eaters as he used to call Geirolf and her too.

She placed her palm center, pretending it was his heart—a cold heart. She sat and didn't notice Hiran behind her. He stood for a while then sat for a long time.

Then she felt the wool blanket over her shoulders, her palm still on the stone, "You're shivering," he said, "Do you want to go home?"

"No, I think I'd like to stay a while longer. But feel free to leave."

"Maybe I'll get us some coffees."

"Yes, that'd be good," she said only intent on her grandfather's stone.

She waited for Etzel's apology all night with several blankets wrapped around her frozen frame. Hiran brought hot coffee and muffins. She wouldn't touch them; she was beginning to understand why Etzel had killed himself. Why he had chosen her to witness his death. Maybe the whole thing had been his only way out. He had the ability to choose death, choose where he died, and who he died with. But a piece of her couldn't forgive him. He'd crushed her just a little. Now she had to leave the Clayfields to shake this feeling. Maybe she'd come back after a faraway college but maybe she wouldn't. Her future unknown where once it had been clear.

ONE YEAR LATER

LATE FALL

Hunter's Moon

Epilogue

A bright tablecloth was draped over two tables. The cake, dishes, silverware bound for it, but then Chickpea kept crawling beneath, begging Terra to come find him.

"Peek a boo, Bean," she said and lifted the cloth an inch, grabbed at his feet.

"I got your toes."

Cheese spreads and fresh breads, butters, and salads were sct out for guests.

"Can you grab the door." Helen whisked in and picked up the little boy, "since you and Emile threw this thing together."

"You love all the visitors don't you, Bean?" Terra grabbed the boy's toes again as he hugged his mother's side. He lay his cheek on her shoulder and smiled at Terra, a finger in his mouth.

"It's good for all of us," Terra said this time to Helen. Then she strode to the door where Meg and Paul stood with presents and balloons.

"Where's my little pea?" Meg crooned as she walked inside with Paul following behind her. Chickpea called back in answer, so Helen had to set him down. He toddled toward his grandmother. Helen watched, not as stiff as she had been, mildly smiling at the interactions of adults and children. Even Paul was crouched on the floor, cooing more than speaking.

Helen seemed happy that Evan couldn't make it. She'd heard people had called him, Emile or Meg, she wasn't sure. And Meg apologized again, saying Evan had a big gallery opening. And everybody nodded like they believed the excuse. Then it was the door again.

"Hiran," Terra said as she opened it, "I didn't think you'd make it."

She took a small brown bag from his hands and hugged him. He looked over her shoulder and then around the room, pausing briefly on Meg and Paul before Terra said, "She's not here yet, and I'm not sure she can come."

Terra remembered Lupine's expressive letters that still sat on her bureau. Lupine was on some scholarship program in Vermont making cheese and learning about large herds of dairy goats.

Hiran's face sagged a little then. His eyes seemed tired.

"How are you, Hiran? How's the University of Iowa?"

His smile was generous, "Good. Real good. I'm also working at the care center which is even better than studying Biology. It's the real deal, ya know. I'm considering geriatric medicine. I think it may be where I belong." He looked at Terra. "How are you doing these days? How's the farm?"

"It's a wild time 'round here," she said, flipping one hand toward Chickpea who struggled and laughed under Paul's hat.

"Honestly," she circled her hand round Hiran's upper arm and squeezed, "I'm really happy. Not happier than with Simon, but full in a way that's new, you know." She looked again at the small person, the honored guest.

"I guess sometimes it makes me just a little sad that we, Simon and me, couldn't have done this together. But, then

I wouldn't know Helen or Chickpea, so I guess it's the way things worked out."

"Yup, things are as they should be," Hiran said.

Another knock sounded. He moved to talk with Helen, Paul, and Meg. Helen had allowed a smile, and it became larger when she noticed Hiran stride toward them.

Emile and Jed were on the porch with two Ziploc bags of frozen blueberries like purple jewels. Terra couldn't help but rest her eyes on Emile's thickening waist, the tight shirt. It was too soon to tell, but she suspected Emile wasn't long for the Junction Bar. Jed was happier than she remembered him at his wedding. He grabbed Terra's hand with his own and pulled her in to an embrace. Terra wasn't used to hugging and awkwardly patted his wide back.

"Good to see you," he spoke into her knitted shoulder.

"Give her some room, Jed," Emile broke them apart, "we can't make love to everyone here."

Jed and Emile guffawed together.

"We were gonna make blueberry blenders," Emile shook the gallon bag, "You got the ice cream and blender?"

"Yup," Terra led them back to her kitchen and crouched to dig out the pail full of ice cream they'd made yesterday. She set it on the island in front of Emile and then pulled out the blender.

"Did you have Esther make the cake like I said?" Emile asked her as she cracked the pail top and spooned out ice cream.

"Yeah," Terra said, "she and Katie set up the cake yesterday, but I haven't seen them yet today."

"They're coming together?" Emile smirked lifting an eyebrow. Terra didn't reply.

"I invited Lani and little Ned. Think Ned and Chickpea might have fun together. Hope you don't mind that, Terra?" She flashed large white teeth and her eyes crinkled in a fetching way.

Jed rubbed Emile's neck and back, a gesture too intimate for Terra to watch. She nodded, skirted around them and out the kitchen. Their voices were low behind her as they measured out blueberries, basil, lemon, and ice cream into the blender.

Back in the living room, Terra nudged Helen's elbow, but she was in deep with Hiran. Chickpea, Paul, and Meg were on the floor, and it seemed the easiest place for Terra to be. They could talk around any issue as they played with the little boy. She wouldn't ask about Evan's disappearance, and they wouldn't tell her. They wouldn't ask how long Helen planned to stay, and Terra wouldn't allow herself to consider Helen leaving. None of them would mention missing Lupine's largeness. Chickpea smiled at any person who talked to him. He made everything better. He wrapped his arms around Paul's neck as he crawled with him on his back, knees be damned. Chickpea noticed Terra squatting beside him and crowed, "Ma, Ma, Ma." Paul hunkered beside her, and Chickpea reached out to yank her silver braid.

Katie and Esther came inside the front door without knocking. People glanced at them. Lani and Ned walked in behind them with a box of blocks, which Ned dropped on the floor beside the door. The thump had Chickpea looking toward the door.

Outside the red farmhouse the smoke lifted into the cold sky—gray as when Chickpea came last autumn. Snow sifted down in a fit of beginning winter. The fields were cleared of corn stalks and beans. Stubs appeared like a badly shorn head of hair, where the fields had yet to be rolled. Only here and there were a handful of haggard corn stalks left by farmers who'd missed the window between rains. Not a mile from Goat's Back Ridge, cylindrical silver bins spun grain.

Winter was in the wind. Crop farmers were drinking coffees at Marie's on Main, chatting about the wet fall and corn prices.

Acknowledgments

Thank you to everyone who made this book possible. To Cornerstone Press, for your interest in my hillside, and Dr. Ross K. Tangedal for choosing *The Clayfields* for your Legacy Series. Thank you, Brett Hill, for your support and guidance throughout this project, and Grace Dahl. Amanda Leibham, thank you for the lovely cover.

Robin Boles, Kate Maude, and Beth Schommer, you created a room of our own. Remember: "If poetry were pottery," I'd invite you to my shed out back where you could buy a poem or two.

Steph Johnson, I so appreciate your calm, insightful monthly critiques and writing talks.

Professor Ruth Wood, thank you for your honest, considerate critique.

Thank you to my wolf pack, Oskar, Theo, and Cedrec; you are my biggest champions. And Mom and Dad, thank you for supporting all my pursuits and instilling my joy of reading.

Elise Gregory received her MFA from Eastern Washington University. An earlier chapbook version of *The Clayfields* was selected as a semi-finalist for *Black Lawrence Review*'s Black River Chapbook Competition. Gregory's poems and fiction have appeared in *Stoneboat, Rock & Sling, Sweet, Women Arts Quarterly, GHLL,* and elsewhere. She is the author of two chapbooks of poetry, *Domestic Spiral* and *Aftermath,* as well as the co-editor of an anthology, *All We Can Hold: Poems of Motherhood* (with Emily Gwinn). She lives in western Wisconsin.

www.ingramcontent.com/pod-product-compliance
Lightning Source LLC
Chambersburg PA
CBHW021435310726
48971CB00005B/1370